COLD BLACK EARTH

ALSO BY SAM REAVES

A Long Cold Fall

Fear Will Do It

Bury It Deep

Get What's Coming

Dooley's Back

Homicide 69

Mean Town Blues

Nonfiction:

Mop Cop: My Life of Crime in the Chicago Police Department
(Fred Pascente with Sam Reaves)

COLD BLACK EARTH

SAM REAVES

THOMAS & MERCER

Published by Thomas & Mercer, Seattle

www.apub.com

Amazon, the Amazon logo, and Thomas & Mercer are trademarks of Amazon.com, Inc., or its affiliates.

ISBN-13: 9781503944343
ISBN-10: 1503944344

Cover design by Stewart Williams

Printed in the United States of America

Readers familiar with western Illinois will recognize the county I have fictionalized to serve as the setting of this story. I have changed place names while attempting to convey a sense of life in a real community, partly to take a few liberties with topography but mostly to emphasize that the story and all characters are pure invention. Any resemblance between the characters in this story and actual people is decidedly coincidental.

1 |||||||

From the train the land looked tired, stubbled brown fields and spindly black trees, vast acres stripped of their riches and left supine under a slate-gray sky, waiting helplessly to be covered by snow. That's the pathetic fallacy, Rachel thought: You're the one who's tired.

When she opened her eyes the land was still there, Illinois in late November, the crops in and Thanksgiving past and the farms settling in for the winter. The quiet time was beginning.

It had taken the California Zephyr an hour to claw free of the metastasizing Chicago exurbs. Rachel had been stunned by the extent of it, mile upon mile of new developments, ranks of identical slapdash prefabs covering up the best farmland in the world. Her father had told her that: This was the best farmland in the world. But her father was gone and the land would be gone soon, too.

The sun went down and she dozed, her head canted against the window, and thus missed a hundred miles or so of lights passing in the dark. She was awakened by the conductor coming through the car calling out Warrensburg, the last stop before the train crossed the Mississippi to set out across the Great Plains. Rachel gathered her things as the train slowed, then stooped to look out at the lamplit town grinding to a halt outside.

Matt was waiting on the platform, and Rachel's heart soared a little when she saw him, aging at last and growing heavy but essentially unchanged, the image of their father in his visored cap but also of the intrepid boy she had idolized. They embraced, and Rachel held on to him for a few seconds after she could feel he was ready to release her, then stepped back to smile up at him. "Hello, big brother."

"Sis. Been a while." His smile faded and he bent to grab her bags. "Hope you don't mind the pickup. Billy's got the Chevy out someplace, running around."

"I'd love to ride in the pickup. I haven't ridden in a pickup truck since, well, since the last time I was here." It was cold out here on the prairie but Rachel didn't care. For the first time since she'd set out on her long journey a week ago, she was sure this was where she should be.

"I think we got a new one since you were here." Matt led her through the echoing station lobby and down the steps outside. The truck was a Ford, massive by the standards of the old Chevy Longhorn she remembered from her childhood, and it was a real working truck, scarred and dusty, with fence posts and a folded tarp and miscellaneous detritus in the bed. Matt slung her bags behind the seat and they climbed in.

The route home took them down Main Street. This had been the big town when Rachel was a girl, but she had seen her share of big towns since then, and now it was just a county seat out in corn and soybean country, with a grain elevator, a couple of intersecting rail lines and some minor industrial plants, now derelict. Downtown was a courthouse, some churches and a line of storefronts, a lot of them shuttered. "Oh my God, the bakery's gone," Rachel said, tracking the decline as they sped down the empty street.

"Years ago. Where you been?"

"Oh, all over. I'll tell you about it sometime."

They laughed a little but there was discomfort there, too, and she knew that when the time was right they would have to talk about it all. "So, Billy have a girlfriend?"

Matt grunted. "I wish he did. Might keep him out of trouble. Nah, nobody steady. He's in his tomcat phase, I guess. Still running around with that Stanfield kid, just raising hell. He's gonna wind up in jail or dead by the side of the road one of these nights."

That was a little gloomy for the brother she remembered, but she supposed he was entitled, after all that had happened. "And how's Emma?"

"OK, far's I know. We don't talk a whole lot. She says Ray's business is hurting. Peoria's not exactly the economic powerhouse of the nation these days."

"I don't think there is one these days."

"No, I guess not. But people gotta eat, so I guess the farmers will do OK. Long as we can stay a step ahead of the government." Matt sounded weary, and Rachel wondered if everyone all over the world was as tired as she.

The last time Rachel Lindstrom had come home, her parents had both been alive. Her father had still been the Colossus, chipped at by arthritis and the weight of years but still bestriding the earth in his Red Wings and his Deere cap; her mother had gone gray and started to stoop but still ruled the house with the quiet assurance of the éminence grise.

A treacherous heart had taken the one and a savage, rapid cancer the other. Rachel had been engaged in serious matters on the other side of the world. She had not set foot on the farm in eight years. For Rachel it was still the lost Eden, and she was afraid of finding it changed. But she was out of excuses for not coming home. There was no more career, no more marriage, no more obligations. She was no longer important, no longer committed, no longer needed anywhere.

All she was was tired: worn out, run-down, bled dry. All she wanted now was to rest in her old bed in her old room, with a view of the tossing branches of the oak and the vast prairie sky beyond it. She wanted to sleep twenty hours a day.

Matt turned off the highway and Rachel's heart quickened; these roads threaded her earliest memories. Farmsteads passed by in the dark, placid and tidy under their halogen lights. "Oh, no! The Swansons tore down that beautiful old barn."

"It was falling down. I don't know how much farming Bob's doing anymore anyway. I think he sold off half the acreage. Mostly he's living off the railroad job these days."

More turns, the road starting to dip and rise. Local undulations veined the prairie, channeling water toward the great river forty miles to the west. Trees loomed in the dark, filling the folds in the land. Matt braked as something raced across the road just ahead, fur flashing in the headlights.

"What was that?"

"Coyote. They're all over the place."

"Coyotes?"

"They've come back big time. They sneak around and pick off people's chickens and farm cats. Pain in the ass. I've shot a few. You hear 'em yowling at night a lot."

"That's scary."

"They're just wild dogs. But a pack of them can cause a lot of trouble."

They crossed a creek on a narrow bridge and made another turn. "Wow, when did they blacktop this?"

"Four or five years ago. I'd been yelling at Jim Hanson for years about it."

"Jim Hanson? Debby's little brother?"

"Yeah. He's been on the road commission since about ninety-five."

"Little Jimmy. He'll always be thirteen years old in my mind."

"He's got the farm now. Their dad passed away five or six years ago."

They topped a rise and the headlights fell on a figure two hundred yards ahead, walking by the side of the road. "Who the hell's that?" said Matt. A distant face turned briefly to them, pale and indistinguishable in the hood of a sweatshirt. The car dipped into the hollow and the lights showed only blacktop. "Somebody's car broke down, maybe."

"Did we pass a car?"

"Could have been on one of the side roads. I didn't recognize him, though. Don't think it was anybody I knew."

The road began to rise again. Matt slowed. "Well, we'll see if he wants a ride."

They climbed out of the hollow, the land opening out, and there was nobody there. "Where the hell'd he go?" said Matt.

Ahead of them was a level stretch. The headlights lit the road ahead and the ditch on either side for a hundred feet or so; beyond was the dark.

Matt had slowed to about twenty. Rachel peered out the window on her side, seeing nothing but corn stubble going by. "That's weird. He just vanished."

Matt gave it a few seconds, then accelerated gently. "We didn't hallucinate that, did we?"

"We both had the same hallucination, anyway. There was a guy there."

"He must have jumped into the ditch, laid down flat. Why in the hell would he do that?"

They hadn't come up with an answer by the time they turned onto the gravel road that led to the Lindstrom place, settled in 1854 by one Swan Lindstrom of Östergotland, Sweden, and worked by his descendants ever since. The land now consisted of something over a thousand acres, lying fifteen miles north and a little east of the county seat and marked by a USDA *Centennial Farm* sign.

Matt wheeled into the drive, gravel crackling under the tires. He parked close to the kitchen door. While Matt reached behind the seat for her bags, Rachel walked away from the house to stand for a moment and look around, seeing details that had changed—a flower bed that hadn't been there, a concrete slab where an old pump had been—but mostly the topography she'd grown up with, ghostly under the lamp high on its pole: house, barn, sheds; beyond them the wide fields, invisible now in the dark.

How many times have I come home late at night like this? Rachel was presented with a brief vision of a thousand arrivals: sleepy in her mother's arms, fleeing from disastrous dates, sneaking in tipsy and giggling. She turned and followed Matt into the house.

Here much was changed: new wallpaper in the kitchen, a stainless steel refrigerator in place of the old Frigidaire, sky-blue paint in the hallway, a new runner on the stairs. Rachel recognized her dead sister-in-law's hand at work and was saddened. "Did you eat?" said Matt.

"Not really. I had a sandwich before I got on the train."

"We may have some leftover pizza."

Rachel wondered who if anybody was doing the cooking in this house now. "Whatever you have is fine. Give me those." She took her bags from Matt and made for the stairs. "Can you put on a kettle for tea?"

"Not sure we have any tea. I'll look."

Upstairs, she threw her bags on the bed in her old room and stood at the window looking out at the oak tree, just visible in the glow from the yard light, and the blackness beyond. She went and sat on the toilet, glad for the familiar shabbiness of the bathroom, then washed her hands, avoided looking at herself in the mirror and passed quickly through the hall, haunted by ghosts.

They sat at the kitchen table. Matt had found a tea bag he said had to be a decade old; it produced a passable cup of tea. Matt opened a beer. After some halting small talk they fell silent and then Matt said, "You missed a lot."

She nodded. "I know."

"Mom was kind of upset that you couldn't make it back when Dad went."

She stared into her tea. "I'm sorry. We went through all this."

"Yeah. I'm just saying."

"I know." Attending her father's funeral would have required the commitment of scarce logistical resources and deprived a besieged American embassy of its best Arabic linguist at a time of exploding crisis, so Rachel had had to make do with constrained, inadequate words with her mother and brother over a satellite telephone link. A year after that she had come halfway around the world on emergency leave to say good-bye to her mother as she lay dying in a Peoria medical center, then flown directly back to Iraq. "I missed both my parents' funerals. I'm not proud of it. That's just the way it worked out."

"Don't worry about it. Far as that goes, none of us managed to make it to your wedding."

"Well, Lebanon's a long way away. It's just as well, considering how long the marriage lasted."

"I stuck up for you, believe it or not."

"I believe it." Rachel raised her eyes to her brother's. "Matt, I'm so sorry about Margie. I can't tell you how much."

If there was pain in there somewhere, Matt had gotten just as good as their father at hiding it. He nodded once, ponderously. "I never should have moved back here. She didn't want to. She wanted her own house, even if it was a dump. But I wanted to keep the damn house in the family after Mom died. What the hell did I know?"

"It made sense to me."

Matt drank from the beer and frowned at the label. "I thought it was going to be fine at first. She did a lot of remodeling, all this." He waved at it. "But then after about a year the depression got worse. And then one day I came in and found her."

"Oh, Matt." She was whispering now, consumed by guilt; after her sister-in-law's suicide she had not even thought of coming home.

"Now I'm wondering how long I want to stay. This house has seen too much. I can't even go in the bedroom anymore. I been sleeping in the den down here."

They traded one of those looks only two people who have grown up together can trade, long and candid, and Rachel found herself hurting for him.

"So," he said. "What about you? What happened over there?"

Rachel sighed. "Everyone knows what happened over there. We blew it. We took the country and then when we had it, we messed it up beyond repair. And I got tired of helping mess things up. So I resigned."

In the silence she could hear the old kitchen clock ticking. "And what happened with Fadi?" said Matt.

She shrugged. "We just discovered there wasn't much of a marriage left, that's all. The separation killed it. I thought it would survive, but it didn't. Seeing each other two or three times a year wasn't enough."

"Yeah, I guess that would be hard."

"It's always tough to make an international marriage work. Especially with two careers going head-to-head." And most especially when one partner is locked up in a fortified compound in a war zone and the other is roaming the nightspots of Beirut, she thought.

Time went by and Matt said, "So what are you going to do now?"

Rachel just blinked at him. "I don't know. Rest, for a start. Just rest. Get to know my family again, look up some old friends. Then look for a job. Where, I don't know. I've got money saved, so it won't be urgent for a while."

Matt drained the beer and stood up and went and put the bottle under the sink. "Well, you can stay here as long as you want. Maybe you can teach us to cook." He headed for the back door.

When Rachel finished her tea and went to find him, he was standing outside in the chill ten feet from the door, listening. Through the crisp, still air they could hear a dog barking, angrily and insistently, somewhere to the east.

"Wonder what's got him riled up," Matt said. He turned toward the door. "Billy's got a key. Make sure you lock up when you come inside."

2 |||||||

In the morning there were no ghosts, only a quiet house beginning to seem familiar again. Matt had left a note on the kitchen table: *Gone to town. Back for lunch.* There was coffee in the pot and bread in the fridge, and Rachel was able to cobble together as much of a breakfast as she ever had. For a moment she was at a loss without a newspaper to read. She looked in vain for the radio on the counter, the one on which her father had listened to the noon market reports on WGN for as long as she could remember. She decided she'd had enough of world news for a while.

When she had eaten she put on her coat and went outside. It was a clear cold day, with just a breath of wind stirring. She stood with her hands in the pockets of her coat, taking in the immensity of the sky and the long views: the scattered distant farms, their closest neighbors a half mile away, the line of trees along the sunken creek bed a quarter mile to the north, the endless empty fields. The sighing sound of traffic on Interstate 74 three miles away, shooting north to the Quad Cities, came clearly across the hard black earth. High above her a jet had left a contrail on its way west.

Rachel made a quick tour of the old farmstead: The barn was mostly empty now that there were no cattle or hogs, the chicken house long since converted to a storage shed. The old corn crib had been replaced by a pair of cylindrical steel grain bins with a grain leg and a dump pit. She still missed the old crib; instead of watching the place evolve, she saw abrupt changes on her infrequent visits, and it was always traumatic. She peeked into the equipment shed to take stock of a million dollars' worth of toys: tractors, combine, planter, semi and trailer for hauling grain. A farm was a considerable business, as Rachel had explained many times to urban sophisticates impressed with her having risen so far above her background.

She walked the perimeter of the acre of grass and trees surrounding the house. This had been all the world she had needed when she was small, exploring this vast realm, obeying strict instructions not to go near the road. Some trees had grown and some had gone; the patch of ground she had been given for a vegetable garden when she was ten was just a change in the texture of the grass now. Standing by the road at the head of the drive, Rachel looked at the handsome frame house Swan Lindstrom had built and his descendants had expanded, now the seat of an established western Illinois corn and beans operation, a family farm hanging on in the age of agribusiness. Rachel was home, and her heart was desolate. She had come halfway around the world again, this time to find comfort in the familiar, and there was no comfort here.

She walked back up the drive and made for the far corner of the lot. Shielded from the house by the barn, Rachel stepped to the fence and managed to get herself up and over without serious damage to her jeans. Pleased she could still handle a barbed wire fence, she set out across a field full of corn stubble toward the trees lining the creek.

The creek had carved a meandering hollow across the land. It was the northern limit of Lindstrom land and prized outlaw country for farm kids. Matt and his friends had tried to dam the stream and built a fort of fallen limbs on its bank. In the tangle of brush beneath the trees were a few places clear and level enough for an adolescent girl to sit and read a book or just poke a stick in the water and brood.

It was rough going over the field and Rachel almost turned back, but her native stubbornness kicked in. By the time she reached the trees she was sweating. In summer the creek bed was a thicket, but now it lay exposed, fallen branches and dead leaves clogging a meager trickle of water, bare trees clinging precariously to the slopes.

She made her way along the edge of the gully, looking for the old paths down and not finding them. Finally she managed to descend, slipping on the hard earth, grabbing onto branches. At the bottom she stood on the bank with her hands in her coat pockets, kicking at shards of ice that had formed along the edges in the night. What am I doing here? she thought. Nothing, she decided, and that was good enough for now. She began walking east along the creek, stepping carefully.

After a hundred feet or so she stopped, looking in vain for something familiar. Wherever her brooding place had been, it was gone now. Trees grew and fell and rotted in twenty years; the land changed. Once as a girl she had decided to see how far she could walk upstream. She had walked for what seemed miles, then climbed up out of the gully and been dismayed to see the back of the Larsons' house, their closest neighbors.

I will walk until I get to the bridge where 400 East crosses the creek, Rachel told herself, and then I'll climb up and walk home by the roads. It would be a circuit of about three miles and a good morning's workout. She had on her running shoes, and even if she got her feet wet in the creek it wasn't going to kill her.

She made a couple of hundred yards without too much trouble. She remembered this part, where the gully widened a little and the trees grew bigger. On a level patch of ground traces of a fire showed that thirty years after she had grilled hot dogs on sticks with Matt and the Larson girls, the spot was still in use.

The creek bed bent and narrowed and the walking got harder. Rachel was having second thoughts again—a foolish middle-aged woman stumbling along a brush-clogged streambed, searching delusionally for her lost youth. She had to cross and recross the stream, slipping on rocks.

She stopped at the sound of something scrabbling in the brush, just around the bend ahead. She remembered the coyotes and felt positively foolhardy, with an edge of alarm now. The scrabbling stopped.

You can at least peek around the bend, she thought. She searched until she found a sturdy stick. Rachel Lindstrom wasn't going to let a puny coyote or two spoil her morning's walk.

When she rounded the bend, it took a moment for what she was seeing to resolve itself into something she could identify. The coyotes were still milling around it, though they had retreated to the far side of the stream; there were half a dozen of them, and only a meal this big could have brought them out in daylight.

Rachel had seen her share of dead animals and even, to her great regret, a few dead people. There was no particular reason why the sight of a dead animal in the bed of a stream should trigger this slow suffusion of dread.

Except that this animal had been flayed, brutal reds and violets veining the pale, headless trunk, the stumps where the limbs had been hacked off. Something had stripped the hide from the raw flesh and left the carcass to the scavengers at the bottom of the gully.

She stood stupefied, trying to make sense of the sight. What animal was this? The answer lay ten feet away on a pile of dead leaves, where the deer's head, propped back on its antlers, presided obscenely, the eye gazing vacantly upward, truncated veins and the severed backbone visible in the cross section of the neck.

Rachel's grip on the stick tightened. Could coyotes do this? Tear the head off a deer?

A hunter might do it if he intended to take the meat—but who would kill a deer and skin it, only to leave the meat for the coyotes? She scanned the rim of the gully on either side, looking for something that would explain this pointless butchery. She saw nothing but a tangle of brush and trees, cover for coyotes and perhaps larger things. Suddenly she was aware that she was well out of sight and hearing of any friendly being and a long, stumbling run from any kind of help.

The coyotes were creeping back. Rachel retreated, hastening to put the bend in the gully between her and the slaughtering place. She stumbled, losing her stick, then rose and thrashed through brush. At the first opportunity she charged up the slope, pulling herself up through clinging branches, toward the sunlight.

At the top she broke out of the trees and stood panting, looking across fields at the Larson place, tranquil in the winter sunlight. A few hundred yards back was the cluster of buildings that were her home, unfamiliar from this angle but marked by the towering oak.

Rachel cast a look over her shoulder, shuddered and began walking along the grassy border of the field. Hunters, she thought, who'd skinned the deer on the spot and went to fetch a truck or a tractor to haul the carcass home.

Leaving the meat unprotected from coyotes? It made no sense. Or perhaps they intended the meat for the coyotes? To keep them fed and distracted from domestic animals? That didn't seem very likely. If you didn't want coyotes to eat your animals, you shot a few pour encourager les autres and kept the .223 handy.

Rachel made tracks, resisting the thought that came trailing after that one: Some people hunted just because they liked to kill things.

When Rachel came into the kitchen, it took her a moment to recognize the man sitting at the table as her nephew Billy. He was a different person from the eleven-year-old she'd last seen: Testosterone had lengthened and roughened his features and furred his upper lip and chin.

He had his mother's dark good looks, but hadn't taken especial care of them. Long stringy hair hooked over an ear with a ring through it, and a wary look came up at her from under dark brows as he slouched at his place in an oversized white T-shirt.

This one fancies himself a bad boy, Rachel thought. "Hello, Billy," she said.

"Hey, Aunt Rachel." He smiled, but he didn't knock over any chairs leaping up to embrace her. His body language said he might respond positively if she cared to cross the kitchen, but that was about it. Rachel contented herself with pulling out a chair opposite him. The smile had helped; if this was a bad boy there would be no shortage of girls anxious to reform him.

"Out late last night?"

Around a mouthful of Cheerios he said, "Mmm. Takin' the back roads home from Peoria. Dodgin' state troopers."

She decided it was best not to ask for details. "Visiting your sister?"

That was funny, apparently; Billy nearly choked on the Cheerios and shook his head. "Nah, Emma doesn't approve of me anymore. Just listening to a band. In a bar down there."

As far as Rachel knew, they hadn't lowered the drinking age to nineteen in Illinois, but she had a feeling that wouldn't deter Billy. She failed to find a follow-up and felt the conversation screeching to a halt.

Billy looked up and said, "You haven't changed."

"That's nice of you."

He shrugged. "Just callin' it like I see it. You quit the State Department, huh?"

Rachel nodded. "It hasn't been much fun the past few years."

"Saw a lot of shit over there in Iraq, huh?"

"A lot of shit," she said, surprising herself. "Mostly I just got worn out."

Billy shoved the bowl away. "Weren't you married?"

"I was. The divorce just went through last week. I said good-bye to my ex-husband in Beirut, flew to Washington via Paris, had a very unpleasant couple of days there talking to my former bosses, then flew to Chicago yesterday."

The bad boy was giving her a surprisingly thoughtful look. "Well, after all those places I got a feeling you're gonna find it a little quiet around here."

Rachel had to smile. "That's what I'm hoping," she said.

Matt brought home groceries and news. "They had one get loose out at the prison yesterday. There's sheriffs' cars all over the roads."

Rachel pulled frozen dinners out of the bags, looking for food. "Anybody dangerous?"

"They're not saying who on the radio. I know they got some tough characters locked up over there."

"I thought it was just a medium-security facility." The prison had been built in the eighties, the town catching a break as the plants closed, getting in on a growth industry.

"What, you think that means everybody in there's harmless? Plus, they got the psychiatric unit over there, with all the crazies."

Her eyes met Matt's. "You don't think that's who we saw on the road last night, do you?"

"Well, I did call the sheriff's office to report it. But I'd be surprised. We're eighteen miles from the prison, and I don't think he covered that on foot. And if he caught a ride, stole a car or whatever, then he's in Chicago or St. Louis by now. He's not going to hang around here. I think that was just somebody fooling around. One of the Collinses stumbling home from the tavern 'cause he lost his car keys. It's been known to happen."

"All right," Rachel said. "I won't worry about it."

"They'll grab him in a day or two. They never get too far. A few years ago two of them made a break for it and got as far as the rail yards. They found them in a box car, hungry and ready to give up. Billy around?"

"Some friend came by and they went off together."

Matt shot her a look, a handful of TV dinners poised to go into the freezer. "Dammit, he was gonna help me fix that auger. I bet he ran off just to get out of it."

"Maybe he forgot."

"He didn't forget. It's a constant fight, trying to get him to pull his weight around here." He jammed the dinners deep into the freezer and slammed the door.

"Seems to me I remember you and Dad tussling over work a few times."

"Not like with this kid. I keep telling him, you're tired of farm life, that's fine. Get your ass back down to Macomb and finish college, go join the Marines, whatever you want to do. But as long as you're living off me, you'll do your share of the work around here. And I have to fight him about it, every day."

"Maybe he'll be back in time." Here I am playing peacemaker, Rachel thought, just like my mother.

"Don't hold your breath. I'm going to have to hire somebody again next year. I was hoping Billy would commit to the farm, at least for a couple of years till he figures out what to do with his life, but it's not happening." Matt drank a glass of water at the sink, looking out the window. "He took it real bad, Margie killing herself like that. That's the worst thing about it. That's what I can't forgive her for. Killing yourself is about the cruelest thing you can do to your loved ones, especially your kids. I don't know if that's what she intended or if she was just too sick to think. But it hurt those kids, that's for damn sure. Billy especially."

The silence went on for a while. Rachel came back from thoughts of cruelties done to her and said, "Can I have the car to go into town? I've got some visits to make."

"Far as I'm concerned."

"I thought I'd start with Susan. And I'll cook tonight. I'll get what I need on the way back."

Matt turned from the window and smiled. "That'd be good. I got a whole side of beef down in the freezer, already cut up. I can bring up some steaks."

"I think I'll save them for tomorrow. Tonight I'm going to cook you something exotic."

"Exotic? Like what?"

"Something other than meat and potatoes."

"What's wrong with meat and potatoes? You forgotten you're Swedish?"

"Nothing wrong with meat and potatoes. Or TV dinners, once in a while. But even the Swedes throw caution to the winds sometimes and have vegetables."

Matt shrugged. "Suit yourself. I got a freezer full of meat, and I don't know who's gonna eat it all."

3 |||||||

The country high school Rachel had gone to served four little farm towns in the northern part of the county, each with the type of unlikely name that betrayed where the pioneers had come from or what they admired: Ontario, Bremen, Regina and Rome. Each town had maintained its own high school until the fifties, when the districts were merged, producing a consolidated high school with a population close to three hundred, just big enough to field a football team.

Susan Stevenson, née Holmgren, had been Rachel's best friend at North County High. Distance and diverging paths had never quite extinguished the friendship, though it had been reduced to a flicker at times. The advent of e-mail had resuscitated it, and through the teeth-grinding times in Iraq, Susan's messages from a blessedly humdrum world had helped keep Rachel's sanity more or less intact.

Susan had married a CPA and moved to Warrensburg, where she had raised three children, run the PTA and the First Lutheran Missions Committee, and in general done what generations of prairie women had done before her—namely, make civilization possible.

"Honey, you haven't changed a bit." Susan stepped back from their embrace and held Rachel at arm's length.

"Don't lie to me."

"All right, you haven't gained an ounce. How's that?" Susan had gained quite a few; she wore them reasonably well, but the willowy young blonde whose looks Rachel had secretly envied was history.

"That's stress, not virtue," Rachel said. "Eighteen-hour days and the occasional explosion don't do much for the digestion."

"Was it awful?"

Susan led her into the kitchen, where a pot of tea was steeping on the table. Through a window Rachel could see trees, a patio with wrought-iron furniture, a garage. Susan lived in the nice end of town, in a house she had described to Rachel as *Addams Family* meets *Home Improvement.*" To Rachel it looked like heaven, a big creaky comfortable Victorian with the pleasantly untidy look of a place where the raising of children had worn down standards of organization.

"Some of it was awful. Some of it was just tedious. All of it was pointless after a while."

"And you just up and quit?"

"Not exactly. My last job over there was to go around throwing unbelievable amounts of money away on projects that made no sense. People were desperate for power and water and we were setting up beekeeping projects. I sent a very skeptical report back to the embassy and got called in for a dressing-down. I lost my temper and either resigned or was fired, depending on who you talk to."

They settled at the table and Susan poured the tea. "I thought of you every time we read about bombs going off."

"There were some bad times. But we were protected. We had an army unit with us everywhere we went. The ones who suffered were the poor Iraqis." Rachel shuddered. "Don't get me started. I'm still trying to process it all."

"There's a book in there somewhere."

"Maybe. Everybody I knew over there talked about writing a book. Now all I want to do is rest. And figure out what to do with the rest of my life."

Susan sipped tea, watching her over the rim of the cup. "And the husband?"

"Now the ex. The naysayers were right. Though I probably could have saved the marriage if I'd ditched the career."

"And what would you be doing if you had ditched the career?"

"Living in Beirut, the idle wife of a rich Christian businessman. I'd have two or three spoiled children, probably bilingual in Arabic and French. I'd vacation in Paris. I'd have made it back here for my parents' funerals."

In the silence Susan reached across the table to put her hand on Rachel's. "Nobody blamed you."

"*I* blamed me. But I'm over that." She heaved a sigh. "I guess I can't really complain. It's been interesting."

"I guess so. Paris, Beirut? I think you get the prize for longest distance traveled from the farm."

"And it's all because of Mrs. Avery's French class. Who'd have thought?"

"Oh, God. You were such a star. I never got much past *keska say ka sah*."

"She forced me to learn it. Said I had a talent. God knows I didn't want to learn French. I was going to be a nurse, remember?"

"I do. And I was going to be a psychiatrist, as I recall."

"If I'd known I'd wind up in a bunker in Baghdad I'd have stuck with the Future Homemakers of America. Didn't you win the Crisco Award for best recipe one year?"

It felt good to laugh; it had been a while. Rachel laughed until the tears came, and then suddenly her eyes were squeezed shut and her shoulders were shaking and Susan had come around the table to put her arms around her. "Oh, Rachel. Honey, it's all right now. You're home."

Susan found her a Kleenex and Rachel dried her eyes. "Sorry about that. Don't know where that came from."

"Well my God, I may not be a psychiatrist, but I know enough to recognize stress when I see it. You've been through the wringer."

"I suppose so. And I guess I always thought I would have a marriage to go back to when it was over. But I didn't."

"I'm so sorry."

"It was a bit of a fairy tale all along. We had three good years in Beirut. But he had a roving eye, even then. The night I left for Baghdad I remember thinking, he's going to cheat on me. Can we survive that? And it turned out the answer was no."

They looked at each other over the teapot for a time, and finally Rachel smiled. "As for being home, I think the jury's still out on that."

--- --- --- --- --- --- --- --- ---

Rachel stopped at the supermarket at the north end of town and managed to assemble the ingredients for a passable lamb couscous, including, somewhat to her surprise, the couscous. Having spent so much of her life outside the United States, she was sometimes startled to find that things progressed when she wasn't there. The most exotic item she could recall seeing in the supermarket as a girl was garlic.

She put the groceries on the back seat of the Chevy, shoving a welter of wadded-up napkins, greasy wrappers and empty cups onto the floor to clear a space. Billy had failed to inherit his father's mania for cleanliness, apparently, or was actively suppressing it. Rachel made a note to spend a morning soon making the car habitable.

The sky was a gray wash above her as she drove north through the darkening afternoon. Could I capture that with watercolors? she wondered. Her hobbies had fallen by the wayside over the years. The thought that she had time now to paint excited her but at the same time gave her butterflies. The rest of my life is wide open, she thought, amazed.

Having a cry had been good for her. She could feel the knots easing. You could only go for so long lying to yourself about how you felt before it caught up to you. Stress was only half of it; some time soon Rachel was going to have to break down and tell somebody how it had felt to be betrayed by the man she had sent all those passionate longing e-mails to, hunched over her laptop in a cramped trailer in the desert.

She switched on the radio. *". . . Illinois State Police are saying the likelihood is that Ryle has left the county, though they warn residents to be on the lookout and to secure their homes and places of business, as he is considered extremely dangerous. Ryle escaped from the psychiatric unit at Mills Correctional Center in Warrensburg sometime yesterday and has been the object of an intensive manhunt for the past twenty-four hours. In 1998 Ryle was convicted of killing his wife and children in Bloomington and dismembering the bodies. At the correctional center, an inquiry continues into how the fifty-two-year-old Ryle managed to escape from the high-security psychiatric unit . . ."*

Rachel stabbed at the button, killing the radio. After three years in Iraq, it hardly seemed fair that horror should pursue her here. She thought again of the man on the road and decided that if Matt and the state police both thought the madman had left the county, that was good enough for her.

When she pulled into the drive an unfamiliar pickup was parked on the gravel near the kitchen door. She came into the kitchen with her groceries to find Matt and another man at the table with beers in front of them. She plunked the grocery bags down on the table, groping for an identity for this ruggedly handsome face she couldn't quite place. "Oh, my God."

"Well, I'll be. It's little Rachel," the man said, rising.

"Danny?"

"Boy, nobody's called me that in a while." He opened his arms for her, a big strapping man with the frame of an athlete, gone a little heavy around the middle but still imposing, graying at the temples and in the goatee and moustache that set off his square jaw. They hugged briefly, and he stepped back to look down at her from his six-foot-three perspective. "You haven't changed."

"Oh, please. I have a mirror."

"I mean it. You look great."

"Thanks. Twenty-five years ago I'd have killed to hear you say that."

He grinned. "Ah, jeez, don't hold that against me. I barely knew who you were."

"I know. That's what hurt." Dan Olson had been in Matt's class, two years ahead of Rachel, the three-sport star and the freshman girl's dream and her first serious crush. "But that's OK. I forgave you." She took her bags to the counter and started emptying them. She found herself wishing she'd ducked into the bathroom first to check her face, then scowled at herself for caring. "And what are you rascals up to this afternoon?"

Matt said, "We're just recovering from all the hard work we did at drill."

"Drill?"

"For the Rome, Illinois, volunteer fire department. I didn't tell you I'd joined?"

"No, I'm impressed. And what do you do at drill?"

"Well, usually we practice first-responder stuff. CPR and all that. Sometimes we even set shit on fire and try and put it out."

Dan chuckled and said, "But today we just went around stringing up the town Christmas lights."

Rachel smiled. "Well, it's dirty work but somebody has to do it. How's . . . let's see. You married Sandy, didn't you?"

"Far as I know, she's fine. She's up in Moline now with the slick bastard she ran off with."

Rachel grimaced. "I'm sorry."

Dan shrugged, smiling. "It's all good. She wasn't cut out for farm life. At least she stuck around long enough to get our kids raised."

"And how are they?"

"The kids are great. I got a boy in the Navy out in Norfolk, a girl married and living in Seattle, and my younger boy finishes up at Macomb in the spring. They're good kids. What about you? You home for good?"

"Boy, that's a great question. For good? Probably not. But for a while, anyway."

"You all done with government work, then?"

"Well, I burned all my bridges at the State Department. I'd like to think there's something I could do with my experience. Maybe teach somewhere. But I don't have to think about that for a while." She turned from the counter. "Now, who's going to be here for dinner?"

She served the couscous at the kitchen table, and she almost laughed at the looks on the men's faces as they peered at it. Matt and Dan had added a few empty beer bottles to the ranks under the sink, and Rachel had permitted herself one. The cooking and the banter had relaxed her, and she had managed to slip away to the bathroom and check that she looked OK and wonder again why she cared.

"This is what they eat in Iraq, huh?" Dan said, pronouncing it "Eye-rack," the way the military guys did.

"No. This is a North African dish. I learned to make this when I was living in Paris."

Dan poked at it with his fork. "You lost me there. I thought Paris was in France."

"It is. There are lots of North African immigrants in France, and I had an Algerian boyfriend. That's what first got me interested in learning Arabic."

"An Algerian boyfriend, huh? I had a girlfriend from Aledo once."

Rachel laughed. "That's pretty exotic."

"She had some fairly exotic sexual practices, for a nice country girl. But we don't need to go there. You know, this ain't bad."

"Thank you. I learned how to make a lot of Lebanese dishes, too, when I was living in Beirut. And that's pretty much all I have to show for twenty years living abroad. I can bring something different to the church potluck."

"Bring this to my church and they'll gather around it in a circle and wait for the minister to try it, see if he keels over." Dan took a drink of beer and said, "Lebanon. You sure like to go where the trouble is, don't you?"

"I just went where they sent me. Once I learned the language, that sealed my fate. I wasn't going to get Paris or London after that."

"Well, that's what you get for hanging out with foreign guys."

"I tried to tell her," Matt said. He aimed his fork at Rachel. "It all started when you went to the homecoming dance with that exchange student we had—what the hell was that kid's name? He was from Chile or some damn place."

"Oh, God, Eduardo. What a disaster that was. He was so nervous he forgot all his English. I had to grab him and kiss *him* at the end of the night. And then he was too embarrassed to talk to me after that."

"But the damage was done. You had tasted that forbidden fruit."

She giggled. "Oh, right. I developed a craving for swarthy pimpled youths who couldn't talk."

Dan reached for his beer. "And somewhere in South America, the man-eating blondes of Illinois are a legend to this day."

It was absurd but it made her laugh again, and it felt good to laugh. "Well, I'm done with foreign guys now, I'll tell you that."

"Now you're talking," said Dan. "We'll get you hooked up with some nice divorced farmer around here."

Rachel cocked an eyebrow at him. "Slow down, Tiger. I may be done with guys altogether for a while."

"Did I say anything about me? I'm too old to chase girls anymore."

"And I'm too old to be a girl, so we should get along just fine."

"I'll drink to that," said Dan. Rachel picked up her bottle to clink with his, and when Danny Olson winked at her she found it was easy to give him a cool indulgent smile in return.

4 |||||||

Winter was the quiet time, the slow time, but there was still work to be done: next spring's seed and fertilizer orders to finalize, financing to arrange, insurance needs to analyze, machinery to repair, infrastructure to upgrade, all the things left undone in busier times. Rachel hadn't owned a pair of work boots in twenty-five years, but she put on her sneakers and followed Matt out to the barn.

"I been trying to figure out what to do with all this space ever since I got out of hogs. Now I'm thinking organic dairy cows."

"Cows? Why cows?"

He gave her a sidelong look and a grin. "You want to know the truth? Since I got rid of the hogs, I miss having animals around. Too quiet."

"So what happened to the hogs?"

Matt shook his head. "Hogs got too big. The size of the operation, I mean. When the price tanked back in the nineties, only the bigger outfits survived. Now you need a CAFO and all that shit."

"What's a CAFO?"

"Stands for 'concentrated animal feeding operation.' You know, a big factory building with fifteen or twenty thousand hogs penned up together. That's what you do if you're serious about hogs now. You take on a corporate partner, have them build the plant, become an industrial farmer. Or a serf, the way I look at it. But you can make a lot of money as a serf these days. You specialize in farrowing, weaning or finishing, and that's all you do. Economies of scale and all that."

"Yuck."

"That's what I say. To hell with it. I'm looking at something small and sustainable." He pointed at the vacant north end of the barn. "I can put a New Zealand–style milking parlor in here. Start with twenty cows or so and go from there, see if it flies."

"What's New Zealand style?"

"You milk the cows in groups. Line 'em up at a trough, hook 'em up to the pumps from a pit below them. I can put in the troughs right here, dig the pit about here. Cost a few thousand bucks for all the plumbing. A lot cheaper than a conventional milking operation. So I can get into it without too much start-up cost. Turn a few acres up by the creek back to pasture, start growing some hay again, figure out the business without staking too much on it."

"It all sounds nice and green."

"Yeah, me the tree hugger. Who'da thunk it? But it makes sense. Chuck Anderson over by Bremen went all organic a few years ago. I don't know that I'm ready to go the whole way. Ravaging the land with fertilizers and pesticides has been a pretty good deal for us. But I'm starting to fall in love with the cow idea. What the hell, it's something different."

Rachel looked at her brother's profile and felt a stir of affection, watching him survey and calculate and dream, just as their father had. "I never thought about the responsibility when we were kids," she said. "How does it feel to be in charge of all this? You're running this thing that got built up over generations. You ever feel the weight?"

He shrugged. "Sometimes. I guess I'd feel more weight if there was somebody to hand it off to. But Billy doesn't give a shit. And Emma's not going to come back from Peoria to run a farm. I think I'm the last generation on this land."

Shocked, she put a hand on his arm. "No, don't say that."

Matt turned his head to fix her with a look. "What, you mean you're going to take up farming? Is that why you came home?"

Rachel blinked at him. "Are you sure about Billy? You don't think he's going to settle down?"

Matt shook his head. "When he does, it won't be here. I'd be real surprised."

"But what'll happen to the place?"

"I'll cash it in, sell everything off and go live in a condo in Florida. Don't worry, you'll get your cut."

"That's not what I was thinking."

"Nah, I know." His look softened. "What, you think I want to be a lonely old man here? Sleeping in the den for the next twenty, thirty years, whatever I got left?"

Rachel just stared at him, ambushed by images of an unsuspected future. After a while she said, "I'm sorry, Matt. I've been living in a fairy tale, I guess. Where the farm goes on forever and I can always come home for Christmas and find it just like it always was."

"Nothing goes on forever," Matt said, turning away. "Thank God."

"You don't have any outstanding warrants on you, do you?" Rachel said, toiling at the kitchen sink.

She had said it as a joke, but there was real alarm in Billy's eyes as his head jerked up from his lunch. "How come?"

Rachel nodded at the window over the sink. "Because a sheriff's car just pulled up out there."

Billy shoved away from the table and came to stand beside her. Outside, Matt had emerged from the shed and was strolling toward the cruiser, hands in the pockets of his overalls. A uniformed deputy had gotten out of the car and was ambling toward Matt, adjusting the set of his gunbelt. Neither of them seemed in a hurry.

Billy made a whiffing noise. "That's just old Roger Wilco. If he's here, it can't be anything serious."

Rachel's eyes narrowed. "Roger Black?"

"Yup. He's kind of famous around here for being a doofus. My dad calls him Barney Fife. Nobody takes him seriously."

Outside, Matt and Roger shook hands, then settled on their heels to talk, two men passing the time of day. Rachel started to laugh. "Roger Black, my God."

"What's so funny?"

"I went to the prom with Roger once."

"You're shitting me."

"No. I was just a sophomore, and I had no idea he liked me. He cornered me in the hall one day and asked me to go with him, and I was so dumbstruck I failed to say no."

"He's an idiot."

"I don't know if he's an idiot. He was kind of quiet, not real glib. But he was a nice guy. He's not exactly . . . what am I trying to say? He's not Hollywood material."

"You mean he's a goofy-looking doofus."

Rachel laughed in spite of herself. "Let's just say he was not well-favored by nature." Roger Black had been an awkward, angular boy, with a long equine face and an uncertain complexion, redeemed slightly by kindly eyes and a crooked smile. Watching him now in profile, Rachel saw that he had gained weight and assurance with adulthood, but he was never going to be the type to set women's hearts a-flutter.

"Oh, perfect. He's gonna come in." Matt had motioned in the direction of the house, and the two men were coming toward it. "Gonna ruin my damn lunch." Billy went back to his place at the table.

When Roger came into the kitchen he and Billy traded a quick glare, and then Roger's eye lit on Rachel and he grinned his crooked grin. "Well, hello, Rachel. It's been a long time."

"Hi, Roger." Rachel didn't know what to expect, but to forestall any extravagant gestures she put out her hand. "It has been a while, hasn't it?"

Roger shook her hand as if he were meeting the president. "Only about twenty-three years, by my count."

"That long? Wow."

Roger's brow furrowed. "The last time I saw you was at the Dairy Queen up in Kalmar, a couple of years after you graduated. I think you were home from college. You were with Sue Holmgren and Tammy McMaster, I recall. I was working for Don Holland at International Harvester at the time. I came over to say hi."

Rachel stared openmouthed. "I can't say I remember it."

"Wouldn't expect you to." Roger grinned again and looked down at Billy. "I took your aunt to the prom one time, did you know that?"

"Yeah. I think that's why she's in therapy now," said Billy.

"You watch your mouth," Matt said, scowling.

"That's OK." Roger waved it off. "Billy and I have had our issues, but that comes with the territory. You keeping out of trouble, son?"

Billy gave him a pitying look. "You think I'd tell you if I wasn't?"

"Billy." Matt's tone was flat and hard.

Roger smiled. "He's jokin' with me, that's all. Forget I said anything, Billy. Just remember, there's reasons for the laws we got."

Billy got up and took his plate to the sink. "Sure thing. See you in the rearview mirror some time." He left the kitchen.

Matt sat down heavily, took off his cap and passed a hand over his face. "I'm sorry, Roger. I don't know where he got the mouth from. I didn't raise him that way."

"It doesn't matter. He's a good kid. He's just going through a tough time, that's all."

"I know you've cut him a couple of breaks. I appreciate it."

"Because he's not malicious. He's just a little wild. I just hope he doesn't hurt himself before he comes out of it."

Matt sighed. "Whatever. Anyway, Rachel, Roger wants to know about the guy we saw on the road the other night."

Startled, she said, "I don't know what I can tell you. I didn't get any more of a look at him than Matt did."

Roger said, "You didn't notice anything, an article of clothing, hair color, something like that?"

She frowned, recalling. "He had on a hooded sweatshirt, with the hood up and pulled tight around his face. But really, we just got a glance at him, for a couple of seconds in the headlights before the road dipped. And then when we got closer, he was gone. That was the funny thing—like, where did he go?"

"Sounds like he was hiding from you."

"That's what I thought," said Matt. "That's why I called you."

Rachel said, "You think it might be this guy that escaped from the prison?"

Roger shrugged. "Well, we have to check it out. I'll tell you one thing—if he is around this neck of the woods, you want to lock your doors, because he's one dangerous individual."

There was a brief silence. "I heard about what he did," said Rachel.

"Sick bastard," Matt muttered. "I remember when it happened."

Roger nodded. "He's one for the textbooks, all right. Classified as unrestorably incompetent, suffering from schizoid personality disorder, delusional disorder, multiple paraphilias, psychopathic narcissism." To Matt and Rachel's astonished looks he said, "I did some reading up on him. What it boils down to is, Matt's right. He's a very scary guy."

Rachel nodded. "And there's no sign of him."

"No sign. We hope that means he's a long way away by now. Of course, all that means is, he's somebody else's problem. Nobody's going to rest easy until we haul him in."

"Maybe we'll get lucky and somebody will shoot him," said Matt.

Roger shook his head. "We can't be thinking along those lines. Doing a good professional job would mean catching him and taking him back to jail."

Matt shot a quick look at Rachel, with a hint of a smile. "OK, Barney. We'll be on the lookout."

Roger smiled, briefly. "Go ahead and laugh, I don't mind. Now, have you seen anything unusual, anything out of the ordinary?"

"What kind of thing?"

"I don't know. Anything that didn't look right. A door on an old barn left open, signs of a campfire somewhere. Unusual animal behavior. Fugitives disturb the environment. They leave signs. You might have seen something."

Matt shrugged. "Can't say I have. Things are pretty quiet around here."

A repugnant image fluttered in Rachel's mind. "I have. I saw a deer somebody had skinned and left for the coyotes."

They gaped at her. "Come on," said Matt.

"Seriously. Down in the creek bed, north of here." She told them about it.

Roger shook his head. "I've seen hunters do some crazy things."

"Maybe they intended to come back, couldn't get it up out of the creek or something."

"That's what I thought," said Rachel. "Anyway, that's the only unusual thing I've seen."

"I can go take a look. I'd be surprised if it had anything to do with Otis Ryle. More likely some hunters who had too much to drink." Roger squared his shoulders. "Well, Rachel. It's a pleasure to see you again. You just in for a visit?"

"An extended visit, I guess. I'm kind of between jobs right now. I'll be here through Christmas and New Year's, anyway. After that, we'll see."

Roger's mouth shifted in the crooked smile. "Well, it's nice to see you. You take care, now." He looked down at the floor, the awkwardness suddenly there, then turned abruptly toward her brother. "Matt, good to see you. See if you can talk that boy of yours into going back to school. He's too smart for that crowd he's hanging around with."

"I'm working on it." They shook hands and Roger left, casting one last look at Rachel before he ducked out the door.

"You're going to be very popular around here," said Matt as the cruiser pulled away from the house.

Rachel made a face. "Oh, please. The last thing on my mind when I came back was to reconnect with all the guys I knew in high school."

Matt laughed softly. "Well, you gotta remember. It's different around here than it is in a big city. In a small community there's a limited supply of people. Believe me, it's something us divorced and widowed guys are aware of. The pool of potential partners is small. And you just added one to the pool. You're sending out ripples."

Rachel tried to see through the amused look on his face, but he rose from the table and turned from her. Loneliness was an aspect of her brother's life she had not considered. Suddenly she hurt for him again, but she could see he wasn't going to sit still for her pity. Rachel turned back to the sink. "You know, I don't think Roger's as much of a fool as everyone seems to think."

"Roger? No, he's no fool." Matt was rooting in the cupboard. "I may rib him with the Barney Fife thing, but I never thought he was stupid."

"Did he ever get married?"

Matt brought out a can of soup and closed the cupboard. "His wife left him a couple of years back. Took their daughter and moved to Colorado."

"My God, did we all make a mess of our marriages?"

"It's harder than they let on when you're young," Matt said, frowning at the label on the can. "They don't tell you what happens when the honeymoon's over."

5 |||||||

WQAD in the Quad Cities had the Ryle story on the five p.m. news. A powder-puff blonde was doing her best to look grim while saying, "Authorities believe Ryle may have left the area, but are warning residents to be on the lookout, as he is considered extremely dangerous." Over her shoulder a picture hovered, a mugshot of a slightly disheveled middle-aged man, mostly bald with a tuft of hair sticking up on top, staring into the camera with a yearning look. "State police and local sheriffs' departments are mobilizing extra units in an intense manhunt for the fugitive. They are warning people not to pick up hitchhikers and to report any unusual activity or suspicious individuals to their local police department."

On the screen a burly state cop in his Smokey hat appeared, a microphone in his face. "The main thing to be aware of is that an individual like this has to seek shelter. It's a little cold to be sleeping under the stars. We're concentrating our search on abandoned buildings, but if he gets cold enough and desperate enough he's going to be knocking on doors or trying to grab somebody's car."

The blonde came back and said, "An investigation at Mills Correctional Center in Warrensburg, where Ryle was incarcerated, has shown that the fifty-two-year-old inmate obtained an unauthorized pass to a receiving area at the prison where outside deliveries are made. He then apparently exited the prison by hiding in a vehicle, somehow avoiding security checks designed to foil just such an escape. An investigation of all vehicles that made deliveries at the prison on the day of the escape failed to yield any indication of which vehicle he may have used or where he exited the vehicle subsequently. Authorities at the prison are promising a thorough review of procedures."

"Slam that barn door shut," said Matt. "The horse is gone."

The blonde wasn't done; she looked her viewers in the eye and said, "Ryle, a former Bloomington resident, was convicted in 1998 of killing and dismembering his wife and two children." Her glossy lips pursed in a moue of distaste, the blonde turned over a page, brightened abruptly and went to a commercial.

"He didn't just dismember them," said Matt, muting the television. "I got the scoop from Roger when it happened."

Rachel looked at her brother in the depths of the old recliner where their father had reigned for so many years. "Do I want to hear this?"

Matt shrugged. "Only if you want to know just how sick this guy is."

"Not really. But I know you want to tell me."

Matt hauled himself to his feet, picking up his empty beer bottle and heading for the kitchen. As he passed Rachel he said, "He ate them."

Rachel turned from the window and looked at the room where she had grown up, essentially unchanged in the last thirty years. Bed, dresser, desk, closet, the armchair by the window where she had sat looking out at the old oak and the fields beyond, dreaming of the wide world she would go out and conquer some day. Her eye fell on her bookshelves, jammed with hoarded favorites. She stepped over and ran her finger over the spines, looking for comfort. Here were *Winnie the Pooh*, *The Wind in the Willows*, *A Wrinkle in Time*, *The Outsiders*, *A Tree Grows in Brooklyn*, *Gone with the Wind*, *Wuthering Heights*. And over here *Anne of Green Gables, One Hundred Years of Solitude, Pride and Prejudice, Island of the Blue Dolphins.*

She turned away. *Wuthering Heights?* Rachel couldn't think of a more depressing book. Isolation and abuse, cruelty and despair. Why on earth did people read the damn thing?

I don't want to be here, she thought. I want to be in Georgetown tonight, listening to wicked gossip about the Secretary over my fourth or fifth cocktail at Martin's Tavern. I want to be in Paris, in Chantal's flat up under the mansard roof, ten or twelve of us crowded in under the eaves, passing the bottle, something cooking on the stove, the slamming of trains behind the Gare du Nord drifting in through the open window.

Instead I'm here.

Rachel moved out into the hall, looking for her parents. Her dead sister-in-law had expunged most traces of them, but here was their wedding picture where it had always hung, at the head of the stairs, a big strapping country boy stuffed into a suit next to his pretty little bride, clutching a bouquet, fifty years before.

Since coming home Rachel had avoided looking into the master bedroom, but now she tiptoed over to the door and gently turned the knob. She stepped into the room and closed the door behind her. The bed was stripped to the mattress. The pictures were gone from the walls; the blinds had been drawn over the windows and the curtains removed. The room was as sterile as a furnished apartment between tenants. If there had ever been a mess from Margie's suicide, somebody had done a thorough job of cleaning it up. There were no ghosts here. She stood looking for a moment and then backed out of the room.

I'm going to go mad, she thought, back at the head of the stairs. She could hear the television going in the living room below. That's what my life is going to be here, she thought. Watching Jay Leno with my brother every night.

When Rachel walked into the living room Matt said, "Dan's coming over. He wants to take us to the bar."

Rachel stopped in her tracks. "What bar?" she said, stupidly.

"Up in Alwood. That's our usual joint. Unless we go over to Logan's, there on 150. They got a pool table up at Alwood, so we usually go there."

"Oh." She stood looking at the television until Matt glanced up at her. "That's nice," she said. She was surprised to find that it did, in fact, have a certain appeal. "When's he coming?"

"Any time." Matt looked back at the TV. "I might let you two go by yourselves. I'm kinda tired."

Rachel thought about that for a second. "Forget it, Matt. If you're trying to play matchmaker, it's not happening."

"I'm not trying to play anything. I'm just tired. You don't want to go, call him and tell him to forget it. I'll give you the number."

Rachel folded her arms, watching Jay Leno smirk. "No," she said. "That's OK. I could stand to get out of the house."

Rachel had left for college before she reached legal drinking age, and thus had little experience of country saloons. This one was dark enough for anonymity but cheerful enough for comfort, especially with the Christmas lights strung up behind the bar. Besides the pool table it had a muted TV with a basketball game on, a jukebox playing Waylon Jennings, three video game machines and a bottle-blonde barmaid on the down side of fifty. It's not Martin's Tavern, but I'll take it, Rachel thought.

"What are you drinking?" Dan said, sliding onto a stool. He had dressed for the occasion to the extent of buttoning his flannel shirt and tucking it into his jeans. Down the bar, male heads were turning, and Rachel thought of ripples in a pool.

"Gin and tonic."

"I don't know if they can handle anything that complicated here," Dan said. "Mostly us hicks drink beer."

The blonde gave him a sour look. To Rachel she said, "Honey, I can make anything you want. You want a mai tai or a martini, I can make it."

"Gin and tonic's fine."

"Well, I'm a hick," Dan said. "I just want a beer."

The blonde went to fetch the drinks, and Dan traded jabs with a couple of the men at the bar, mostly middle-aged and with a preponderance of denim, Deere caps and paunch. Dan made no attempt to introduce her, and Rachel was grateful.

"Here's to ya," Dan said, clinking his glass against hers. "Nice of you to come and hang out with us hicks."

Rachel gave him the dead-at-ten-paces look. "Look, Dan. I may have been away for a while, but that doesn't mean I brought back any kind of attitude."

He smiled, looking sheepish. "All right, that's good to know. I'm trying hard not to be intimidated, all the places you've been, the stuff you've done."

"Everybody's got to do something. I just had an idea and ran with it."

"You went and saw the world. I've never done that."

"It's not too late."

He took a drink of beer and shook his head. "Yes, it is. I'm not going anywhere at this point in my life. Once I washed out of football at the collegiate level, it was over. That was my shot. But you had your shot and made it count. You went and did exciting stuff in exotic places."

Rachel concentrated on stirring her drink. She had spent years defending the dignity of farm life, and the last thing she was going to do was exalt her experiences over those of somebody who had stayed home to work the land. "It's still just life, wherever you go. I messed up a marriage in another country, big deal. I still messed it up."

"Takes two to mess up a marriage. That's what I decided."

"Sometimes it takes three. Or, in my husband's case, half a dozen."

"Are you kidding me?" Dan gave a shake of the head. "Jesus. With you at home? What was that man's problem?"

"Mainly the fact that I wasn't at home, I think. But thanks for the vote of confidence."

"Well, hell. I'm just calling it like I see it. Anybody that's running around on you needs to get his eyesight checked or his priorities straight. Or both."

She rolled her eyes. "It'll take a couple more drinks before I start falling for lines like that."

"And it'll take a couple more drinks before I can come up with another one."

They laughed. Rachel was determined to keep it light, but it was nice to be flattered; it had been a while.

"I'm worried about your brother," Dan said.

"Why's that?" Rachel said, looking into her glass.

"He's depressed. Look at him tonight, sitting there watching TV instead of coming out with us."

Rachel had her suspicions about that, but she said, "Yeah, that surprised me a little."

Dan frowned into the mirror behind the bar. "He never has bounced back from Margie killing herself."

"Well, that would be a tough thing to bounce back from."

"Yeah, but you would. You'd have to. You gotta go on with life. I don't think he's fighting hard enough."

"He had a lot to absorb in a short time. My folks and Margie all went right in a row. He's worried about Billy, too."

Dan waved a hand in dismissal. "Billy's OK. Matt's too hard on him. He's forgotten what it's like to be eighteen, nineteen. We did some running around, too. Billy's a damn good kid. He did some work for me a couple of years back, helping me put up a shed. He's a good worker when he wants to be."

"I think Matt's worried about the company he keeps."

"What, the Stanfield kid? OK, the kid's a little rough. But I don't know that they're getting up to anything too awful."

"What are they getting up to?"

Dan drank, not looking at her. "All I know is the rumors."

"Which are?"

"Don't take my word for it. It's all just hearsay."

"Has Matt heard it?"

"Sure. OK, look, the Stanfield kid got busted for selling drugs a couple of years back. Got probation, didn't have to do jail time. But people don't figure he got out of the business. And Matt's scared Billy's in it with him."

"What drugs?"

"Dope. Pot, weed, whatever you call it. There's worse things."

"Sure. Still, it's not what you want your kid doing for a living."

"No. But I can't see Billy getting involved in it, not real deep anyway. He's a pretty sensible kid. But what Margie did knocked him for a loop."

Rachel searched Dan's profile. "What happened to Margie? She seemed pretty stable, happy enough, the last time I saw her."

Dan let out a long whistling sigh. "Don't ask me. Matt always just said she was depressed. She was on medication when she died. I think there were some issues there, about her not taking it all the time or something. It was just bad news, the whole thing."

"I could use some good news one of these days."

They listened to the jukebox for a while, somebody singing about somebody else dragging his heart around. Dan said, "Well, the good news is, your farm's in pretty good shape. Matt's a damn good farmer. He's worked his ass off and been careful and a little lucky, and he's got a good operation going. With what your dad and Margie left him and what he rents on top of it, I think he's making a pretty decent living."

"Margie had land?"

"Yeah, she'd inherited some acres from her grandpa or something, over there just south of Ontario. She was renting it out, but Matt started working it after it came to him when Margie died. Anyway, I think he's got about eighteen hundred acres in all now, and he's doing OK.

He's not one of these five-thousand-acre CEO-type farmers, like your cousin Steve, but he's a respected guy, with being on the Farm Bureau and the school board and all that. Matt Lindstrom's got a hell of a lot of friends around Dearborn County. Me, for sure. He's helped me out a couple of times when I wasn't sure how the bills were gonna get paid, hired me to drive or help him get the corn in or whatever."

Rachel hesitated and then decided that sounded like an invitation to inquire. "You farming your parents' place?"

Dan shook his head, grimacing. "I'm not even really farming anymore. I help out Matt or my cousins when they need it, but what pays the bills is driving a truck for the hog plant up at Kalmar. I'm just about the only non-Mexican employee left up there. Keeping western Illinois supplied with pork chops and sausage, that's what I do. That and haul grain for people when they need it. A trucker's license is a good thing to have."

Rachel stared at him, astonished. "What happened to your farm?"

"We lost it. My old man never did get out from under all the debt he took on back in the seventies. He bought a lot of land when crop prices were up and interest rates were low, and then got walloped when things went to hell in the eighties. All the time we were growing up, he was always hanging on by his fingernails. He finally gave up and went into Chapter 7 and liquidated, in eighty-nine. I think you were gone by then."

"Oh, my God. I'm so sorry. What happened to your parents?"

"Dad got a job at Maytag in Warrensburg and worked like a dog till he dropped dead in ninety-nine. My Mom moved out to Arizona to live with my sister. My brother Jim's coaching high school basketball down in Kentucky. Me, I'm the only one left around here. I'm still in our old house, anyway, over by Bremen. That's about all we managed to keep. I can look out the window at all the land we used to own."

Rachel shook her head, remembering a long-ago Christmas party in a big warm farmhouse, the handsome Olsons having a few neighbors in for *lutfisk* and *glögg*. "That's so sad. Your family's been around here forever, like us."

Dan shrugged. "Hey, shit happens. It all went down about the time I got married, which was kind of disappointing, but that just meant I had to scrape for land to rent like all the other young guys. It ain't for the faint of heart, I'll tell you. And it doesn't always make for a lot of presents under the tree at Christmas. But I did OK. We managed to get the kids raised, Sandy and me, and then when they were raised she took off. When you get down to it, I can't complain too much. I never went hungry and I never had to go to work in town." He grinned at her, and the old charm was there, a little scarred and a little worn but still with enough wattage to make Rachel wonder for a second what she'd ever seen in foreign guys.

She looked down at her drink. "I never heard my parents talk about money. When I got old enough to ask how we were doing, my dad would always tell me not to worry about it. And then I went away."

"Well, they weren't all good years. I know your dad and Matt were kinda close to the edge a few times."

Rachel nodded. "I could never understand why he and Margie never came to visit me in Europe. He would say they couldn't afford it, and I always thought he was just a stick-in-the-mud, making excuses."

"He was probably telling you the truth. But like I say, I think he's OK now."

"I guess I missed more than just a couple of funerals. I'm just starting to realize, I basically checked out of family life for twenty years."

"Well, you're home now. It's not too late to get interested in farming again."

Rachel had to smile. "I don't know. If it's too late for you to see the world, it's probably too late for me to raise corn and beans. But I'm glad I came home. For the people if not for the farm."

Dan clinked his glass against hers again. "Farmers are people, too. People with shit on their shoes, but you get used to that."

Rachel laughed. "Give me time. That might take a week or two."

6 |||||||

"Who the hell is that?" said Matt, looking out through the window in the back door.

At the kitchen table Rachel looked up from her book. In the country the sound of tires crackling on gravel meant company and was generally something you looked forward to. She got up and went to the window over the sink. A white Dodge Stratus had pulled up next to the pickup. "It's Billy," she said as the car door opened. The wind whipped her nephew's hair across his face as he made for the house.

"Where'd you get that thing?" Matt said as Billy came in the door.

"I stole it." Billy brushed past him and grunted at Rachel by way of hello. "You guys have lunch yet?"

"Only about an hour ago. You make a mess, you clean it up."

"Anything left?" Billy was already in the refrigerator.

"There's lentil soup in that plastic container," said Rachel.

"Lentil soup?"

"Broadening our horizons, she calls it," Matt growled. "Be grateful."

Rachel smiled at Billy. "I can make you a salad if you want."

"Nah, that's cool." Billy lifted the lid. "Looks interesting."

Matt was frowning. "So what's with the car?"

"Now that Aunt Rachel's here we need a third car. She can have the Chevy. I got a deal on this one from a guy up in Atkinson."

Matt was glowering, suspicious. "How much?"

Billy poured soup into a bowl. "Couple of thousand."

Matt stared as he put the bowl in the microwave and stabbed at the buttons. "Where the hell'd you get two thousand bucks?"

Billy shot him a glare. "I got money saved up."

"From what?"

"From working."

"What, you mean from when you were at the feed store?"

"And other stuff. Odd jobs, I help guys out. Like when I helped Dan build that shed. I know you think I'm a lazy piece of shit, but I been working since I was sixteen. Not counting all the unpaid labor around here. I got savings." Billy shucked off his denim jacket and hooded sweatshirt and hung them up by the door. He returned to the refrigerator, pulled out a beer and shot Matt a challenging look. "Believe it or not."

Matt stared for a moment longer and then shrugged. "OK. I'm glad. That's real good, that you had that much saved up."

Billy took a swig of the beer, set it down on the counter and strode out of the kitchen. When they heard him go into the bathroom down the hall, Matt said quietly, "He didn't save up any two thousand bucks doing odd jobs." He was frowning again.

Rachel thought of rumors and hearsay. "Do you keep track of everything he does?"

"No, but if he was working that much I think I'd know about it."

"Be glad he's not asking you for money."

"I am. I guess." They heard the toilet flush. "I'd just like to know where he got two thousand bucks."

Rachel assembled her tools: portable vacuum, pail of warm water, handful of rags, trash bag, dishwashing gloves. She put on her coat and hauled her gear outside. The Chevy sat forlornly on the gravel fifty feet from the door. Matt had taken the pickup to the lumber yard in Ontario to price materials for the barn conversion, and Billy had jumped in his new wheels and gone tearing down the drive. Rachel wasn't sure why she'd felt the need to wait until Billy was gone to tackle cleaning out the Chevy; maybe she hadn't wanted to give Matt another occasion to tee off on the boy. But she was damned if she was going to drive the thing around another day with garbage around her ankles.

She pulled the car close enough to the steps that the vacuum cleaner cord would reach with the help of an extension cord. She put on the gloves and started pulling trash out of the car, beginning with the backseat. Fast food wrappers, discarded packaging from batteries and car care products, old newspapers, brown paper bags that had probably held things that shouldn't have been consumed in a moving automobile. Rachel shook her head. When the seats and floors were clear she started probing under the seats, grimacing.

More trash: an apple core, a broken pencil. A roll of toilet paper, crushed and soggy. And, suddenly more interesting, a pair of women's panties, with a red heart just above the crotch, slightly soiled. Rachel wrinkled her nose and stuffed them into the trash bag.

Billy was having a more interesting time in the car than she had suspected. She wondered who the girl was. And how on earth do you wind up leaving your panties in the car? Rachel sighed and probed farther under the seat.

She grasped what felt like the wooden handle of a hammer. When she dragged it out it turned out to be a hatchet. Rachel stared at it unmoving for a few seconds, just kneeling there with an elbow on the back seat.

Something had been smeared and then dried dark red on the blade.

She stood up, bringing the hatchet into the sunlight. Oil, she thought. Someone smeared dirty oil on it. Yet she had never seen oil that shone this deep reddish brown. She raised her free hand to run a finger over it but hesitated.

Rachel tossed the hatchet onto the ground. If it was blood, there wasn't all that much of it. About as much, she judged, as you would get if you cut off somebody's finger.

Maybe a thumb, Rachel thought, and laughed at herself. She remembered Matt killing chickens with an axe, when they had kept chickens. She was fairly confident Billy could explain a bloody hatchet, even if a car was a strange place to keep it.

She glanced at her watch and went back to work. She was expected in town in an hour, and there was a lot of work left to do. Ask him, she thought. Just ask Billy about it. There has to be a reasonable explanation.

"You have lived the life I dreamed about."

Catherine Avery had taken a degree in French at the University of Illinois in the nineteen fifties, married a medical student with roots in Dearborn County and come back with him to settle there. She had proceeded to teach French at North County High School for thirty-five years, beleaguering legions of farm youths with the conjugation of *-ir* verbs and mostly failing to communicate her passion for Flaubert, Rimbaud and Boris Vian.

Mrs. Avery gave a wistful smile as she filled Rachel's cup with coffee. In retirement she was avian and brisk, a small woman with an excess of energy and iron-gray hair pinned up haphazardly in a vaguely Anna Magnani look. Her living room was full of pictures of children and grandchildren, a coffee table volume on Impressionist painters the only visible sign of suppressed Francophilia. "A package tour to Paris every four or five years doesn't really scratch the itch."

Rachel returned the smile. "After about six months it's just the place where you live. You have plumbing problems, and dealing with the syndic is a pain. The romance wears off a little."

"Still, it is Paris."

"Oh, yes. I was happy there." Rachel raised her cup to her lips. "Mostly."

"I guess that's all we can aspire to." The smile faded, but the wistful look remained as Mrs. Avery set down the coffee pot. "I'd have to say I've been happy here, too, mostly. It's not a particularly . . . *stressful* place to live. Unless, of course, you've taken on too much debt, or the factory job that's seeing you through the lean years has suddenly gone to China."

"I grew up with it all, but I've been away too long. It all feels foreign to me now."

"And as the wife of a country doctor I've become more of an expert on the rural economy than I ever dreamed I would. I suppose that's what happens when you marry outside your caste, so to speak. I was supposed to wind up living on the North Shore married to a Chicago financier."

Rachel smiled. "I might have outdone you as far as marrying outside my caste goes."

"I would say so. He's Lebanese, is that right?"

"That's right." Rachel sipped coffee and set the cup down gently. "Lebanese, Christian, from a wealthy family that came through the civil war better off than most. I met him when I was at the embassy in Beirut. He was good-looking, charming, serious and accomplished in business matters, and spontaneous and fun-loving in everything else. He made me laugh, he courted me in an old-fashioned gentlemanly way, finally he swept me off my feet. I ignored everything everyone told me about the difficulties of an international marriage and said yes."

She glanced at Mrs. Avery but found her look of sympathy intolerable and looked out the window instead. "The marriage might have had a chance if I'd given up the career. But when we went into Iraq,

I was suddenly a hot commodity because of my Arabic, and that was when I had to choose, even though I didn't realize it at the time. And I chose the career."

A train rumbled through town, the mournful sound of the whistle trailing off into the distance. The room was growing dim, and Rachel felt her spirits fall.

"It doesn't sound like the best of circumstances for a marriage," said Mrs. Avery.

"It probably wasn't. I used to pride myself on my level-headed judgment, but I'm a little humbler now. Anyway, I wanted to thank you. There aren't many teachers you can say really changed your life, but you changed mine."

The look on Mrs. Avery's face was faintly alarmed. "Oh, dear. For the better, I hope."

"You showed me what was out there. All the rest is what I made of it."

Mrs. Avery brushed a wisp of hair from her eyes and tucked it behind her ear. "Honey, you had a dream and went and chased it. That's more than a lot of people can say. You'll always have Paris, if you'll pardon the cliché."

Rachel forced a smile, teetering suddenly on the brink of a bottomless desolation. Looking at the children in the photos on the piano, she opened her mouth to say she would trade Paris and all the rest for a living room full of pictures, but she thought better of it.

Rachel had meant to bring home a half gallon of milk but forgotten to stop in Warrensburg. Swanson's General Store in Ontario was gone, but the gas station out on the highway now had a minimart attached.

The woman behind the register turned out to be Debby Mays, who had been a freshman when Rachel was a senior, and while Rachel had been manning far-flung outposts of the U.S. government, Debby had been raising children. "I told Amber not to make the same mistake I did. Go and get some schooling, make something of yourself before you start having babies. But she didn't listen." Debby shrugged and drew on her cigarette. "And I gotta say, the babies are cute. I love bein' a grandma."

Rachel smiled at her, though the thought of being a grandmother at thirty-nine depressed her. She was groping for a suitable pleasantry when the bell over the door jingled and a man walked in.

In truth Rachel might not have recognized him but for the hook; but the hook drew the eye just as it had when Rachel was a child, cowering behind her mother's skirts. "Hello, Mr. Thomas," she said.

He stopped in his tracks and stared, a sour-looking old man with wildly undisciplined eyebrows, a Harvester cap on his head and a brown corduroy jacket over old-fashioned engineer's overalls. In place of his right hand he had a two-pronged stainless steel hook. He peered at Rachel as if she had asked him for money.

"I'm Rachel Lindstrom," she said. "Jim Lindstrom's daughter."

It took him a moment but his seamed face finally contorted into what might have been a smile. "Why, sure. Little Rachel, I remember. You've been away a long time."

"I have. How's Ruth?"

The old man dug in a jacket pocket with his good hand. "She died in May."

Rachel gasped. "Oh, I'm so sorry."

"Well, she was seventy-six. I never thought she'd last that long."

Rachel stared at him, appalled. Recovering, she said, "I was very fond of your wife. She was my Sunday School teacher when I was little. And then later she gave me painting lessons. She was a wonderful teacher."

The old man shrugged. "I liked her, too. Ten dollars on pump three out there," he said to Debby, sliding a bill across the counter. "So where you been, little Rachel?" His voice was deep but rough, like the sound of an empty oil drum being dragged across gravel.

Coolly now, Rachel said, "Overseas, mostly. I worked for the government for a long time, in the State Department."

He gave her a look from head to toe that would have been impertinent coming from a younger man. "Home for the holidays, huh?"

"That's right."

"You still painting pictures?"

"Oh, I haven't in years, I'm afraid. But I've always intended to get back to it some day."

"Well, maybe you can come out to the farm and take some of those pictures off my hands. House's full of 'em. I'm just gonna throw 'em out otherwise."

"What, your wife's paintings? Oh, don't do that. You don't want them?"

"There's a couple I'll keep. But there's more'n I know what to do with. And all the paints and brushes, too, if you want 'em. Come out and take a look and take what you want."

"I may do that. What would be a good time?"

"I'm most always home. You know where I live." He pushed out the door and hobbled toward a rusted old light-blue Ford pickup.

Debby said, "So you're friends with old Captain Hook, huh?"

Slightly dazed, Rachel said, "Not exactly. He and my father grew up together. I knew his wife mainly, from church. She was so sweet."

"I guess she had to be, to make up for him."

"Losing a hand might make me a little cranky, too. My father said it ruined Ed." Rachel shuddered. "God. Farmers and corn pickers."

Debby blew smoke, shaking her head. "Used to happen a lot. And they all knew better. But it was too much trouble to stop and shut the thing down, with all those acres of corn to get in. And ninety-nine times out of a hundred they got away with it, reaching in there to unjam it."

Rachel watched through the window as the pickup rolled out onto the highway with an excruciating grinding of gears. "Poor man."

"Well, that's no excuse." She shot Rachel a furtive look. "My mother always told me to steer clear of him, and I always told my daughters the same thing."

Rachel frowned. "I must have missed something. You know something I don't?"

"Well, maybe it was only rumors. I hate to bad-mouth a friend of your family. But people always said he was a little free with that good hand around women."

Rachel shook her head. "I never got that kind of vibe from him. But like I said, he and his wife were friends of ours, so maybe I just didn't see it."

"Or he was careful around you. Because of your dad." Debby shrugged. "All's I know is, there was always that rumor. You didn't want to let him get you alone in the back of the store or whatever. But what do I know?"

Rachel sighed, reaching for her milk. "More than I do, I'm sure. I'm just starting to realize how out of touch I've been."

"Well, that's what Christmas is for," said Debby, stabbing out the cigarette. "Coming home and reconnecting. You have a great holiday, now."

7 |||||||

Rachel hadn't been to a basketball game in a quarter of a century. "The last time I saw a basketball game you were playing in it," she said to Matt.

"The game's moved on some since then," he said. "They don't use peach baskets anymore."

They were in the truck and heading for Ontario. "Who are we playing?"

"Kalmar. Probably the best team we face this year. They got this Peterson kid who's a hell of a player. They say a couple of Division One schools have been recruiting him. Meanwhile all our good players graduated last year. We'll have our hands full."

Rachel had about as much interest in basketball as Matt had in French literature, but the thought of spending an evening alone at the house, brooding on bloody hatchets, failed marriages and vicious old men had made her an instant enthusiast. "Do we get to sit with the grown-ups tonight? I remember there was this strict segregation, adults on one side of the gym and kids on the other."

"Of course." Matt grinned. "Remember how Dad used to sit there with Henry Olson and yell at the refs?"

"Yeah, it was embarrassing."

"Well, when Billy was playing, he came out of the locker room after one game and wouldn't talk to me. Because I embarrassed him, yelling at the refs. I did it, what they warn you about. I went and turned into my father."

Rachel smiled, aware that a large part of what had driven her to Paris and Beirut and beyond was a determination not to turn into her mother. Suddenly she missed her mother with a pang so intense it made her catch her breath.

They were on the outskirts of town now. The lit-up windows of the gym, the biggest building in town, were visible across the railroad tracks. In a farm community social life was built around school events, and Rachel could see a file of cars pulling into the parking lot. She said, "I'm shy all of a sudden. It's like my debut in public or something. I'm going to be embarrassed walking in there."

"It'll be fun. People will be glad to see you."

"Especially the divorced farmers, huh?"

Matt laughed. "Don't worry, there's not that many."

Just enough to make me self-conscious, Rachel thought a few minutes later, walking into the gym, feeling a couple of hundred pairs of eyes locking onto her. The place hadn't changed much—maybe a few more conference championship banners hanging from the rafters—but the players going through their warm-up drills and the cheerleaders prancing at courtside and the students clambering on the bleachers were mere children. Rachel was amazed.

She quelled her desire to turn tail and run, instead following Matt along the foot of the bleachers. She heard her name called and she recognized Ann Gerard, twenty-five years older and twenty-five pounds heavier but still wearing her hair in a basic bob with bangs, unchanged. Rachel waved and moved on. Matt was already heading up an aisle toward a group of men sitting together, Dan Olson among them. Here we go, she thought.

"You don't have to sit with us," Matt said when she caught up. "All we're gonna do is bitch about the officiating and second-guess the coach. You might want to go sit with the gals."

"Which gals would those be?" said Rachel, wishing bitterly she'd thought to ask Susan to meet her there. "I don't know any gals, I'm afraid."

"To hell with that," said Dan, grinning. "Sit here with us. This row's just a whole lot of ugly without you. Remember Phil?" He elbowed the man sitting next to him. Rachel remembered Phil, and beyond him Chuck and Joe and Darrel; they were all recognizable under the extra weight and the grayed hair and the lined faces, the jocks of twenty-five years ago transformed into the pillars of the community, farmers and business owners and county officials. Matt stepped aside to let her into the row, to sit next to Dan. There were greetings and some banter, and just as Phil took on a serious look and leaned toward her Dan said, "We'll try not to bore you too bad. If you get tired of us you can go sit with Janey Phillips over there. Remember her?" He pointed.

Grateful for the deflection, Rachel said, "Oh, my God. With the bleached hair? What happened to her? She was like, the mousiest little thing in high school."

"I guess she decided mousy wasn't working. She's done better as a blonde. Right, Phil?" Phil grunted. Dan said, "Phil narrowly escaped being her second husband."

"She's on her third now," said Phil.

Rachel smiled. "And is that Tommy Swanson I see walking in there?"

"It is. He and Linnea have five kids."

"Linnea Hanson? You're kidding me."

"Nope. She weighs about three hundred pounds now."

"God. She was so pretty, too. And is that . . . Is that Luci Seifert there, by the door?"

"Yup. You notice how all the guys kind of snap to attention when she walks in." The woman in question was a well-lacquered brunette with expensive hair and very tight jeans, tottering a little on spike-heeled boots.

Rachel rolled her eyes. "She is . . . nicely preserved."

"If you say so. We don't notice things like that at our age, do we, fellas?"

This brought a rumble of half-hearted merriment from the row. "Nice heels," said Rachel.

"And they're still as round as ever," said Dan, and the laughter was full-throated this time.

"Goodness, aren't we catty tonight," said Rachel. "Who's the lucky beau?" The man trailing after Luci was thin and blond, with a face that showed some mileage and possibly traces of a few thousand drinks. He wore a long double-breasted coat with a fleece collar, and jeans disappearing into a pair of alligator cowboy boots that must have cost five hundred dollars.

Dan grunted and she glanced at him, sensing a drop in the temperature. "We don't talk about him."

"We just take potshots at him," said Phil, making a pistol with his hand and squeezing off an imaginary shot.

"Why, because he's sleeping with Luci and you're not?"

"Whoaaa," said Dan, leaning away from her. "Who's catty now?"

Sheepish, Rachel grinned. "Sorry. I'm just wondering why this guy's so unpopular."

"'Cause he's a fucking crook," said Phil.

"Watch your language," said Dan. To Rachel he said, "Because he's a miserable low-down piece of shit."

"OK," said Rachel. "I give up. What'd he do?"

Dan and Phil traded a look and Phil shrugged. Dan said, "That there's Mark McDonald. He's not real popular with the farmers around here because he swindled a lot of them out of their money a few years back."

"How'd he do that?"

"He used to run the elevator up at Kalmar. Come to find out, about ninety-nine or so, instead of running it like it should be run, he and his boss were playing the commodities market up in Chicago. With our money. When the Department of Agriculture shut 'em down they had something like a million bushels in positions on the market. That's way over the limit for an outfit like that. And they were losing the bets, and trying to cover up by getting in deeper. So of course they got shut down and went bust, and a lot of people around here lost a lot of fuckin' money."

"Me for one," said Phil. "Could have been a lot worse, without the insurance, but it was bad enough to ruin my damn year."

Rachel watched McDonald run a jaded eye over the crowd, apparently unconcerned about potshots real or imaginary, before settling onto the bleachers next to Luci. "Why isn't he in jail?"

"He was. He got out a year or so ago. What happened was, he pleaded guilty to destroying records and cut a deal to testify against his boss. So he only did two or three years, though what I heard was that the whole thing was his idea. I think the boss is still inside."

"Jeez, you'd think he'd be afraid to show his face around here."

"Yeah, wouldn't you? But he moved back here and got a job and he's been pretending to be an upstanding citizen. But I don't think anyone's gonna buy the bastard a drink anytime soon." Dan pointed with his chin. "Remember Bobby there?"

"Bobby Jacobs? Sure. I wouldn't have recognized him. He doesn't look like the years have been too kind."

"Well, he's had some knocks. His son got killed in a car wreck, along with his girlfriend, a couple of years ago, over near Rome."

"God, that's awful."

"You know how it is. Up in Chicago the teenagers shoot each other. Out here they roll their cars going a hundred miles an hour."

The game started, to Rachel's relief; the local gossip was too depressing. She found herself leaning toward Dan rather than Matt. "When did they start wearing bloomers?"

"That's the style now, big baggy shorts."

"My God, they're wearing girdles underneath."

"Those are called compression shorts."

"If you say so. I liked it better when they wore the little tight shorts."

"The hot pants look? That's good on women, not so good on men."

A fleeting image went through Rachel's mind of Danny Olson in tight basketball shorts, but she suppressed it. The score seesawed a bit, but then Kalmar started to pull away. She laughed at the men, so extravagant in their reactions. It occurred to her that in a culture that prized male stoicism, sports allowed men a rare excuse to suffer and exult. When her attention wandered from the game, she looked at people, recognizing a few more, amazed by the number she didn't. On the other side of the gym the students were an undifferentiated mass, other people's children.

This is what you do on a Friday night if you live here, she thought.

Halftime came. Matt and Dan and Rachel followed the crowd out into the hall, where people milled around the concession stands and spilled down the main hallway of the school. Rachel excused herself and made for the restroom, but before she got there she felt a hand on her arm and turned to find her cousin Steve smiling at her.

"Hey, Rachel. Heard you were home." Steve Ashford was the son of Rachel's father's sister; he had the Lindstrom family gene for height but was otherwise all Ashford: hair at the dark end of the color range, graying nicely at the temples, and a face that had benefited from maturity, crow's-feet suggesting a man who had mostly enjoyed the ride. His corduroy sport jacket was just a shade dressier than average for the crowd. They embraced, and Steve said, "Last I heard you were in Iraq getting shot at."

"Not really. The ride to and from the airport's always interesting, but I don't think they were aiming at me."

"Well, it sounds exciting. I haven't been shot at since deer season. You just home for the holidays, or you come to teach Matt and Billy how to wash behind their ears?"

"They seem to be taking regular baths. I'm home till I decide what to do next, I guess."

Steve frowned. "Did I hear you were married to an Arab guy?"

"You did. What you didn't hear about was the divorce." Rachel flashed a quick smile "How's your mom?"

"She's OK. We had to put her in a home, finally. The last time she fell she cracked a hip, and that was about it for being able to move around and keep house and stuff. She's still sharp as ever, though. You should go and see her. She always liked you."

"I'll do that." As a child Rachel had secretly admired her Aunt Helga's acid wit and slightly subversive worldview, so different from her own mother's steadfast uprightness. She noted the name of the nursing home and then asked the usual perfunctory questions about Steve's kids and finally made it to the restroom.

When she came out she found Matt and Dan drinking concession-stand coffee with a stumpy, thick-trunked man in a Harley-Davidson cap, some years past sixty. He had a gray beard that crawled around the contour of his jaw and a moustache that dived down around both sides of his mouth to join it, and he had a belly that was giving the buttons of his shirt all they could handle. His face had weathered a lot of years and his eyes were shrewd. Danny was listening to him with a somber look but gave Rachel a wink. He put a hand on her arm and said, "Carl, you remember Rachel Lindstrom, Matt's little sister?"

The man frowned at her and held out his hand. "Can't say I do, really, but pleased to meet you. Carl Holmes."

They shook hands. "Carl married my Aunt Peg," said Dan. "After she was widowed a few years back. We had no idea we were welcoming a Green Bay Packers fan into the family, but it's worked out OK 'cause we're tolerant, broad-minded Scandinavians."

Holmes said, "You gotta be pretty broad-minded to root for a team as shitty as the Chicago Bears."

"Rooting for losers builds character, Carl. But then I don't expect a Packer fan to know much about character."

"Yeah, our morals get corrupted by all those trips to the Super Bowl."

It was an old ritual; Rachel had been hearing it since childhood. Having discharged it, the men scanned the crowd, the smiles lingering on their faces. "Well, look at that," said Holmes. "Junior's got a new girlfriend."

They turned to look and saw a fortyish man with a completely shaven head and a tidy moustache passing by in the crowd, hand in hand with a not-unattractive blonde of a certain age. The man looked pleased with himself.

Rachel said, "My God, is that Barry Henderson? What happened to his hair?"

"Yeah, that's Junior," said Matt. "Believe me, the chrome dome is an improvement over the comb-over."

"Since when do you call him Junior?"

"Since he took over the bank. His old man keeled over with a coronary about five, six years ago. And Barry instantly became Junior."

"And proceeded to carry on the old man's tradition of screwing the little guy," said Holmes.

Dan grinned at him. "Now, Carl. Bankers have to make some tough calls. You have to understand the business."

"I understand the business. Foreclose on the little guy and let the big-time operators slide, year after year."

"It's called Too Big to Fail," said Matt. "That's the way the government operates, too."

Holmes made a whiffing sound of disgust. "Well, it ain't right."

"I think we're all agreed on that," said Dan. His gaze was wandering. "Well, I guess I'll go and see if our boys can figure out what that hoop's doing up there on the wall in the second half." He slapped Holmes on the shoulder. "See you around, Carl."

"You get your butt over to the house and see your aunt, son."

"I'll do that, I promise."

Rachel followed Dan and Matt back toward the gym, then veered off to bend over a drinking fountain. When she straightened up she found herself face to face with Roger Black.

8 |||||||

"Hello, Rachel." He was out of uniform tonight, wearing a suede jacket open over a plaid flannel shirt; he looked freshly combed and shaved and smelled faintly of cologne. He smiled his crooked smile, and Rachel thought what a pity it was that some people were given, through no fault of their own, features that were just enough out of kilter to repel rather than attract.

His eyes at least are kind, she thought. "Off duty tonight?"

"Well, I worked today. I been on days for a couple of years now. Didn't expect to see you here."

"It was kind of a last-minute impulse. I decided it was a good opportunity to see people."

"Yeah, this is about it for night life around here." The crowd was starting to flow back toward the gym doors. "Where you sitting in there?"

Rachel's heart sank. "I'm with Matt and Dan and some other guys."

"Would there be room for one more?"

Rachel opened her mouth to say I'm afraid not, but she couldn't do it. "I'm sure we can make room."

"Would you mind if I joined you?"

"Not at all." She was already moving, thinking: This is going to be priceless.

Dan's coterie had retaken their seats. When Rachel came up the aisle with Roger trailing her, they fell silent, watching them climb. "It's the law," said Dan. "What'd we do, Officer?"

"I'm off duty," said Roger. "You could light up a pipeful of meth and I wouldn't care. Can I sit here?"

The look that ran up and down the row told Rachel that Roger wasn't the most popular man in the county, but after some grumbling they all shifted a place to make room for him. Matt stepped out again to let Rachel and Roger in, winking at her as she went by. Rachel sat down with Dan to her right and Roger to her left just as the teams took the floor for the second half.

"Well, ain't this cozy?" said Dan. "How you been, Roger?"

"Busy. Three cars per shift to cover the whole county, and with the harvest over, too many idle hands. Today I had a domestic down near Bates City and then had to haul ass up to Anderson to chase down a drunk waving a gun. Then the paperwork, once we got him back to Warrensburg and locked up. More of the same tomorrow, no doubt."

"Well, cheer up, buddy. Time to leave the job at the office."

"You try looking at the things I deal with every day. Accidents, suicides, guys beating on their wives. You'd be depressed, too."

After an awkward second or two Dan reached across Rachel to slap Roger on the knee. "You're a fun guy to be with, you know that, Roger?"

Roger ducked his head, looking sheepish. "Sorry. Don't mean to bring anyone down. You like basketball, Rachel?"

As a gambit it was lame, but she grabbed for it. "Sure. Makes more sense than football. Put the ball in the basket. I can understand that."

"There's more to it than that. There's strategy and stuff."

Dan leaned forward to peer at Roger. "I want to hear you explain what a matchup zone is."

Roger grinned, knowing he was caught. "Hell, you were the basketball star. *You* explain it."

"Damned if I know. In my day all we had was Coach Hendricks. His idea of strategy was 'Follow your shot, dammit!'"

Roger said, "My dad never let me go out for sports. Too many chores."

Dan laughed. "Well, somebody has to do the work in this world. I guess you got elected."

With a studied casualness, eyes on the game, Roger said, "I did have the Grand Champion Single Barrow at the Dearborn County Fair one year. I guess that was what I did instead of sports."

I am forty-three years old, Rachel thought, and I am sitting at a high school basketball game with two guys competing for my attention. "Look at those fancy sneakers," she said, silencing them both.

Things did not improve for the home team despite a brief surge in the third quarter. Dan split his attention between Rachel and the guys to his right, while after a few banalities directed at Rachel, Roger eventually drifted into conversation with Matt. By the start of the fourth quarter Rachel was stifling yawns, and with five minutes left in the game and the home team losing by fifteen, the gym started to empty.

"We got a tradition," Dan said, reaching for his coat. "After basketball games. We go to the Outback in Warrensburg and sit around and eat and congratulate ourselves on how much smarter than the coach we are. Oh, and we drink a little, too. Usually it's just guys, but we're willing to make an exception for you. You're coming, right, Matt?"

"Sure." Matt stood looking down at Rachel. "Coming along?"

This was another thing Rachel had thought she was done with: having to rapidly assess the social consequences of simple yes and no answers. She could see Roger wouldn't be included in the invitation unless she insisted, and she didn't want any hurt feelings, but she didn't want to be in the middle of another two hours of sparring between suitors, either. "Actually, I'm kind of tired." She turned to Matt. "Can you drop me at home?"

He frowned. "It's a little out of the way."

"I can run you home," said Roger.

Take that, Danny Olson, Rachel thought. She smiled at Roger and said, "Oh, that's so nice of you. Thanks."

They made their good-byes in the parking lot. The look on Dan's face was amused. "You keep your hands to yourself now, Roger," he said. His posse snickered, the cool guys laughing at the doofus.

"I got a feeling Rachel can defend herself OK," said Roger.

"Don't make me slap you again," Rachel said, playing along. Everyone laughed and she climbed into the passenger seat of Roger's Explorer.

For the first couple of minutes they were silent, both of them laboring fiercely to find an opening. "You go to all the games?" Rachel said finally.

"Most of 'em. Not a lot else to do around here."

Tell me about it, Rachel thought. "You ever think about moving, going somewhere else?"

Roger drove for a while before answering, steering smoothly with a hand resting loosely on the bottom of the wheel. "Thought about it. Not sure I got the courage."

"Courage? Roger, you're the one who faces down drunks with guns. I wouldn't think courage is the problem with you."

"Well, there's courage and there's courage. Drunks with guns I can handle." He chuckled, a dry breathless sound. "It's talking to regular people that makes me sweat. You know what I went through just to get up the courage to ask you to the prom that time?"

Please, thought Rachel. Don't let this turn into a declaration of undying passion. "Well, you managed it."

"Yeah, I did. I managed to get married, too, somehow. Not sure how I did it, and it didn't last, but at least I can say I did it. Anyway, I always thought what you did was pretty damn impressive. Musta took guts to go off and live in foreign places like that."

"I didn't feel brave, really. Just curious. I just kept running after things that interested me."

Roger seemed to consider that for a time before saying, "Well, we're glad to have you home."

"I don't know that I'm staying, Roger. I'm just catching my breath."

"So where you going next?"

"I don't know. Ask me in a week or two."

Another silence followed. As he turned onto the road that led to the Lindstroms', Roger said, "See if you can get that nephew of yours curious about something while you're here. Now there's a kid that really needs to get the hell out of Dearborn County."

"Billy? Yeah, I don't get the impression he's a very happy boy."

"No, he's not. He's a smart boy, but he's confused."

Roger slowed, approaching the driveway. As he made the turn Rachel said, "Level with me, Roger. I've heard the rumors about Billy. How much trouble has he gotten into?"

Roger rolled to a stop near the back door, and put the car into park. "Not that much, really," he said. "So far. I've stopped him for speeding. One time he was drunk and disorderly and wound up in the tank." He hesitated, examining a fingernail. "And he was at a party last year where a couple of kids never woke up after taking some bad drugs somebody passed around."

"Oh, my God."

"We never could prove who brought the drugs. Some said Billy had a hand in it, but I'm not sure. I think it was his asshole friends, if you'll pardon the expression. He's got a couple of buddies who've done time, and they didn't exactly come out reformed. Billy's a lot better than the company he's been keeping."

"That's so scary. But I don't know if I have any influence at all."

"Billy just needs to figure out what he wants to do with his life and go do it." Roger turned his head to look at her in the dim light coming through the windshield. "If you can help him figure that out, you'll be doing a good thing."

Rachel pulled on the handle to open the door. "I'll get right on it," she said. "As soon as I figure it out for myself."

The purring of the telephone woke Rachel up. It took her a second to focus: She had dozed off in front of the TV. She groped for the remote to mute it, then fumbled with the wireless phone to answer it. "Did you have to slap him?" said Matt in her ear.

It took her a second to think what he was talking about, and then she was irritated. "You and all your friends have overheated imaginations."

"Relax, will you? I'm joking with you. Did I wake you up?"

"I was just watching TV. Where are you?"

"Just leaving Warrensburg. We ran a little late and I didn't want you to worry."

"You didn't drink too much, I hope."

"Just the usual amount. Don't worry, the highway's pretty straight right here."

"Well, be careful. Listen, Matt."

"What?"

"I'm not in the market for a boyfriend. See if you can put the word out, will you?"

There was nothing but static in her ear for a few seconds, and then he said, "I'm sorry, sis."

She could hear the contrition in his voice. "Maybe I shouldn't be so touchy. How was dinner?"

"The usual. Good for some laughs. We didn't spend the whole time talking about you, I promise."

"I'm sorry, Matt. Thanks for checking in."

"Billy home?"

"No sign of him. Get off the phone and drive."

"You got it. See you in a few minutes."

Rachel sat with the dead phone in her hand, drowsy and dislocated. After a time she rose and put on her coat and went outside and stood in the dark beneath a breathtaking sky, shielded from the barn-yard light by the house, looking at the far-flung stars. I have no place in this world, she thought.

Beirut was just a fading dream, sunlit and turbulent, a pain in her heart. There weren't going to be any children, spoiled or otherwise. Paris was simply remote, a stage for the brave, hungry girl she had been a long time ago. And Washington had never been anything more than the company town, and she was done with that company.

Which left this. Could I live here again? Rachel asked herself. People do. They make their lives here and raise families and are happy. I could come home again. I could teach school and have time to write those books and make my way back into this life I left and maybe even-tually find somebody nice who would rescue me from being a spinster, growing old with her widowed brother in the house they grew up in.

Sound carries a long way in cold air, and Rachel stood listening to the faint scattered disturbances of the night. The clanking of distant hog feeders, a car burning rubber away from an intersection somewhere down the road, the rumble of a far-off train. Rachel frowned, fixing on an angry grating sound just audible somewhere, she thought, to the southeast.

She identified it at last and turned to go back to the house, wonder-ing who on earth was out at midnight using a chainsaw.

9 |||||||

Greenview Terrace did offer a view of green slats in a chain-link fence along the back of the parking lot; in addition Rachel estimated that the concrete walkway along the front of the building might just qualify as a terrace. Beyond its compliance with the truth-in-advertising statutes, however, Rachel did not find much to recommend the institution in which her seventy-eight-year-old aunt had come to rest.

The odor that pervaded the place was a delicate blend of over-cooked food, poor hygiene, chronic disease and inevitable decay, with a subtle undertone of pine-based cleaner. The hallways were starkly illuminated by fluorescent tubes and populated by shambling disheveled ancients supporting themselves on walkers, harried by attendants dressed like hospital personnel but with the dead-eyed stares of prison warders. The place made Rachel want to cry.

"I do miss a good home-cooked meal," her Aunt Helga said, looking out the window at the fence. "The food here isn't fit to give to the hogs." Helga's hair was cobweb-white and imperfectly subjugated with bobby pins placed at random; arthritis, osteoporosis and myriad unguessable afflictions had reduced her to a frail collection of limbs in a chair. But the eyes were still bright and the voice, while cracked, still had breath behind it. Her room was crowded with pictures and knick-knacks but still looked like a hospital room.

"I'm sorry," said Rachel. "I can bring you something if you want."

Helga smiled. "It's not your fault, honey. You didn't put me in here."

"I just meant . . ." Rachel foundered. In truth she was appalled that her cousins had deposited their mother here, but then it was easy for her to pass judgment; she and Matt had been spared the tough calls by the simplifying expedient of death.

"You've been away, haven't you?" said Helga.

Rachel nodded. "I worked for the State Department. I lived overseas for a long time."

Helga raised a crooked index finger. "You told me. I remember now. My memory's going, you'll have to be patient. You were married, I seem to recall."

"I'm divorced now. He was Lebanese."

"And a very handsome fellow. Your mother showed me the pictures."

Rachel smiled. "That's why I fell for him, I suppose."

"You're not the first gal who ever did that." Helga shook her head once, a slow uncertain gesture. "Your Uncle Clay was a handsome fellow, oh about sixty years ago."

"Steve looks just like him."

"Yes, he got his father's looks. And his father's land. Where he got the expensive tastes, I don't know."

"Steve seems to have done pretty well for himself."

"Oh, he's made himself a lot of money. I think he needed to, to keep that wife of his in the style she was accustomed to."

"I don't really know her."

A couple of seconds went by. "Must have been the government that taught you to be diplomatic like that."

Rachel laughed. "It's the truth. I never had a chance to get to know Becky. I missed out on a lot, being gone."

"We were all so proud of you. Your mother would pass your letters around. When something would come on TV about the Middle East we'd all wonder if you were in the middle of it. You should have seen the way your father talked about you. I swear, his chest would swell up. 'My daughter's in the State Department, and she says the PLO's finished.' And people would be so impressed."

"I wasn't a big deal at all. If I had any opinion about the PLO, it wasn't particularly authoritative."

Rachel sat and watched her aunt's gaze wander. Eventually her eyes came back to Rachel's and she said, "And now you've come home. For good?"

"I don't know, Aunt Helga. For the holidays, anyway. And then we'll see."

"Did Matt tell you to come home?"

Irked, Rachel opened her mouth to tell her aunt things didn't work that way anymore, not in her family. She hesitated and said, "No. It was my decision. It was time."

"Well, it's a good thing you're here. That house could use a woman."

"They just need a good nutritionist."

"Such a shame, Matt's wife. To do that, right there in her home. At least he found her, and not the boy."

"I don't know if it was any easier for Matt."

"Better him than the boy. Poor Esther Johnson was never the same after she found her father hanging in the barn. That was before your time, I guess."

"Esther's father killed himself? How awful. I never knew that."

"People do. And they never consider that somebody's got to find them and deal with the consequences."

"I think if you're severely depressed you may have trouble thinking through the consequences."

"Depressed? My heavens, girl. All it is is what they used to call feeling sorry for yourself. They've given it a fancy name, and now if you feel sorry for yourself long enough you get to go to the doctor and get pills. You think I've never felt bad? I used to stand at the sink washing dishes and looking out the window at the fields and thinking all I would ever have to look forward to in my life was more dishes to do and nothing but beans and corn to look at for the whole rest of my life. But you keep getting up in the morning and sooner or later it passes. That girl just didn't have the faith to wait for it to pass."

And I don't either, thought Rachel. "Not everybody's as strong as you are."

"That boy's gone off the rails, too. My Lord, that hair. And running around with a bad crowd. All that started after his mother killed herself."

In the silence that followed Rachel stared out the window and wondered about train schedules. With any luck she could be on a jet at O'Hare within twenty-four hours, taking off for some place that had not yet been soured by death and failure.

"It's good you've come home," said Helga. "The family needs you."

"I don't know about that."

"Oh, yes they do. And you need them, too. You're still grieving."

"It shows, does it?"

"Honey, you look so sad it makes *me* want to cry. You're grieving for your husband, aren't you?"

Rachel could not speak. She nodded, looking out the window, determined not to break down.

"And you're doing the grieving for your parents you didn't get to do because you were far away. You're going to have a hard time for a while, but then it'll get better. And you'll be glad you came home."

"Maybe," said Rachel after a few seconds had passed. "It's early yet."

It looked as if there were snow coming. In the west the sky looked like sheet steel. Rachel was suddenly anxious for a comforting fall of snow, something to brighten the dark earth, soften the hard edges, muffle the sharp sounds. She wanted a white Christmas, lighted windows glowing across the fields, her mother and father silhouetted in the doorway as she pulled up in the yard.

That's all gone, Rachel thought. You could have had that, but you left. She turned down the gravel road that led to Ed Thomas's farm.

After what she'd heard from Debby Mays the day before, this errand had a distinct whiff of being invited up to look at etchings. But Rachel remembered Ruth Thomas too fondly to let her husband pitch her life's work, however amateurish, into the trash. Kindly and patient, Ruth had taught her how to see line and color, how to wield pencil and brush. There had always been cookies at the end of the lesson and affection from a woman who had, inexplicably, no children of her own.

And Rachel could remember Ed Thomas with both his hands and her father's approval, and had always tried to make allowances for his misfortune.

She turned into the Thomases' drive, noting the peeling paint on the barn, a rusting harrow nestled in a patch of weeds, the general dilapidated look of the place. Since his accident nearly forty years before, Ed had been a semirecluse, renting out his land and watching the farmstead slowly deteriorate. The house needed paint as well, and had plastic tacked over the windows; the lightning rod on the roof had fallen and dangled over the eaves, unrepaired. Rachel pulled up under a bare maple and cut the ignition, steeling herself.

There was no vehicle in sight, and she was faintly relieved to think that Ed might not be home. She got out of the car and stood for a moment, listening. There were the usual sounds of vast openness, wind whistling faintly around edges of buildings, but there was something else as well, a scrabbling sound difficult to locate. A brief quiver of distaste shook her.

She quelled it and tried to locate the source. It seemed to be coming from beyond the barn, and she walked toward it. "Ed?"

Her call silenced the noise. She took a few steps and it began again, something rustling, scraping, dragging on the ground. She called out again as she drew near the corner of the barn, not quite as loudly.

She stopped in her tracks as the coyote came out from behind the barn. For an instant she was simply bewildered, thinking wildly that she must be prey to some strange form of déjà vu.

Clutched in its jaws the coyote held a human arm, bone and red meat showing obscenely where it had been severed from the shoulder. It might have taken Rachel a moment to recognize it had it not been for the shreds of cotton twill still wrapped around it and the hooked prosthesis still in place where the hand had once been.

"I heard it. I heard it happening." Rachel had finally stopped trembling, but she felt cold, chilled to the core. Roger had left the cruiser idling and turned on the heater, but it wasn't helping. Outside the car, lights flashed in the dark like a carnival midway along the road to Ed Thomas's farm. Two more sheriffs' cars, an Illinois State Police cruiser, a useless ambulance and half a dozen unmarked cars were clustered at the entrance to the driveway.

Matt sat beside her on the backseat, his arm around her. Rachel wanted to be strong; she had kept a cool head in a crisis many times and she wasn't going to go all girly and hysterical in front of the men. But it was good to have her big brother's arm around her. As a local first responder Matt had been one of the first to show up. He had found Rachel at the intersection of the county hard road and the Thomases' road. That was as far as she'd gotten before she began to think clearly enough to stop and fumble for her cell phone. Matt had gone to look at the scene and come back white-faced to pull her into an embrace. Fifteen minutes after that, Roger had come tearing up from the south, his lights visible two miles away and closing fast, skidding to a halt a few feet from them.

Now Roger twisted to look at her over the seat. "When?"

"Last night. I heard it. I went outside for some fresh air and I heard the saw going, off in the distance. I didn't think anything of it. I just thought somebody was cutting firewood or something. I should have done something."

"Like what?" said Matt. "Could you tell where it was coming from?"

"No. I don't know. I don't know what I should have done."

The feeble dome light gave Roger's long-jawed homeliness a touch of the sinister. "About what time was that?"

"Near midnight, I think."

"Make sure you tell the detectives."

"I know I saw it, too, but I can't remember it," she said. "It's like I erased the image."

Matt and Roger traded a look. Rachel said, "I know I walked around the corner of the barn. I remember exactly what I thought. I thought, Ed is hurt, Ed needs help. When there's an accident you have to help. I didn't want to walk around the corner of the barn, but I knew I had to. So I did. But I don't have any visual memory of what I saw there."

Roger peered at her and then his eyes flicked to meet Matt's and he said, "Traumatic amnesia. It's been known to happen."

It's not fair, Rachel thought. I should have been safe here. "It happened to me once before," she said.

That got their attention. "When was that?" said Roger.

"When I was in Iraq. I saw a family that had been killed in their car at a checkpoint. The father misunderstood or panicked or whatever and didn't stop in time. The soldier who killed them was standing off to the side, crying. I looked into the car and saw them all lying there shot to pieces, the parents and three little kids, but when I got back to the base the image was gone. It didn't come back to me until about three weeks later when I woke up with it in the middle of the night."

In the silence Matt squeezed her shoulder. Roger said, "So this might come back to you, too."

"I guess I have that to look forward to, yes." Rachel stared at the flashing lights. "Poor Ed. Oh, God, poor man."

"He was dead before he got cut up, if it helps."

That hung in the air for a while and then Rachel said, "How do you know?"

"Well, one, there'd have been more blood if he was still alive. Plus, I heard one of the investigators say there was blunt trauma to the head. The guy . . ." Roger paused.

"That's OK. You don't have to draw me a picture. I keep feeling like I'm going to be sick. I wish I could just throw up. I think I'd feel better."

"Roger, can I take her home?"

"Not till the detectives clear it, I'm afraid. I'm sorry you have to wait around. They like to take their time. Rachel, if you really feel sick, I can take you into Warrensburg to St. Mary's, and they can come and chase you down there."

"No. I'll be all right."

Roger nodded. "Not too many people would have had the presence of mind to stay here and make the call. That took guts."

"It wasn't guts. It was just paralysis. If I'd been thinking clearly there's no way I would have sat here waiting for you. It's the crazy guy, isn't it?"

Roger turned to look out through the windshield. "Seems like a good guess."

"And he could be still around. He could be right there in the house, for example."

"I think they checked that right away."

"But he's around here somewhere."

Roger sat unmoving for a long moment. "We'll get him."

Headlights approached from the opposite direction. Roger got out of the cruiser and waved a flashlight beam back and forth across the road, signaling halt. As the van pulled up in the cruiser's headlights Rachel saw a satellite dish on top, the logo of a Quad Cities TV station on the side. "That was fast," she said.

"The buzzards are circling," said Matt, pulling her closer. "They'll be all over us before we know it."

10 |||||||

Rachel stood looking through the window in the back door. The light from the halogen lamp high on the pole barely reached the shed, the barn, the grain bins, all the familiar structures now made sinister in the dark. A man could hide in there, Rachel thought. He could be out there right now.

"Come have some hot chocolate, honey," said Karen Larson behind her.

Rachel turned. Matt had phoned Karen and Clyde Larson to give them the news, and they had insisted on driving the half mile down the road to join Rachel and Matt, circling the wagons. Nobody knew where Billy was.

Clyde Larson was one of those who was going to go on farming until he dropped dead; he didn't need the money but he didn't know what else to do with himself. He had married off three daughters, two to men with no interest in farming and one with land of his own; Clyde had sold off a lot of his acreage but was hanging on to the original homestead that bordered the Lindstroms'. He was past seventy and moving a little slower, but he could still climb up on the tractor. Karen had been close to Rachel's mother and had been at her bedside in Peoria when she died. She was a long-limbed slender woman, bent and gray now, with knowing eyes behind thick glasses.

"Thank you." Rachel took the mug from Karen and held it to her breast with both hands. "I feel like I'll never be warm again."

"Oh, sweetie. To have to see a thing like that." The horror showed in Karen's face.

Something dark and frightening flared briefly in Rachel's mind, something she fled from quickly. "There are people who have to deal with things like this for a living." Rachel thought of the doctors in Baghdad, sorting the living from the dead in blood-slick hospital corridors.

They settled at the kitchen table. From the living room came the low mumble of the television and the muttered comments of the men, surfing the channels for news. Rachel sipped the hot chocolate. "Who could do that? Who could do that to another human being?"

"A sick person. You would have to be, wouldn't you?"

"I suppose so. I *hope* so."

"I heard he did the same thing to his family. Can you imagine?"

I can now, Rachel thought. Out loud she said, "Ed's truck was missing. The detectives think this Ryle must have taken it. They said every cop in Illinois and Iowa will be looking out for it tonight."

"They'll catch him."

"But to think, he was around here, so close, yesterday, last night. Where was he hiding?"

"There are a lot of empty barns around here."

Clyde and Matt came in from the living room. "You got something to protect yourself with, right?" Clyde was saying.

Matt put a beer bottle in the sink. He turned, leaned back against the counter and folded his arms. "I got rid of my guns after Margie killed herself. I swore I would never have a gun in this house again."

Clyde gave him a long grave look. "I can understand that, son. But the circumstances are kind of special, don't you think? And there's other people here you need to protect. I'll lend you my .38 if you want. Or a shotgun. Take your pick."

Matt looked at Rachel. "You want Clyde to bring over a gun? You want to take charge of it?"

Rachel couldn't read what was in his face; it was perfectly impassive. "It's your house. Your rules. I'll do whatever you say."

Matt looked at Clyde. "I think we'll lock the doors and hope for the best. But I appreciate the offer."

Clyde shrugged. "I'm not gonna insist. Let's just hope this joker's in jail by morning. If you need help, pick up the phone and I can be here in five minutes."

"Thanks, Clyde."

"Are you going to be all right, Rachel, honey?" Karen put her hand on Rachel's shoulder.

Rachel smiled at her and patted her hand. She opened her mouth to say yes, but suddenly it was all she could do not to scream at the top of her lungs.

Karen frowned. "What's wrong with me? You poor thing." She looked at Matt. "I'll be staying the night, if you don't mind, Matt."

"OK, sure. We got plenty of beds."

"Thank you," whispered Rachel, tears beginning to come. "Thank you."

Susan came in the back door with a look of amazement on her face. "I didn't know there were that many cops in the state of Illinois. They're all over the roads."

"The more the better," said Rachel. "I wouldn't mind seeing a few tanks."

"Come here." Susan held out her arms. For a long moment they swayed together in an embrace. "How are you feeling?"

"Sick. I feel sick. The best I can describe it is like a moral nausea. The whole world is spoiled."

Susan held her at arm's length. "You look like you haven't slept in about three days."

"I finally dropped off about six, for about half an hour. And this morning we had the police in again. And a couple of reporters. Matt let the cops in and sent the reporters packing."

"Do the police have any leads?"

"They're not saying. They just wanted to hear what I had to say, again. I've been through it with the sheriff's department and the State Police. I'm about ready to get my story printed up on cards I can just hand out."

"I won't ask you to go through it again, then," Susan said, gallantly.

Rachel sighed and turned away, making for the sink. "I found the body. He was cut up with a chainsaw. I saw it but I don't remember it, have no visual memory, I mean. Roger says it's traumatic amnesia. The only thing I'm really afraid of is that I'll remember it suddenly."

There was a shocked silence behind her as she rinsed dishes. When Rachel turned again, Susan had sunk onto a chair and was sitting with a hand over her mouth. "Oh, Rachel," she breathed.

"Yeah." Rachel dried her hands. "You know what I really need? I need to get out of the house."

Susan was still reeling from the horror, but she managed to get her feet back on solid ground and drew a deep breath and said, "All right." Suddenly she was brisk again, the organizer. "You can come with me on my interview."

"What interview?"

"For the living memory project. The County Historical Society commissioned an oral history, based on old folks' reminiscences. Somebody realized the Great Generation is dying off. So they dreamed up this book project and like an idiot I said I'd be in charge of it."

"Sounds like fun."

"It is, mostly. But it turned into a lot of work. You have to transcribe all the interviews, and that's a pain. If you wanted to get involved I would be thrilled. It's a lot of unpaid labor."

"Sure. I could use something to do."

"Great. I was going to talk to the Petersons over in Bremen today. Remember Cecilia? Graduated a few classes ahead of us? These are her parents. They're in their eighties and living in town, and old Wally just about wept with gratitude on the phone. I think he's desperate for somebody to talk to besides the wife."

Rachel stripped off the apron. "Let's go."

It was a relief to be outside. The snow had held off, but a hard gray sky was still clamped down over everything, and a steady insidious wind had dragged the wind chill down below freezing. Rachel found Matt in the barn and told him what the plan was. He nodded, gazing at the chalked layout of his milking setup. "Be careful. You might want to be home by dark."

"I'll be fine. Susan says there are cops everywhere."

"Don't pick up any hitchhikers." He finally looked at her. "You OK? Really?"

"I'm OK. I spent three years in Iraq, remember? I've got some bounce-back in me." It was bravado, but Rachel had had her moment of weakness and wasn't going to show it again.

Matt nodded. "I mean it about being careful. He's out there somewhere."

"You be careful, then. You're the one who's going to be alone here."

"I'm aware," he said.

"See you, then." She turned and went.

In the car Susan had the heater on and the radio tuned to a Chicago oldies station. "We can listen to the news if you want."

"Are you kidding? That's the last thing I want to hear. Turn it up, I like this song." Out in the open now, the car moving, Rachel found herself getting jittery, light-headed. In the distance, about where Ed's place would be, a helicopter hovered.

At a crossroads they passed a parked sheriff's car. The driver was a deputy they didn't recognize, but they waved. "That's reassuring," said Susan.

"They can't have every intersection staked out," said Rachel. "There aren't that many cops. That must mean they think he's close."

The temperature seemed to drop a couple of degrees. "Maybe they'll catch him today."

"That would be good."

They went a mile or two in silence, Rachel feeling for the positive memories associated with the places they passed, trying to banish the air of oppression and menace. She was looking at the isolated farmsteads, the occasional clusters of trees, the great distances. *There are a lot of empty barns around here*, she remembered Karen Larson saying. "Remember when we used to leave our doors unlocked?"

"Different days. Crime was something that happened in Chicago."

"I never felt unsafe out here. Never. Now . . . I'm thinking we're a long way from help if something goes wrong."

"There's help." A State Police patrol car crossed the road at the next intersection, a few hundred yards ahead. "They'll catch him. It's getting colder. Where's he going to hide?"

The answer came to Rachel instantly and she opened her mouth to voice it, but stopped herself because it made her shudder.

Anywhere somebody answers the door, she thought.

Wally Peterson had sold the farm and moved into a brick bungalow in Bremen, a hamlet of four hundred or so souls which sat at the point where U.S. 34 and the BNSF railroad line diverged. Urbanization was thin in towns like this, and the street Wally's house sat on was a country road fifty yards east of his front door.

"I can see corn out the back window, so I feel like I'm still living in the country. But I don't have to pick the damn stuff anymore." Wally still had both his hands but had lost most of his hair somewhere along the way; he combed a few strands over his shining dome every morning in valiant futility.

Susan had set up a little digital voice recorder on the coffee table in front of Wally and his wife, Janet, a plump little woman with tight white curls that looked like lambs' fleece. Janet had let Wally do most of the talking despite Susan's efforts to draw her in, apparently content to sit at the end of the couch watching her husband with reptilian patience and striking like a cobra when he got a name or a date wrong. "It wasn't 1946, it was forty-eight. You were still in the army in 1946." The look that accompanied the corrections was carefully blank, the rolling of the eyes artfully implied. To Rachel the whole thing looked like a long-settled constitutional distribution of power.

The Thomas murder had monopolized the first ten minutes of the encounter, but Rachel had managed to steer the conversation away from it before her central role had emerged, merely acknowledging Wally's probing remark that it had happened "over your way." When Susan had finally focused minds on the task at hand, Rachel had sat queasily trying to follow, wondering how long it would take her to feel right.

"We were living on the old Berger place north of Regina at the time," Wally was saying. "I rented the house from Old Man Berger for ten dollars a month and that was too much. He hadn't done nothing to it since his grandpa built the place after the Civil War. We had an outhouse and a pump. Wasn't no running water. We had electricity for lights but no telephone. Didn't get a phone till sometime in the fifties."

"Fifty-two," his wife cut in. "When Bobby came along. My oldest. I told Wally, 'I'm not sitting out here in the middle of nowhere with a baby to take care of and no way to talk to anybody. I'll lose my mind.'"

"And you did anyway," said Wally, winking at Susan.

Janet shot him a fierce look. "Well, it's lonely out in the country. You try spending your whole day with nobody to talk to. Half the farm wives out here are a little crazy."

That fell flat, the company possibly recalling Rachel's deceased sister-in-law. Wally said, "Not like this Ryle boy, though. There was something wrong with that boy from the start. You could see it." He shook his head.

Everyone just stared at him. "You knew him?" Susan said.

"Well, I think so. How many Otis Ryles could there be? I recognized the name when it came on the news. He lived with his grandma in Regina when he was a boy. Bessie Ryle. The Ryles were kind of a ne'er-do-well family. Bessie lived in a tumble-down kind of a place and cleaned other people's houses to make a living. Bessie's boy, I think his name was Otis, too, had gone out west sometime in the fifties, and then when he came back he brought a wife and a little boy with him. I don't know the whole story, but apparently she turned out to be a tramp and after a few years she ran off and left him with the boy. Well, that didn't last too long. Otis took off, too, after a while, just dumped the boy with Grandma and disappeared. I guess Bessie did what she could, but from what I heard he was a real stinker even when he was little. Bessie couldn't really do nothing with him and then she gave him up. The state came and got him and we never heard no more about him."

Susan and Rachel traded a look. Rachel turned to Wally and said, "Do a lot of people know that? That he grew up here?"

The old man shrugged. "If you're old enough you might know. But that was a long time ago."

"I think maybe you should talk to the police. They'll want to know that he has connections around here."

"Oh, I don't think he has what you'd call connections. He hasn't been around here for forty years. And Bessie's long gone."

"Even so. I think they'll want to know."

Wally shrugged. "I don't think anybody's going to be hiding him, if that's what you're thinking."

"I'm not saying that. But if he lived here, even a long time ago, that could determine where he looks for shelter, that kind of thing. I think it's something the police should know. Would you talk to them?"

Wally laughed, flapping a hand. "Sure, if they want. But I don't know how much I can tell them."

There was an uncomfortable pause. Rachel was framing an excuse to get Susan moving out the door when Janet spoke. "He was a mean little boy. I remember people telling me about him. He caught a rabbit once and poured gasoline on it and set it on fire, just to watch it run."

"Oh, God." Susan made a face. Rachel looked at the floor, lips pressed tight.

"Well, he didn't have much of a start in life," Wally said. "I remember someone saying the boy got whipped a lot. I think Bessie kind of took her bad luck out on him."

So much cruelty, thought Rachel, who had seen Arab children whipped in the street. She said, "I remember reading somewhere that severe abuse of a child, at a certain point, around six or so, produces what they call the 'malevolent transformation,' and after that the child is lost. That phrase just kind of haunted me. 'The malevolent transformation.'"

The room fell silent, everyone staring at Rachel. "That's awful," Susan said finally.

Wally cleared his throat. "Well, that's what happened to Otis Ryle. What you said there. They lost him."

11 |||||||

"We actually knew that," Roger said. "A few people have told us about it. People in Regina remember Ryle. But as far as we know he never came back to the area after he went into state guardianship in 1968. Until they brought him to the psych unit here in ninety-nine."

"Where the hell was he for thirty years?" said Matt. He was nursing a beer. Roger had declined one because he was on duty. Rachel had made herself a cup of tea. Outside, the first snowflakes were swirling on the wind.

"All over the state," said Roger. "Foster care in Peoria, Kankakee, Decatur. Then the juvenile home up in St. Charles, after he attacked his foster mother with a hammer."

Matt made a noise of disgust. Rachel said, "I'm sure that did him a lot of good. I mean, if this was a disturbed child, an institution for juvenile delinquents doesn't sound like the best place to get help."

Roger shrugged. "There's more kids that need help than there are resources to help them."

Matt said, "What do you do with a kid that attacks a woman with a hammer, anyway? It was probably too late to fix him by then."

Roger nodded. "Most likely. This was a pretty disturbed individual. I looked at his file from the psych unit. Reported distant and out of touch with reality as a child, bullied by other kids, sometimes violent in response."

Matt said, "But he wound up married. Who marries a guy like that?"

"Who knows? The wife's not around to ask anymore. When he got out of St. Charles he went to Chicago, and he was their headache for a while. He did a term in Pontiac for assault in the late seventies. But then he seemed to settle down. At least as far as we can tell. He got married and had kids, moved back downstate to Bloomington and got a job. And then one day he snapped. Killed the wife and kids, cut 'em up and ate 'em." Roger looked and sounded tired, slumped at the end of the table.

Rachel felt something black and viscous and heavy settling on her heart. She had come halfway around the world fleeing this dread, and now it was here.

"So where's he hiding?" said Matt.

Roger sighed and ran a hand over his face. "Brother, I wish I knew. We're turning the county upside down. We think he took Ed Thomas's truck, and so we're looking for that. We're checking out every barn, shed and corn crib and abandoned house between Moline and Peoria. But there's a lot of them, and not many of us. We're asking anyone who might know Ryle or have an idea where he'd hide to contact us. We're asking folks to keep their eyes open and their doors locked."

Rachel watched snowflakes dance just beyond the kitchen window. "If he took the truck, maybe he's far away. That's what I'd do, in his place. Just get on the highway and go. Maybe that's why there's no sign of him."

"Well, there's a bulletin out on him coast to coast. If that's what he's doing, somebody ought to pull him over before too long. We can hope." Wearily, Roger pushed away from the table and stood up. "Gotta run. We can hope, but we can't let our guard down. Take care, Rachel. Thanks for the call and keep your eyes open."

"Oh, yeah," she said. "From now on I'm sleeping with my eyes open."

Rachel was lying on her bed in a fetal position, wrapped in a blanket and trying desperately to recall images of sunnier climes and easier times, when she heard a vehicle pull up on the gravel outside. A minute later she heard Dan Olson's voice downstairs.

She gave it a minute or two before she threw off the blanket and went into the bathroom to wash her face and comb her hair. I don't care who it is, she said to herself in the mirror. I need the company.

When she came into the kitchen Matt and Dan were at the table, the beers open in front of them. The look Dan gave her had none of the usual levity in it. "How you doing, Rachel?"

"I'll live." She filled the kettle with water and lit the stove. Turning to face him with arms folded, she said, "I hope Matt gave you the story, because I'm tired of telling it."

Dan nodded. "I'm sorry you had to see it. Must have been a shock."

"So much of a shock that I can't remember it, actually. I guess that's a blessing, till it comes back to me, anyway."

"Jesus."

"It wasn't any fun. But I'll get over it."

"Yeah, you will. When I was a kid I saw my Uncle Rollie get crushed under the rear wheel of a John Deere Model B. I couldn't sleep for a week. It was the sound more than the sight that did it."

Rachel winced. "Oh, thanks for sharing that."

"But I got over it. So did he, by the way. He never walked too well after that, but he lived."

"I think this is a little different," said Matt.

Dan waved a hand. "Shit, I know. I'm sorry, Rachel. I'm just running off at the mouth. I don't know what to say. I'm freaked out. I mean, what the fuck? Is this the crazy guy? What the hell's going on here?"

"Roger says the detectives are starting with that assumption. But they're not ruling anything else out."

They all looked at that for a second. "Who else would it be?" said Matt.

"Old Ed didn't have too many friends," said Dan. "But I don't think anyone would have sliced him up with a chainsaw just because he was a liar and a cheat."

Matt gave him a sharp look. "What are you talking about?"

"I mean the way he screwed guys who rented his land."

Matt shrugged. "I heard a couple of things. Everyone grumbles about landlords."

Dan's frown deepened. "It happened to Pete Harris once. They had a handshake deal for Pete to plant eighty acres of his, down south of Ontario. A week later Ed calls Pete to tell him he's given them to somebody else because he was willing to pay him ten dollars an acre more. So much for the handshake."

Matt sat back on his chair with a sigh. "Yeah, I know he wasn't everyone's favorite neighbor. Hell, I'm not gonna apologize for him just because he and my old man were friends. But Jesus, that shouldn't happen to anybody."

"No, I'm not saying it should. I just . . . I don't know what I'm saying. Let's just hope they catch the fucker."

The three of them sank into a glum silence. Rachel made her tea and brought it to the table. "Did you know Otis Ryle lived in Regina when he was little?"

Dan peered at her. "Are you shitting me?"

"No. His grandmother raised him. Till the state took him, anyway. Her name was Bessie Ryle."

"Ryle. I don't know of any Ryles still around here."

"Me neither," said Matt. "But you gotta know the police are gonna track down everyone she might have been related to."

Dan scowled at him. "Good God. If anybody around here would hide a guy like that, after what he did, they oughta be shot."

Rachel said, "I can't imagine anyone taking him in. Unless he threatened them or something. Some old relative or something, somebody he can intimidate."

Matt said, "Would he know who to go to? I mean, if he hasn't been around here in forty years or whatever? Who does he even remember? I can't see it."

"Me neither," said Dan. "More likely, if he is still around, he's hiding in some old abandoned house or something. There's a bunch of them. There's the old Miller house down by the creek across from my place. I saw a couple of sheriffs' cars down there yesterday, checking it out. There's got to be twenty or thirty abandoned farms between Rome and Bremen."

Rachel sat down at the table. "Roger said that's what they're checking first, vacant houses. But I'm betting on the getaway attempt in the truck. I think some state trooper's going to pull him over somewhere today. Maybe already has."

Dan took a drink of beer and cocked his head, considering. "I don't know that I'm so confident of that that I'm gonna leave the doors unlocked tonight."

"Me neither," said Rachel. She shuddered, and it was visible enough that both the men stared at her.

"You sure you're OK?" said Matt.

"No, of course not. But I'm not going to freak out and cry or anything."

The look of real concern on Dan's face caught her by surprise. She managed a smile and said, "Does sleeping with a light on help?"

His look softened. "TV helps. I remember after my uncle got hurt my mom let me fall asleep on the couch with Johnny Carson on for a few days."

Matt said, "It always works for me. Puts me out like a light. We'll set up a cot in the living room if you want."

They fell silent then, and Rachel could tell they were all thinking about the same thing: the need, sooner or later, to climb into bed and lie there listening to the night.

Rachel came awake in the dark; she didn't know where she was or what had woken her up. She was aware only that something had brought her up from sleep and that there were bad things in the dark. She listened.

The house was silent, though Rachel knew it had not been, a moment before. There was a reason she was awake. She knew now that she was on the couch in the living room and that somebody had put a blanket over her. The last thing she could remember was watching something idiotic and soothing on the television, Matt in the armchair across the room.

Like a wave of physical sickness, knowledge came flooding back.

Something moved in the dark. A floorboard creaked, clothing rustled. Rachel knew now that it was the sound of the back door opening that had woken her up.

Steps came softly up the hallway from the kitchen. Her heart thumped. He was watching, Rachel thought. He was watching when I found Ed.

The footsteps paused in the doorway. Rachel held her breath. As the seconds went by the silence became unbearable.

Somebody took a step into the room. Rachel cried out, thrashing at the blanket, jerking upright. In the doorway, faintly backlit, the shape of a man loomed. "What the fuck," it said.

"Who's there?" Matt's voice boomed from the den.

"It's me, for Christ's sake," said Billy. "Hold your fire."

Light flooded the room as he switched on a lamp. Rachel had slid off the couch onto the floor and was propped on one elbow, her heart kicking wildly. Matt came lumbering out of the den, in T-shirt and briefs, and stood gaping at him, not quite awake.

"Jesus Christ," said Billy, scowling at them. "A little nervous, are we?" He wore a black leather jacket over a hooded sweatshirt, and there were flakes of snow on his shoulders and in his long stringy hair. He looked like a Hun on the steppes, scanning the horizon for plunder.

Rachel laughed, covering her face with a hand. "Just a bit, Billy. Just a little bit."

In the morning the world had changed. There hadn't been quite enough snow to soften all the hard edges—corn stubble poked through a layer of white, and the wind had scoured clear patches on the slopes—but the dark earth was brightened and Rachel's mood with it. A few hours of genuine sleep with no dreams had taken her another few steps away from the horror, and she could feel the tiny pilot light of her native optimism rekindled, deep in her inner workings. She fixed a big farm breakfast for herself and Matt, knowing that keeping busy was the best way to avoid brooding. Cleanup and laundry and an hour's worth of news on CNN took her up through late morning. Matt had gone to look at dairy equipment in Kalmar. Then she heard movement upstairs, the hiss of the shower and finally Billy's step on the stairs.

He passed through the kitchen with strands of wet hair splayed out on bare shoulders, jeans sagging low on his hips revealing the plaid of his boxers. "Morning," he said, making for the basement steps.

"If you're looking for clean clothes, they're in the living room. I did a couple of loads and folded them in there."

He muttered something and did an about-face, his eyes fleeing hers as if suddenly embarrassed by his naked torso. He was lean and wiry, with just a wisp of hair on his chest. Rachel rose and went to the refrigerator. When Billy came back in he was buttoning a flannel shirt. "Sorry I scared you last night," he said.

"That's all right. Want some bacon and eggs? Your father and I went for the big artery-clogging breakfast today. We can't do it too often, but you're too young to worry about that."

Billy shrugged. "Sure." He poured himself a cup of coffee. He fiddled with milk and sugar while Rachel heated the skillet and laid strips of bacon in it. "So you found the body," Billy said.

"That's right." Rachel poked at the bacon, not looking at him.

"Must have been a shock."

"It was." She glanced at him over her shoulder. "I knew Ed Thomas. He was a friend of your grandfather's."

Billy nodded. "Everybody knew him. He was a real creep."

Rachel shoved the bacon to one side. "How do you like your eggs?"

"Aw, just scramble 'em. I'm not too particular."

"Pancakes?"

"Nah, don't bother. I'll just have some toast." He fished out a couple of slices of bread and put them in the toaster. "I know you're not supposed to bad-mouth people when they die. But I don't think anybody's gonna be too sorry he's gone."

Rachel tended to the eggs and bacon. When they were done she put it all on a plate and brought it to Billy at the table, then sat back down with her cup of tea. "Why's that?" she said.

Billy shrugged, swallowed and took a mouthful of coffee. "Like I said, he was a creep."

"You mean the feeling up girls?"

Billy gave her a sharp look. "Not just girls."

"You're kidding me."

"Nope. Friend of mine did some work for him once and at the end of the day the old bastard propositioned him."

Rachel gaped at him. "That's unbelievable."

"That's what I said. But my friend swore it was true. Not that he came right out with it. It was, like, subtle. Like, 'Why don't you stay and have supper with me and we'll watch some movies.' Nothing you could take to court or anything. But the dude said the message was pretty clear."

"Yuck." Rachel set her cup down. "Yuck. That's awful. I have to say, I never heard anything like that. That's disturbing."

"Well, you been gone a long time. Maybe he wasn't that way when you were around. I don't know. But that's why nobody wanted to work for him. Word gets around."

Rachel sat with her eyes closed, hand to her face, feeling the horror again. When she opened them she saw Billy staring at her, looking worried. "I'm sorry, Aunt Rachel," he said. "Whatever the hell he was, I don't mean to make light of it."

They exchanged a long look, and Rachel could see the pain in her nephew's eyes; he had his own horrors to remember. "How long does it take before you feel normal again?"

That was not a good move, Rachel thought, watching Billy's expression harden. She was groping for common ground, but she could see she had blundered. "What," he said. "After you find somebody dead? I don't know. I didn't find my mother. I just went to the funeral. All I can tell you is, I ain't felt normal since."

"I'm sorry, Billy."

He shrugged, tucking into the eggs. "Not your fault," he said, and Rachel could tell she had lost him.

12 |||||||

"There's a lot we don't know," said Roger. "Starting with why he chose Ed Thomas." He was warming his hands on the mug of coffee Rachel had set in front of him, his fur-lined trooper's hat on the table at his elbow. "It was before the snow and the ground was close to frozen, but the state forensic guys are pretty good. They found tracks from two vehicles, yours on the drive and one other which was all over the place. That's got to be Ed's pickup. If Ryle was there, he either walked in or he rode in with Ed." Roger hesitated, looking at Rachel, then said, "The amount of blood around the kill site helped them. They found two sets of footprints and were able to identify Ed's, so they've got something to go on."

Coolly, Rachel said, "I think I managed to avoid stepping in it. But I'd be happy to let them look at my shoes."

Roger's eyes fled hers. "They haven't asked. What we're thinking is that maybe Ed picked him up hitchhiking."

"Would he do that?" said Matt. "I'd say he was more the type to run a hitchhiker off the side of the road."

"Who knows? The killer got there somehow. Maybe he flagged him down on a pretext, like his car broke down or something. But then why would Ed take him back to his place?"

"For gas? I think Ed still had a tank in the yard. But I'm having trouble seeing Ed putting himself out for anyone like that."

Roger shrugged. "Well, there's other reasons you might bring someone home." He stared into his coffee with a look of distaste.

Rachel and Matt traded a look. "Like what?" said Matt.

Roger took a sip of coffee. Eyes on the tabletop, he said, "Just speculating here. But when we searched Ed's house we found what I'd call a fairly large stash of pornography. Not all of it, uh, heterosexual."

"Oh, God, poor Ruth," Rachel breathed.

"She may not have known anything about it. He probably kept it hidden as long as she was around. Anyway, it's all speculation, like I said. Just one reason why he might have brought a hitchhiker home. And then had him go off on him. It would fit the profile for Ryle. According to what I've seen, sexual abuse as a child was a big factor in his pathologies. But we really don't know anything. For that matter, there was no sign anybody besides Ed had been in the house. The door was unlocked, but there was no disturbance inside. Beyond the general mess, anyway. Ed wasn't much of a housekeeper."

Rachel wondered if she was the only person in Dearborn County who hadn't seen through Ed. "Awful, awful," she said quietly.

"Funeral's tomorrow," said Matt. "Closed coffin. I guess we have to go."

"Of course we have to go," said Rachel. "Whatever else he was, Ed was our father's friend. And his wife was my friend."

"We may be the only ones there."

"That would surprise me," said Roger. "That would surprise me a whole lot."

The last church service Rachel had attended had been her wedding in Jezzine, Lebanon, in a five-hundred-year-old church, smoky with incense and echoing with strange chants. There wasn't going to be any of that at Trinity Lutheran Church in Ontario, but as far as Rachel was concerned the simple white frame construction with its squat steeple and vista of open fields beyond was all a church should be; she was through with exoticism.

There were four TV station vans parked within a block of the church. One was from Peoria, two were from the Quad Cities and one had come all the way from Chicago. "He did it," said Matt, easing to a stop down the block from the church and throwing the pickup in park. "Otis Ryle put us on the map."

"I have a feeling it's a map we don't want to be on." Rachel made no move to get out of the truck. "Will they know who I am?"

"Not until somebody points you out to them. Which should take about a minute."

"Terrific."

Matt gave her a long look. "We can turn around and go home if you want."

She thought about it. "No. I'd feel like I chickened out. I'm here for Ruth." She reached for the door handle.

A sparse crowd of perhaps two dozen people milled in front of the steps. Matt had put on a suit, but he was a rarity. Nobody dresses up for church anymore, Rachel thought. The best-dressed people in the crowd were the TV reporters, two men and a woman, identified by the mikes in their hands and an air of fretting about their hair. There was apparently no filming going on at the moment, the cameras sitting idle on their tripods and the crews—the most slovenly of all those present—peering at their equipment or blowing cigarette smoke up into the wind.

They went slowly up the sidewalk, a few heads turning as they approached. "Do you still come every Sunday?" Rachel asked, prey to a sudden devastating sweep of longing for a certainty she had lost years before.

"I don't make it in every week," Matt said. "And I stopped trying to make Billy go when he was about fourteen. But I get to feeling guilty if I miss too much."

Rachel had given up feeling guilty as her faith waxed and waned; she figured the ongoing torment of doubt was between her and God and required no public adjudication. "I stopped going years ago," she said.

"Well, you'll be the belle of the ball. Old Martha Erickson was asking about you just the other day. She seemed to be under the impression you had become a Muslim."

Rachel had to stop and turn her back on the throng, her frazzled nerves giving way.

"You OK?" said Matt, full of concern.

Rachel stood hunched with her face in her hands, giggling uncontrollably. "A Muslim," she managed to gasp.

Matt put an arm around her shoulders. "I told her you only had to wear the veil on Fridays."

Rachel had to ride out another spasm of suppressed laughter before she recalled what was lying in the coffin inside, killing the mirth instantly. She took a few deep breaths. "I'm OK," she said. Matt handed her a handkerchief and she wiped her eyes.

A benefit of the attack was that she had given a perfect imitation of grieving distress in full sight of the crowd, and they shied away from her as she approached the church steps.

Except, of course, for the TV people. The Peoria crew had gotten the jump on the others, and a well-groomed youngster in a camel-hair coat came trotting down the sidewalk, microphone in hand and look of professional gravity on his face. "Ms. Lindstrom?" he said, accosting her.

"Please," she said. "I don't have anything to say."

She might as well have spoken in Arabic. "I'm told you were the one who found the body."

"Fuck off," said Matt, and they brushed past him. Rachel saw that a camera was trained on her and lowered her eyes. The two other reporters made tentative approaches as she and Matt navigated the crowd, but Matt fended them off. They stopped to shake a few hands. Nobody had anything to say beyond the greetings; the atmosphere was strained, like a party where something embarrassing had just happened. They went up the steps and into the church.

Here in the vestry were more people they knew: The Larsons were there along with a few other neighbors, mostly elderly. Ed Thomas had shed friends over the years, but they were turning out now, whether from loyalty or morbid curiosity Rachel could only wonder. A man Rachel had never seen before, stooped and gray in an ancient polyester suit, was introduced to her as Ed's brother Dick from Warrensburg. He looked dazed, blinking wetly at everyone and occasionally mumbling something nobody bothered to ask him to repeat. After an uncomfortable round of platitudes, Rachel followed Matt into the sanctuary, where the closed coffin sat on a bier at the front.

Her mind wandered during the service. The pastor was in his thirties, plump and high-voiced. There was no eulogy and his message was brief, a hasty rehashing of the scripture, "I am the resurrection and the life." Nobody appeared much comforted. The church was barely half full and most of the congregation had seen the backside of sixty. Rachel tried to focus, to find solace in the ritual, but found it hard.

Afterward the church emptied fast. Standing on the steps in the chill, Rachel saw that all three television crews were occupied, interviewing people they had snagged from the congregation. She and Matt made their good-byes and started down the steps. Ed Thomas's brother was in a knot of people at the foot of the steps talking to a man in a trench coat; Rachel knew she'd seen him recently but couldn't place him. "Who's that talking to Ed's brother?" she said when they had cleared the crowd.

"Mark McDonald," said Matt. "We saw him at the basketball game."

"Right. What's he doing here?"

Matt cast a look over his shoulder. "From the look of things, I'd say he's trying to get his hands on Ed's land. And if I had to bet I'd say he's going to get it. Ed's brother doesn't look like the type of man to drive a hard bargain."

"Where does a convicted felon get the money to buy farmland?"

"It's not his money. He works for DAE."

"What's DAE?"

"That's the big ag company that's trying to buy up all the land around here. Dearborn Agricultural Enterprises. The word is they're gonna grow corn for ethanol. They've been throwing money around the county, driving up land prices. I heard they made Ed an offer and he told them to go to hell. You'd think if anybody would sell, he would. Cash in and go live in Florida. But he was a stubborn old bastard. Go figure."

On the drive home Rachel sat thinking of Ruth Thomas, married but childless, watching her husband grow bitter and vicious as the years went by, devoting herself to other people's children. She wiped a tear from the corner of her eye.

"I know," said Matt, glancing over. "He was a jerk, but Dad liked him. It's like losing a little bit of Dad that was left."

"It's Ruth I'm crying for," said Rachel.

"Ah," said Matt. He sighed.

And myself, Rachel thought. I'm crying for me, too.

13 |||||||

The world outside was bleak: pale sky and mottled earth, wind rattling the windows and trailing dustings of snow across the frozen ground that stretched away into a colorless nothing at the horizon. Matt had gone to town again, on errands unknown. Billy had gone rocketing down the drive in the Dodge and wheeled east, sliding on the gravel. Rachel cleaned up the lunch dishes, puttered aimlessly, turned the television on and then off again, and finally gave up. She put on her jacket, went upstairs, walked to the end of the hall and opened the door, and mounted the narrow stairs that led to the attic.

It was cold up here and darker than she remembered; as she reached the top of the stairs, stooping so as not to hit her head on the rafters, she saw that the light from the round window at the far end was blocked by stacks of boxes. The attic had filled up since she had last been up here, no doubt the result of her dead sister-in-law's makeover of the house. Here was her father's trunk, there her mother's garment bags, thrown carelessly in a corner. She picked her way through the maze toward the window, light growing as she neared it.

There was still open space by the window, and if anything the place was more private than ever, shielded from the stairs. Rachel settled on the floor with her back against a wall of boxes, turned up the collar of her jacket and hugged her knees, and looked out the round window across the fields. She could make out the water tower in Rome, two miles distant. Beyond that was the limitless earth.

Rachel had dreamed of Fadi early that morning, a beautiful dark-eyed golden Fadi, laughing at her and holding out his hand, on a terrace in an impossible, precipitous city hanging far above a turquoise sea. Rachel had awakened in the cold gray dawn and lain in her bed finally certain that the man she had loved and the world he had given her were gone forever.

The sobs she had been suppressing for weeks came as great heaves. Rachel sobbed until she ached, looking out across the fields through her tears, in despair as vast as the world outside.

She cried to exhaustion and fell silent, head against the wall, cheeks glistening with tears, mucus running down onto her upper lip. The air was cold enough that she could see her breath, and she watched it rise through the light from the round window. A step creaked on the attic stairs.

She held her breath. She had not imagined it. Someone was coming slowly up the stairs. Her mind began to work rapidly: Had she locked the door after Billy left? Would she have heard someone breaking in? Had she been heard?

Why else would someone be creeping up those steps?

Her heart was thumping madly. Keep silent and he won't know you're here, Rachel thought, knowing that was infantile even as she heard the steps come softly across the attic floor. Fight then, she told herself, seeing Ed Thomas's sundered arm in the jaws of a beast and knowing she would never win a fight with the man who had done that.

Then you are going to die, she thought. The adrenaline made her stir at last, sucking in breath as she discovered she very much wanted to live. She had gotten one leg under her, preparing to rise, when Billy stepped out from behind the boxes.

They stared at each other for what seemed like a long time. "Hello, Billy," she said.

"You OK?" He was a bad boy, gaunt and menacing in his black leather jacket with his hair framing his long face, but the look in his eyes was alarmed.

Rachel closed her eyes briefly, took a deep breath and tried to smile. "Not really. But I'm not going to kill myself. I promise." She sniffed, wiped at her eyes with the sleeve of the jacket, and then stalled, awkwardly, face covered with snot and nothing to wipe it with.

"Here." He produced a blue paisley bandanna from inside his jacket. "It's clean."

Rachel took it and blew her nose, wiped her face clean. "I'll wash it for you."

"Don't worry about it." He was staring down at her with an absorbed look.

Her heart rate was beginning to subside. "I'm sorry. That was a callous thing to say. If you want to sit down I'll try and tell you why I'm falling apart up here."

Somewhat to her surprise, Billy shoved a box out of the way with his foot and lowered himself to the floor. There was just enough room for them to sit facing each other with their knees drawn up and touching side by side, feet tucked against the other's hip. Billy reached inside his jacket again, and this time he brought out a stainless steel half pint flask. He twisted off the cap and offered it to her. "Here you go. Good for what ails you."

Bad boys have their uses, Rachel thought, putting it to her lips. It was bourbon and it burned a little, but it was good. "Thank you," she said, handing it back. "I was about to ask you a really stupid question."

Billy took a sip and replaced the cap. "What's that?"

"I was about to ask if you'd ever been betrayed by someone you loved."

He laughed at that, a short ironic grunt. "Yeah, you could say that." He frowned out the window, the westering light showing up the fine lines of his face. "Brain chemistry," he said.

"Brain chemistry?"

"Yeah. That's the only way to look at it. It was just brain chemistry. She couldn't help it. She wasn't really trying to punish us. It just seemed like it."

"I think that's probably about right," Rachel ventured.

"But it was Dad's fault, too. Shit, we were happy in the other house. I was, anyway. I couldn't see any reason to move. But he was like, no, we have to keep the house in the family. The Lindstrom farm, the century farm, all that shit. So we moved over here. And the house I grew up in is just standing there empty."

"Well, the farm's really important to him."

"Yeah." Billy's tone of voice told her what he thought of the farm.

Rachel hesitated and then said, "When you're handed something like that, built up over the generations, you don't take it lightly. And that's all I'm going to say in his defense."

"Nah, I know." He looked away out the window again. "But I didn't ask to be born into this family. None of this was my idea. But somehow I'm supposed to say, oh sure, I'll be happy to take over, spend the rest of my life staring down bean rows, never get more'n twenty miles away from where I was born." The look on his face had gone sullen. "Fuck that."

Rachel waited a while and said, "So what do you want to do?"

A look of great weariness passed over Billy's face. "Fuck, Aunt Rachel, I don't know. Why do I have to do anything with my life? I ain't hurting nobody. If all I ever do for the rest of my life is party, who gives a shit?"

They looked out the window together for a time, just watching the snow drift gently across the land. "I think this is where I'm supposed to give you the lecture," Rachel said. "But having screwed up my own life to the point where I'm blubbering in the attic at age forty-three, I don't think I have a lot of credibility. So I'm just going to ask you for another drink." He handed her the flask and she drank. "Maybe adulthood isn't all it's cracked up to be."

"That's the impression I'm getting." He took the flask back. "So, who stabbed you in the back? Your husband?"

"Yeah. I started to get the picture when I would come home to Beirut on furlough and find other women's cosmetics in the bathroom."

"Damn. Welcome home."

"Yeah. I guess I pretty much asked for it. I knew when I married him, or I should have known, that I wasn't marrying into a culture that valued a woman's career prospects. When I put my career first, that was pretty much it for the marriage. And then I went and flushed the career down the toilet, too. So now where am I?"

"Sitting in the attic getting drunk with your no-good nephew."

Rachel had to smile at that. "There are worse fates," she said, holding out her hand for the flask.

- - - - - - - - - - - - - - - -

When Matt came in he stopped in his tracks by the back door to stare at them sitting at the kitchen table, cards and small change scattered over the tabletop. "What you playing?" he said, taking off his coat.

"Gin rummy." Billy was dealing. "I hate to be the one to tell you this, but I just gambled away the farm."

"Suits me." Matt pulled out a chair. "Let somebody else worry about it for a while."

"Aunt Rachel says she'll let you stay, long as she gets that rent check in Paris every month."

"Should just keep me in that nice little flat on the Île St. Louis," Rachel said, deadpan.

Matt's eyes narrowed. "You two been drinking?"

They burst out in giggles and Rachel knew she was cutting a poor figure for a grown-up woman, but she didn't care. "Couple of God damn schoolkids," said Matt. "Well, is there any left?"

"I'm afraid not," said Billy. "We killed the bourbon. But I think there's beer."

Matt shook his head and went and got himself one. Rachel gave him a sheepish look. "What can I say? Never could hold my liquor."

Matt opened the bottle and sat down. "Well, while you two been sitting here getting drunk, there's a manhunt going on out there."

That killed the mood fast; Rachel and Billy exchanged a look and then Billy tossed his cards down on the table. "They coming up with anything?" he said.

"I don't know, but there's cops all over. The word is, they found a place where he might have been hiding out, over toward Regina. There's an abandoned house right by the strip mines down there where they found signs somebody'd been in there in the last couple of days. There was food and stuff in there, and a couple of blankets, and somebody'd built a fire in the fireplace."

"That doesn't mean it was him," said Billy. "There's a million abandoned houses around here. People get in there and do drugs and shit. Or just camp out. There's homeless people out here in farm country, too, you know."

"I know. I'm just telling you what the grapevine's saying. Ron McKay's brother farms down there, and he had state cops out beating the bushes behind his place."

"The grapevine. You been hanging out with the geezers at the Snack Shack again?"

Matt gave Billy a cool look and Rachel tensed, but after a moment Matt smiled. "I'm one of the geezers now, boy. Watch what you say. Anyway, hanging out with the geezers is how you get the news around here."

Billy let it go. "Seems like all they got to do is look for that truck. There can't be too many of those old Fords still around."

"Yeah, and if he's still around that's probably how they'll spot him. I think they got tire prints from Ed's place, and I bet the state cops are smart enough to compare 'em with anything they find."

Billy frowned, fiddling with coins on the table. "What would he be doing hanging around here, anyway? If I was him, with a set of wheels, I'd be in fuckin' Mexico by now."

"Watch your language, will you? Who knows how a sick mind like that works? Maybe he's got old grudges to settle, or thinks he does. You know Ed Thomas grew up near Regina and knew the Ryles, right?"

Rachel and Billy stared at him. "Listen to you," said Rachel. "Pulling that out of your hat, like you knew it all along. Who told you that?"

"That's what Ron says. He says not too many people remember the Ryles because they lost their land and moved away a long time ago, like forty years ago, but according to him, and he says he got it from his dad, the Ryles and the Thomases knew each other back in the day and didn't get along too well."

"Meaning what?"

"I don't know. All Ron said was, they didn't get along. Ed's father and Bessie's husband had some kind of a feud or something, way back in the fifties. That's all he knew."

"Ron told the police this, I'm assuming."

"Oh, yeah. I think they're all over it."

Billy said, "So the guy comes back forty years later to whack old Ed? Dude's got a long memory."

"Hold on," said Rachel. "Otis Ryle was just a little boy when the fifties ended. I'm having a hard time believing he would have even known anything, much less cared, about some feud his, what, grandfather had? Bessie was his grandmother, right? And it doesn't sound like he was exactly invested in the Ryle family honor or anything. I can't see it."

Matt spread his hands. "Yeah, I don't know. All I'm telling you is what Ron told me. That's the scuttlebutt. Make of it what you will."

Billy shoved back from the table. "Sounds like a lot of horseshit to me. I think the dude went off on Ed because Ed propositioned him.

And now the dude's long gone. The cops are wasting their time poking around people's barns."

"Ron said they got all the meth cooks in the county upset. They're not used to cops going around turning over rocks."

"Yeah, well, I wouldn't know anything about that." Billy headed for the hall.

"I hope not," said Matt. "I certainly hope not."

14 |||||||

Rachel found her Aunt Helga in another resident's room, bending over an old man with twisted limbs lying on his back in bed, staring up at her and thrashing feebly. His eyes watered and the tendons in his neck strained with the effort to speak. On the wall a television was blaring, a studio audience shrieking with laughter. "Don't wear yourself out, Ralph," Helga was saying. "I know. I hear you." She clasped one withered hand in hers and squeezed, then detached herself and pushed away from the bed, leaning on her walker. Her eyes met Rachel's, and Rachel was startled to see the anger that blazed there.

They made their way slowly back to Helga's room. "That's what a stroke does to you," Helga said when she was settled on her chair, panting a little. The anger was gone, replaced by a haunted look. "That poor man lies there all day and can't even tell the girl when he's wet himself. The television's on day and night, driving him crazy, and every time I turn it off the staff comes and turns it back on again. He's got a sister who comes and reads him devotional passages every day. That would be enough to make anyone into a pagan. I had Steve bring me a volume of Zane Grey stories so I could go in and read him something different once in a while, but the sister put an end to that. She said he couldn't follow the stories anyway, which any fool can see isn't true. His mind's still there, which is the real tragedy. I hope God's got a nice place reserved for that poor man when he finally goes, because he's in hell now."

She was breathless when she finished, and Rachel sat and watched as the heaving of her sunken chest slowly subsided. At last she said softly, "What about you, Aunt Helga? Are you in hell?"

Helga appeared to consider the question seriously, but when her answer came it was with a dismissive gesture. "Oh, no, honey. I'm all right. I'd rather still be at home, but then I'd be completely dependent on people who have their own lives to lead, and that's not very agreeable, either. I don't like it, but I can't say I don't belong here. It's just another thing to make the best of."

Rachel nodded. She wasn't sure why she was here; it certainly wasn't because she had expected laughter and high spirits. Maybe it was because she had sensed Helga could help her make the best of things. "Are you lonely?" she said.

Helga gazed at her for a moment. "In here, you mean? No more than I was before. I've got children and grandchildren, and a telephone. But from the look on your face I'd guess you are."

Rachel looked out the window. "Not yet. But I'm afraid of it."

"Yes, it is the most terrible thing there is, isn't it? But you did the right thing. You came home."

"Yes. Just in time for a murder."

"You mean Ed Thomas." Helga searched her face. "Steve told me you found him."

"I found him, yes."

"You've not had an easy time recently, have you, child?"

"I've had better months."

"And they think it was the Ryle boy? Otis?"

"He seems to be the main suspect. Did you know him?"

"Knew the family. But Otis would be, let's see. He would be in his seventies by now, maybe eighty. He was only a few years younger than me. I'm surprised he's still alive, the kind of life he led."

Rachel frowned. "You must be thinking of the father. The one who escaped from prison is in his fifties."

Helga's eyes went a little vague. Rachel had opened her mouth to explain further when Helga said, "Otis had a son? I never knew that."

"Yes, but apparently he abandoned him, dumped him with his mother, Bessie."

"Bessie Ryle, goodness. There was a nasty woman. I remember Ruby Hart telling me about Bessie screaming at her in the general store in Regina because she thought she had cut in front of her. I don't think Bessie was quite stable. And Otis left his son with her? Poor child."

"Yes. But she gave the boy up to foster care after a few years. And he never came back until they brought him to the prison here."

"Another Otis Ryle, imagine that. One was enough. He was what they called a hell-raiser. But I never heard anything about him after he went out to California, goodness, must be sixty years ago."

Rachel waited for more, and when nothing came she said, "Aunt Helga, what do you know about a feud between the Thomases and the Ryles?"

"Oh, goodness. I don't know. Seems to me I remember hearing something about that, but I couldn't tell you what. Something to do with land, probably. That's what farmers fight about around here, when it isn't women. I remember hearing that Bessie claimed the Ryles were cheated out of their land. But nobody seemed to take that seriously. As far as I ever knew, they lost the land to the bank because they weren't very good farmers. Why, do they think that has something to do with what happened to Ed?"

"I don't know what the police are thinking. It doesn't seem likely to me. This Otis Ryle was just a little boy when all that was going on. But who knows?"

"You never know about people. I always felt sorry for Otis's sister."

"He had a sister?"

"Yes, and she wasn't like the rest of them. I didn't know her very well. But she seemed nice. And a little ashamed of the rest of her family. She came to our church a few times, I remember. She married somebody up

Kalmar way, if I recall, and I never heard any more about her." Helga seemed to drift away again. "So many people over the years. I've lived a long time."

I could live another forty-three years, Rachel thought, terrified. That's a long time to be alone. "Can I bring you anything? Is there anything you miss, anything you need?"

Helga came back from wherever she was and focused on Rachel. "Just all those years, child. If you could bring them back I'd be the happiest woman on earth. But you can't. Nobody can."

"I'll let the detectives know, but I don't think it means much," said Roger. "That was a hell of a long time ago and Otis Ryle was just a kid. I can't see it. I think it's a coincidence. "

Cell phone to her ear, Rachel stared out through the windshield of the Chevy at drawn blinds at the back of the nursing home. "OK, I just thought I should pass it along."

"I appreciate it. We can use all the help we can get."

"No progress, huh?"

"Just if eliminating possibilities is progress, which I guess it is. We've covered just about all the abandoned farmsteads. Found a few things people didn't want us to find. But no Ford pickup, no Otis Ryle."

"Maybe he's far away."

"That's what we're hoping. But we're not ready to sound the all clear. The fact remains that whoever killed Ed Thomas is still at large. And there's absolutely no guarantee he isn't still in Dearborn County somewhere. There's a lot of square miles out there, with a lot of places to hide. So keep your doors locked."

"OK, thanks, Roger."

"Thank *you*. I'm glad you called." There was a brief pause. "Say, Rachel?"

Something in Roger's tone of voice made her heart sink. "What?"

"I was wondering if I could take you out to dinner sometime."

Oh, God, Rachel thought. Why me? She groped frantically for an excuse. Seconds went by, and she knew her paralysis had gone past the point of mere surprise and into awkwardness. Roger said, "Just dinner. No pressure, no nothing. Just to catch up a little bit."

She could hear the tension in his voice. Put him out of his misery, she said to herself. And then she caved. As she said it she knew it was cowardice and cursed herself, but she said, "Sure. That would be nice."

"All right. What about tomorrow night? I'll take you to that French place in Rock Island if you want."

A French place in Rock Island? Rachel couldn't picture it. But having already conceded the essential, she had no grounds for resistance. "That sounds nice, Roger. What time?"

When Rachel was a small child she had been afraid of the dark because it might be hiding anything she could imagine. Now she was afraid because she knew exactly what it was hiding. In daylight she felt merely shaky, fragile, as if she were getting over the flu. With sundown the dread returned.

I am going to go mad, Rachel thought. Isn't somebody supposed to offer me counseling? Where are the solicitous social workers, the psychologists, the grief counselors and the therapists? Where is that pompous little pastor?

Rachel knew if she needed help she was going to have to go looking for it. And she didn't know where to start. Once she had had a husband who would have taken her in his arms and comforted her, but that was all gone. Matt was being kind, dancing around the edges of her distress like a good stolid Scandinavian brother, but there were limits to what he could do. Rachel was on her own.

Matt had gone to bed, fatigued after a day's labor in the barn, surveying and staking out the location of his milking operation. Billy had not been seen all day. Rachel put on a nightgown and bathrobe and flopped on the couch with the TV on. She wore out the remote surfing channels and then gave up, killed the TV and picked up *The Crystal Cave*, which she had pulled off the shelf hoping for escape. She read a few pages but could not focus and tossed the book down on the couch beside her and put her face in her hands.

By way of distraction she returned to her annoyance with herself at failing to fend off Roger. She had said nothing to Matt about Roger's invitation, and then been irked by her own embarrassment. She had had enough practice in her life deflecting come-ons, especially in the brutally skewed male-to-female ratios she had been used to in Iraq, that it should have been child's play to put Roger gently back in his place. But she had said yes.

Tires purred on gravel outside and lights swept over the snow on the yard as a car turned into the drive. Rachel was mildly surprised at the small leap in her spirits at the thought of Billy coming in. She waited for the sound of his key in the door.

Instead, after half a minute or so a sharp rapping sound came from the back door. Rachel froze. She had managed to forget escaped madmen and butchered farmers for a few minutes, but now her heart was suddenly pounding. She waited for Matt to stir, to come out of the den and take charge, but there was no sign of him.

The knock came again, half a dozen quick raps on the glass. Rachel rose from the couch. Homicidal maniacs don't knock, she told herself as she started down the hall. This is Karen Larson come to see if I need company, or Dan Olson, come to take me to the bar again.

Dan would have called, she knew. Probably Karen Larson would have, too. And what better way for a homicidal maniac to gain entry than simply to knock?

Rachel stopped in the dark hallway. Where was Matt? She nearly turned around to go and wake him.

And then she was angry at herself again, for playing the helpless female. The door was locked and there was a window in it; she could see who was standing there without putting herself in danger.

The thought of Otis Ryle standing at the door, patiently knocking, halted her in her tracks. He could smash the window in her face, reach through and seize her by the throat.

The knocking came again, tap-tap-tap-tap on the glass. She was closer now, and its proximity made the sound more mundane. You are being a fool, she told herself. Go and see who is at the door.

The kitchen was dark, but she made no move to turn on the light; she wanted to be looking out into the lamplit yard from darkness. She felt her way through the kitchen carefully and went down the three steps to the entryway. As she passed the household tool bin that lay at the foot of the steps, she reached down on impulse and grasped the first wooden handle her hand fell on. She came up holding the hatchet she had put there after cleaning out the car.

She could see a figure silhouetted in the lamplight outside the door. She stepped closer. The figure moved, light from the halogen lamp high on its pole falling on its face.

It was a girl, long black hair framing a pale face, dark eyes rimmed with black, a black scarf up to her chin, a black jacket. She had opened the storm door to rap on the glass of the inner door. Now she had sensed Rachel's presence and stood staring through the window, wide-eyed. For a moment Rachel just stared back. Then the girl leaned forward, pressed her forehead against the glass, shading the side of her face with a hand, and said, just audibly through the door, "Is Billy there?"

Rachel exhaled. "Just a moment." She replaced the hatchet in the tool bin and then stepped back to the door. She raised her hand to the deadbolt. This close to the door she could feel the chill coming through the glass, seeping under the door. She hesitated a moment longer, then turned the deadbolt and pulled the door open a few inches, stopping it with her hip. An icy breath of wind hit her. She said, "Billy's not here."

The girl was no older than twenty and looked as if she could use a good home-cooked meal. She was dressed in black from head to toe, wearing high leather boots with spike heels. Her face was deathly pale and she was shivering in the cold. She said, "Shit." Beyond her on the gravel was a car Rachel didn't recognize, some kind of muscle car.

Rachel wondered if this was the girl whose underwear she had thrown away. She almost gave in to an impulse to pull the door open wide and tell the poor girl to come in out of the cold. Something in her vaguely disreputable look stopped her. She said, "Sorry."

"Do you know when he'll be back?"

"I couldn't say. Billy doesn't really check in with us. Do you have his cell phone number?"

The girl just stared at her. Then she did something that puzzled Rachel: She looked to her left, off into the darkness at the side of the house, as if consulting someone. Rachel, uneasy, narrowed the gap in the doorway by a couple of inches. She said, "Do you want me to give him a message?"

The girl turned back to her and said, "No, that's OK. Forget it." She turned on her heels and went tripping down the steps. She walked toward the car as Rachel closed and locked the door.

When the girl reached the car she halted, turned, and looked again at something Rachel could not see. As Rachel watched, a man came into view, long-haired and leather-jacketed, slouching, with a furtive air. He looked over his shoulder at the door, and the face Rachel saw was a real bad-boy face, bony and feral, without Billy's redeeming handsomeness. The man got in the driver's seat and the girl got in on the other side, and after a moment the lights came on and the car spun around and went tearing down the drive and turned east on the road.

Nice friends, thought Rachel. She stood there in the chill wondering why any friend of Billy's would need to lurk just out of view. Then she thought of worse things out there in the dark, checked the locks and hastened away from the door.

15 |||||||

"What the hell did you do to my hatchet?"

Matt stood in the doorway brandishing it like a tomahawk, glowering at Billy where he sat at the kitchen table with Rachel. The dark stains did not look particularly gruesome in the morning light.

Billy frowned at him, coffee cup halted halfway to his mouth. "Where'd that come from?"

"The tool bin, where else?"

"I found it when I was cleaning out the car," Rachel said. She cast a guilty look at Billy; she had neglected to ask him about it, and now she felt obscurely at fault, seeing him in hot water with Matt once again.

Matt was rubbing the blade with a thumb. "What'd you do, kill somebody with it?"

"The turkey," Billy said. "I took it to Pete's at Thanksgiving, remember? Instead of a store-bought turkey he had one he'd been raising. And that's what we used to kill it. Turned out to be harder than you'd think."

Matt stared at him with distaste. "Especially when you're drunk, huh?"

"Hell, we weren't drunk yet. It's just a big damn bird, that's all. Put up a fight."

Matt looked at Rachel and shook his head. "He ditched the family at Thanksgiving and went off and partied with his buddies. He came back two days later, hung over."

"Didn't do nobody no harm," said Billy. "Except the turkey." He shot Rachel a covert grin.

"Well, you think you might have cleaned off my hatchet?" said Matt. Billy's face went sullen. "I meant to but I forgot. I'll do it."

"I'll put it by the back door." Seeing the look Matt gave Billy and the boy's stony expression in response, Rachel had to suppress an urge to play peacemaker; she knew from experience that was an ungrateful role. What they really needed, she thought, was to have their silly heads knocked together.

Rachel hadn't been to the Quad Cities since she stopped seeing her orthodontist three decades before. Outside Illinois she had never come across anyone who hailed from there or who had ever heard of them, and yet here they sat, a cluster of industrial towns on a westward bend of the Mississippi that had merged into an urban area big enough to have a federal arsenal, a minor league ball team, and, Rachel hoped, a decent French restaurant.

The restaurant was in downtown Rock Island, a few blocks from the big lazy river, and looking at the menu in the tastefully muted lighting Rachel realized that, provincial or not, this was going to cost Roger a pretty penny. "This looks wonderful," she said.

"You're going to have to help me out," said Roger. In his V-neck sweater over a striped Oxford shirt he looked like a man who didn't dress up much, making an effort. "I've never had French food before." He looked up from the menu, mouth twisted in a smile. "I figured this was my best chance, with somebody that speaks the language."

"I'll try to steer you to something good." Conversation on the half-hour drive up 74 had been just a touch strained, sticking to banalities and avoiding any mention of murder or police work. Despite the awkwardness Rachel's spirits had been raised just by moving, seeing countryside go by. "Do you like seafood? Coquilles St. Jacques are good."

"Whatever you say. You're the expert. How in the heck do you pronounce this, anyway? I've always wondered."

He goggled in disbelief at Rachel's pronunciation of *hors d'oeuvres* and failed to replicate it; Rachel talked him out of ordering beer and then felt bad watching his face as he looked at the prices on the wine list. "Usually if you ask, you can get a cheaper house wine by the glass," she said.

Roger smiled, handing her the list. "Heck with it. Order us a good bottle and don't worry about the price. Money's no object tonight. I got nobody to spend it on and it just piles up."

All right, pal, you asked for it, Rachel thought. She negotiated the ordering process, and when they each had a glass of a mid-range Pouilly-Fuissé in hand, they clinked glasses and drank. "Mm. That's good." She set her glass down and said, "Roger, this is so nice of you. But before we go any further I really have to make one thing clear. I'm just not in the market for romance at this stage of my life. I'm home for a few weeks to rest and catch up with my family, and then I'm leaving again. I don't know where I'll end up, but it almost certainly won't be here. So I'm happy to revive a friendship, but that's really all it's going to be. OK?"

He looked grave for a second or two, and then nodded. "I appreciate your being frank, Rachel. I don't know if I gave off the wrong signals or what, but I never intended to come on too heavy. I always liked you, I won't deny that, and when you came back I might have gotten a little excited, but I'm a grown-up and I understand where you're coming from. Far as I'm concerned, it's just a pleasure for me to go out for a nice dinner with a pretty woman and hear about all the adventures she's had. So there's no strings attached to any of this, and I'm just glad for the company and the education."

Rachel returned his smile, feeling the tension ease a little. Up to this moment she'd had her fears about how this was going to go. "Well, the education goes both ways. You've got expertise in things I've never dreamed of, I'm sure. More practical things than ordering a bottle of wine."

"Like how to break up a bar fight? Yeah, I've pretty much earned a graduate degree in that at this point."

They laughed and the easier mood carried them through the Coquilles St. Jacques and into the Sole Meunière. Rachel did most of the talking, Roger following intently as she covered her trajectory from college language major to Foreign Service recruit to experienced officer with half a dozen countries under her belt. "Your turn," she said after a lull. "How did you wind up on the sheriff's department? I would have thought you'd be farming, like your dad."

Roger washed down a mouthful with wine and sat frowning at the glass. "Long story," he said. "Family feud, is what it boils down to."

"Oh, I'm sorry to hear that. Who's got your dad's land?"

"Somebody I don't even know. I haven't set foot on it in twenty years." He looked up at Rachel and the corner of his mouth twitched, just a little.

"What happened?"

"Remember my sister Marcia?"

"Sure."

"Well, my dad gave her power of attorney when he got sick. Her, not me. Just because she'd gotten her degree at U of I and I'd dropped out. I guess he figured she was the smart one."

"Ouch."

"Well, I didn't think too much of it. Until she sold all the farmland about a week before Dad died."

Rachel's jaw dropped. "How could she do that?"

"She had power of attorney."

"I mean, ethically, how could she do that to you? Without consulting you?"

"Oh, she consulted me. She sat me down and told me she didn't think I was responsible enough to run the farm. See, I'd been running around a little bit right before then, doing some traveling and sowing wild oats or whatever. My idea was to get all that out of my system before I came back and took over the farm, 'cause I knew Dad was fading. But Marcia said I'd shown I wasn't steady enough to take the place over and I'd be better off taking my share of the proceeds and investing it and finding something else to do. Of course, what that meant was, her share was bigger. Because the will said I was supposed to get all the farmland, she was supposed to get the house, and we were supposed to split any money in the bank half and half. Well, there was a hell of a lot in the bank, but it was all from the land I was supposed to get. And she got half of it, and there wasn't any land left. And then she went and sold the house, too."

"But that's outrageous. Couldn't you contest it?"

"Well, I got a lawyer, and all he did was charge me thousands of dollars and negotiate a little money back from Marcia. But it was all done aboveboard, perfectly legal."

Rachel just stared wide-eyed for a few seconds, and then she put a hand on his arm. "Oh, my God, Roger, I am so sorry. How could she do that to you?"

He shrugged, lifting the glass. "I always figured it was her husband's idea. I never did think much of him. They took their half of the cash and went to Texas and we don't communicate much anymore. Last I heard, she'd divorced him after all that."

Family conflicts over land were not unheard of, but Rachel had never seen one this ugly up close. "You got screwed."

"Yeah, I guess I did. But I did have the money, and I used some of it to go back to college, and that's where I met my wife, so I guess it worked out. I did a couple of other things for a few years and then applied to the department and here I am."

Rachel held his gaze for a few seconds; she felt freer to like Roger now that she was confident the terms of their friendship were clear, and she was conscious of a certain reservoir of affection she had had for him since that single slightly awkward prom date, which could have gone so much worse. Roger had been good-humored and perfectly gallant, and at the end of the night he had gratified Rachel by making clear both his gratitude for her company and his awareness that there would be no sequel. "Matt said you have a daughter."

"Yeah. Lindsey. Wanna see a picture?" Roger dug in his hip pocket and produced a wallet, from which he extracted a school picture of a freckled blonde girl on the cusp of puberty.

"Oh, she's pretty. How old is she?"

"Twelve. She's in seventh grade. Out in Colorado Springs with her mom. I don't get to see her more than a couple times a year." He gazed at the picture for a couple of seconds before stowing it away. "That's kind of hard."

"What happened with your wife?"

Roger shrugged. "Night shifts, strange hours, missed dinners. She didn't want to be a cop's wife. Not out in corn county, anyway. She was from some suburb of Chicago and she hated small towns. She wanted to go out west. So she found a guy who would take her there."

"I'm sorry."

"That's life. What about you? What killed your marriage?"

Rachel told him about Fadi and the nightspots of Beirut, which took them through dessert. "And here we are," said Rachel.

They smiled at each other, but Rachel was careful not to maintain the eye contact too long; she knew it was the wine that was making her so big-hearted. She pushed her plate away and tidied her napkin. "Thank you, Roger. This has been wonderful. I'm glad we had a chance to reconnect."

"Me, too." He was frowning now, fidgeting a little and looking uneasy, and Rachel guessed he was beginning to think about the three-figure tab. Abruptly he said, "I'm sorry you had to get involved in this killing. I hope it's not affecting you too much. You seem like you're doing OK." He looked almost shamefaced.

You sure know how to round off a romantic evening, she thought. "I'm OK. I'm just sorry for Ed," she said.

Roger's look sharpened. "He didn't suffer too much. He really didn't. The autopsy established that. The blow to the head killed him. All the rest was . . ." He waved a hand vaguely.

"Yes, well. We don't really need to think about that tonight, do we?"

"No, sorry." Roger threw up both hands. "Shouldn't have brought it up. It just bothers me, that's all. I won't be able to rest easy till we catch the guy."

"Me, neither," said Rachel, drily. "Believe me."

Roger was starting to realize the dimensions of his gaffe. Flustered, he looked around and said, "What do you have to do to get 'em to bring the check?"

And that, thought Rachel as she watched Roger's taillights draw away down the drive, was one of the stranger evenings I've spent. She threw the deadbolt and turned to face the empty house, sagging back against the door.

She had known the house was empty as soon as Roger turned into the drive. Neither the pickup nor Billy's Dodge was in sight, and the two lights that were on, one in the living room and one in the kitchen, were the ones Matt always left on when he was out. If he had been home, most of the first floor would have been lit up.

Roger had sensed her uneasiness and asked if she would be OK; by reflex she had said sure, not wanting to prolong an evening that had run its course. Now, listening to the empty house, she wished she had asked him in.

There is nobody here, Rachel told herself. There is no sign of forced entry. There is no reason to believe that the man who sawed Ed Thomas into pieces is waiting for me at the end of that hallway or at the top of the stairs. I have come home to this safe, familiar house when it was empty many times in my life, and I have never been afraid.

Rachel's heart had accelerated and her knees had gone weak; her breathing was shallow and rapid. She strained to listen and heard, at long intervals, the faint random creaks that are always there in an old house. She had lived with them for years. Now each one sounded like Otis Ryle's soft tread.

You are being childish, she told herself. Still, she dared not move. She listened for another minute. That, surely, was a careful placement of a foot in the upstairs hall. And yet there was nothing after it, only silence.

I want a gun, thought Rachel. I want Clyde Larson's gun. With a gun I would not be afraid to march through the house, opening doors, looking in closets.

Leave, she thought. Run out to the Chevy, jump in and drive to where there are people. Drive down to the Larsons'. Karen will give you hot chocolate and Clyde will give you a gun.

16 |||||||

"I know it's irrational," said Rachel. "But I couldn't stay there. I was too scared."

"It's not irrational at all, dear. Good Lord, with that man still on the loose? I've been scared to death myself the last few days." Karen Larson was in her bathrobe, hair in a net and ready for bed, but she had rallied to the cause. "I am *so* glad you came over." She set the mug in front of Rachel and squeezed her shoulder. Rachel closed her eyes, on the verge of tears, overcome with gratitude. Mother me, she thought. Please mother me.

The chocolate was too hot to drink. She slurped a little and set the mug down. "I'll call Matt and find out when he'll be home."

"You can stay here as long as you want, honey. Spend the night if you want."

"Thanks, but I think I need to get back on that horse. Let me see if I can raise Matt." She rummaged in her purse until she came up with her cell phone. When Matt answered she said, "Hey, it's me. Where are you?"

"I'm at the bar, where I'm supposed to be. Where are you?"

"I'm at the Larsons'. I was too scared to stay in the house after Roger dropped me off."

"Why, did something happen?"

"No, I was just scared to be in the house alone. I'm just still a little freaked out, that's all."

A few seconds went by. Rachel expected jocularity, dismissal. Instead Matt said, "Sit tight, I'll be right home."

"I don't want to spoil your evening. I can stay here for a while."

"Nah, I was about ready to leave anyway. You want me to pick you up?"

"I can make it a half mile down the road by myself, I think. I just want you to be there when I get home. I want you to check all the closets and make sure nobody's hiding under the beds. I'm just having an attack of old-fashioned crybaby-scared-of-the-dark."

"Well, I can understand that. Give me ten or fifteen minutes. I'll call you when I'm home, OK?"

"OK. Thanks." Rachel clicked off and sat with a hand over her face, eyes closed. Karen pulled out a chair, sat and gently grasped her other hand.

Rachel looked up when Clyde came into the kitchen carrying a revolver and a box of shells. He sat down and said, "You've handled firearms before, right?" He was looking at her with concern, having second thoughts maybe about entrusting his Smith & Wesson Model 10 to a mere slip of a girl.

Rachel shrugged. "I've shot the .22 a lot. Handguns, once or twice. I could use the safety lecture."

Clyde gave it to her, showing her how to break out the cylinder and load the shells, then emptying it again and explaining how the double action worked. "You can shoot it when it's not cocked, but it takes a hard pull. Once you cock it, though, it'll go off if you look at it funny. So be careful."

Rachel nodded. "Thank you, Clyde. I'm fervently hoping I never have to use it."

"That makes two of us. Just remember, shooting it's the easy part. The real trick is anticipating, getting the thing out and pointed at the right person, heading off trouble if you can, so you never have to pull the trigger."

Rachel loaded the cylinder, swung it home and pushed the box of shells back across the table. "I think if I need more than six shots I'll be in trouble so big, a gun won't help me."

The look on Clyde's ancient seamed face was dead serious. "If you need more than one, you better hope the cavalry's coming."

When Rachel pulled up at the back door, Matt's truck was parked there and lights were blazing in the house. Feeling foolish, she paused on the step with her key in her hand and her purse dangling heavier than usual on her arm. Leave the gun in the car, she thought, and then remembered her dread of the creaking empty house. Keep it with you, she decided. Under your pillow, cradled at your breast.

A noise penetrated her awareness and she turned to look out over the vast black countryside with its thin scattering of lights. A high distant keening was just perceptible far off in the night; it puzzled her but after a moment she decided it was a car horn, blaring away stupidly. Stuck, no doubt; nobody would stand there leaning on the horn for minutes on end. The driver was probably frantically trying to cut it off. But it was disquieting; quickly she went inside.

Matt was on the computer in the den, bringing up data on the commodities markets. Without looking away from the screen he said, "So, did he try and kiss you?"

Rachel laughed. "No, he was a perfect gentleman, start to finish. Of course, I drew a line in the sand as soon as we sat down."

"Probably scared him to death."

Rachel set her purse on the floor, flopped onto the bed and leaned back against the wall. "I think Roger's probably pretty hard to scare."

"If you're a meth head or a drunk, maybe. I think women terrify him."

"Could be. I think he's very lonely."

"Well, losing a wife can do that to you."

Rachel watched him for a moment and then got up and went and put her arms around him, bending over him. "I'm sorry, Matt."

He shoved away from the computer. "Well, there's no crying in baseball. I'm OK. I get Billy straightened out, I'll be happy."

Rachel sank back onto the bed. "Roger says Billy's basically a good kid. He says he's too smart for the people he's hanging out with. I think that means he'll come to his senses."

The look Matt gave her was weary and completely free of illusions. "He can start anytime, far as I'm concerned. Now, you're sitting right where I hope to be laying in about a minute and a half. I'm calling it a night."

Rachel picked up her purse, heavy with the weight of the gun. She started to tell Matt about the gun but hesitated.

"What?"

"Nothing." She leaned over and kissed him on the top of his head. "Good night."

"Night. You OK, for sure?"

"Yeah."

"Come knock on the door if you need company."

Suddenly she was overcome with love for him; all that pain he must have inside him and here he was, offering to comfort her. Rachel opened her mouth to tell him how much she loved him but all that came out was "Thanks. I will."

Rachel awoke in the depths of the night. For a moment she was bewildered; darkness was universal, and she could have been anywhere on the face of the earth. A great fear roiled, black and lethal, just below the level of her awareness.

Then she was fully awake in her bed, the old woolen blanket rough against her cheek. A door had opened and closed, downstairs. The back door, she thought. Someone has just come into the house.

Over the thumping of her heart she told herself it was Billy coming in, and she was a fool to lie here trembling like this. A short time passed; there was a distant murmur of voices. Rachel checked her watch: Three o'clock had come and gone. The voices sounded again, low and terse. She lay in bed trying to identify them: One was Matt's, but whose was the other?

She got up and put on a bathrobe and slippers. She stood at the head of the stairs in the dark, listening, until she was sure. Matt and another man were talking quietly somewhere below. She could not make out the words. There were footsteps and then the sound of running water.

Rachel tightened the belt on her robe and descended the stairs. The hall light was off, but light shone in the kitchen at the end of the hall and spilled from the bathroom halfway along it. Someone was running water at the bathroom sink. Rachel stepped softly down the hall and halted at the door of the bathroom.

Dan Olson stood bent over the sink in a T-shirt, washing something from his hands and forearms, the muscles of his arms rippling. Pink water swirled in the white porcelain sink. On the floor at Dan's feet lay a sweatshirt, mottled red.

Rachel sucked in a sharp breath. Dan's head snapped toward her, his face grim and haggard. "Jesus, Rachel!" He leapt back from the sink, wet hands held away from his body. "You scared the shit out of me."

They gaped at one another. Breathless, Rachel said, "What are you doing here?"

Dan opened his mouth and nothing came out. Matt appeared in the doorway from the kitchen. Dan said, "I gotta wash my hands."

"For God's sake, what happened?"

After a long second Dan said, "Somebody else got killed."

Rachel put a hand on the doorjamb to steady herself. Matt said quietly, "There's been another murder. We got the call."

"Who?" said Rachel, her voice nearly failing her.

Dan answered. "Carl Holmes," he said, bending to the sink again. "My uncle."

- - - - - - - - - - - - - - - -

Rachel had made herself a cup of tea. Dan and Matt had sucked down a beer apiece and started on a second. "Bob Dayton found him," said Matt. "About three miles from here, on the Bremen road. He heard the horn going off and got in his truck to go see what it was. He was so freaked out he took off down the road, got all the way to Bremen before he pulled over and dialed 911. County emergency calls get routed to the local first responders, which is us. Dan got there about a minute after I did, and then Tom Carlson and Andy Wilson showed up, and then finally a sheriff's car. We hung around till the detectives showed up."

"Wish to God I was never there," said Dan, staring at the tabletop.

This is knowledge I don't want, thought Rachel, but I have to share the load. "He was in his car?"

"In his pickup," Matt said. "When I shone the light on him"—Matt squeezed his eyes shut, grimacing, rubbed his face with both hands—"I couldn't figure out what the hell I was seeing at first." He opened his eyes and looked at Rachel. "His throat was cut."

"He was halfway out, like he'd gotten the door open and tried to run," said Dan. "But he never made it. He just kind of twisted and got, like, wedged with his elbow against the horn. The cops yelled at me for moving him, but I couldn't stand there and listen to that noise. That's when I got the blood on me. There was a fuck of a lot of it."

Rachel rose from the table. She walked to the sink and stood with her arms crossed, looking at her reflection in the window. "Sorry," said Dan behind her.

Matt said, "The guy must have flagged him down, hitched a ride or something. The truck was in the ditch just shy of the stop sign at 600 East. The guy must have waited for him to slow down, then cut him and got out and run."

"Run where? Where's there to run to?"

Matt said, "The closest house is the Nylands', a couple of hundred yards north. The sheriff's guys checked there right away, as soon as they got some backup. Everybody was OK there, no sign of trouble. They're checking all the farms around there. Nobody knows where he went."

"How could he just disappear?"

Nobody had an answer for that. "I gotta go tell Aunt Peg," said Dan, his voice ragged. "I told the sheriff's guys I'd do it. What the fuck was I thinking? I can't do it. It'll kill her. This'll put her over the edge. Ah, *shit*." He took a pull on his beer. "I gotta go tell her."

Silence reigned. Dan made no move to get up. Rachel swayed a little, her eyes closed. How strong can I be? God, if this is a test, give me the strength to pass it. She opened her eyes and said, "Three miles from here?"

Matt looked up. "That's right."

"So he could be right outside by now. He could be watching the house."

"He could be, I guess. If he's invisible. There are a lot of cops on the roads right now."

Dan said, "He could be going across fields. Nobody'd see him from the roads."

"Then he's leaving tracks. And the cops'll find them. Soon as daylight comes. They were looking when we left."

"He had to have a vehicle," said Dan. "He's still got Ed's truck, I bet. Maybe he staged a breakdown, flagged Carl down, pulled the knife and cut him, then took off in the truck. Who the fuck knows?"

Matt sighed. "If he's driving Ed's truck around, I'm not so worried about him hanging around outside the house. It means he's got a hiding place somewhere."

They all thought about that for a few seconds. Rachel said, "Clyde gave me his gun. I've got it upstairs by my bed."

A look of weariness, or maybe resignation, passed briefly over Matt's face. "Keep it there. I think we're OK as long as we keep the doors locked. I don't know that this guy's going around breaking into houses."

"Not yet," said Dan. "Shit, I gotta go tell Aunt Peg." He shoved away from the table and stood up.

Matt watched him as he stood up. "You OK to drive? You look like hell."

"I feel like hell. But I'll make it."

In pressure-cooker situations in Iraq Rachel had found that sometimes the worst part was seeing what stress was doing to other people. Dan looked dazed, unfocused. Rachel saw his hand trembling a little where it rested on the back of the chair. "Be careful," she said.

"Oh, yeah. You know it." He turned to her and spread his arms, and they embraced.

"I'm sorry," she whispered.

Dan released her and made for the door. "Hang in there, pal," said Matt, and he hugged Dan as well, throwing in a couple of thumps on the back. "You want me to come with you?"

"No, I got it. My job. I shoulda done it first thing. What the fuck time is it? Christ, she's probably woke up and gotten worried. She's probably trying to call him on his cell phone. I gotta roll."

When Dan had gone, Matt and Rachel sat at the table staring at nothing. "This is bad," said Matt after a while. "This is really, really bad."

Rachel was thinking about a beach in a sheltered cove on the island of Cyprus, where she and Fadi had lain in the sun and been happy. I want to be anywhere but here, she thought.

Tires crackled on frozen gravel outside. Matt and Rachel traded an electrified look. "Billy," she said.

"Maybe. Go get that gun."

"Come on, Matt. It's Billy."

They listened as the car pulled up, the engine shut off, a door slammed. When the key went into the lock in the back door, Matt exhaled. "Shit," he said. "I'm freaked out now, too."

Billy came into the kitchen with his keys dangling from his fingers, wide-eyed. He stopped still when he saw them at the table. "You heard?" he said.

Matt nodded. "We heard. Where you been?"

"Trying to convince a couple of sheriff's deputies I didn't have anything to do with it. They're all over the place out there. What the fuck's going on around here?"

"You tell me, son," said Matt, shaking his head. "You tell me."

17 |||||||

When Rachel awoke groggy and unrested after a couple of hours of fitful sleep, it was past ten and the sheets of snow on the fields outside were gleaming in the sun. She came downstairs to find Matt in the kitchen talking to two strangers, obvious cops despite the plain clothes. One was heavy-set and gray, the other thin, fair and intense with a short military haircut. Introductions were made but Rachel forgot their names immediately, retaining only the fact that they were from the Illinois State Police. Matt sat at the head of the table bleary-eyed and bedraggled, and Rachel wasn't sure he'd been to bed at all.

"I was about to come and get you," Matt said. "The, um, officers had a few questions. About Ed."

"Oh." Rachel made for the coffeemaker. "OK. I made a statement already. I thought the guys I talked to were from the State Police."

"They were," said the older man. "And we've got their report. We just wanted to go over a couple of things."

Rachel poured herself a cup of coffee and brought it to the table. "Like what a coincidence it is that both murders were discovered by people from the same family?" There was an awkward silence, glances darting around the table.

With a hint of a shrug the younger detective said, "Well, technically speaking your brother didn't discover it. He was the first on the scene after the call. But we don't have any reason to believe it was anything but coincidence. If you've got any ideas about it being otherwise, we'd like to hear them."

Rachel shook her head. "No. Though I'm starting to wonder why our family seems to have a black cloud hanging over it."

It was Matt who answered the looks of keen interest from the detectives. "We've had some deaths in the family over the past few years," he said.

"Sorry to hear that," said the older detective, managing to look sympathetic. He waited a second or two and said, "Actually, what I wanted to ask you was whether you had remembered anything more. The report says you were unable to remember what exactly you saw at the scene." He was working hard to keep his expression neutral, but Rachel could see the skepticism there.

She drew a deep breath. "I'm told it's called traumatic amnesia. I can remember everything up until I went around the corner of the barn. I turned the corner and saw something terrible, and then the next thing I remember I was in my car, driving away. It's hard to explain. I know I saw it, but I just have a blank there where there ought to be a visual memory."

The detective nodded. "You use the term *traumatic amnesia*. Is that a professional diagnosis? Did you get counseling, see a doctor about this?"

She shook her head. "No. That's not a professional diagnosis. It's amateur speculation."

The detectives traded a look, and Rachel knew what was coming. "I think you should see somebody," the younger detective said. "Consult a doctor."

Rachel clasped her hands under the table to stop them trembling. "So I can remember what I saw? I'm not sure I want to."

"In case you saw something that might be of importance," said the older man.

"I saw exactly what she saw," said Matt. "I was there in a few minutes. And then within half an hour the place was overrun with cops. There's no need to make her go through something traumatic again."

"With all due respect, Mr. Lindstrom, you can't guarantee she saw exactly what you did. Not if there was a gap of a few minutes."

"I can tell you what I saw," said Rachel. "I saw Ed Thomas's body cut up in pieces. I know that intellectually. I just don't have the visual memory, that's all."

Again the detectives consulted each other silently. This time the older one said, "All right, we'll leave that for the time being. I was wondering if I could go over a couple of other points with you." He took her through her story, from hearing the chainsaw in the night to seeing the coyote. "You're fairly certain about the time, when you heard the chainsaw going?"

"I think it was close to midnight. That's about all I can tell you. I looked at the clock in my room when I went to bed a few minutes later, and it was around twelve fifteen."

The cop nodded. "That correlates pretty well with what other people have told us."

"You mean I wasn't the only one who heard it?"

"Oh, no. Lots of people heard it, and they all pretty much agree on the time. That's pretty helpful, actually, in pinning down the time of the attack."

Rachel felt a knot of tension ease deep inside her. She was not alone; this was not just her nightmare. "I wish I'd known what I was hearing," she said.

"By that time it was too late to do anything," the older cop said.

"Except maybe increase the chances of catching the guy."

"Don't second-guess yourself. Nobody else did anything, either. They just thought somebody was cutting up wood." He put away his pen and flipped his notebook shut. "We'll get this guy before too long.

As I was telling your brother, we're in the process of putting together a task force to investigate these killings. ISP, Dearborn County Sheriff and Warrensburg PD are all contributing personnel. That gives us plenty of manpower to track this guy down."

Rachel frowned at him over her coffee cup. "You're sure it's Otis Ryle, are you?"

The cops exchanged a brief look and the older one said, "Nothing's for sure at this stage except we've got two people dead in close proximity. But we're working on a strong presumption it's Otis Ryle, yes. Sometimes the obvious is actually the case. Most times, in fact."

"So where is he?"

"Good question," said the younger cop, as they both stood up. "We don't know. But considering you've had two killings within a few miles of here, I think the answer has to be, 'Not far'. I say that not to frighten you but to make you careful. Keep your doors locked, check the car before you get in. Don't for God's sake pick up any hitchhikers or even stop to help somebody at the side of the road, unless it's somebody you know personally. If you see anything suspicious, don't investigate, don't be a hero. Call 911 and get to a safe place. This guy's very, very dangerous."

All Rachel could do was nod. Matt said, "I think we're pretty clear on that point."

When the detectives had gone Rachel said, "Why did they say to check the car before I get in?"

Matt sighed, massaging his forehead. "When they looked at the blood splatter, and the angle of the cut and all of that, it looks like Carl was attacked from behind."

"From behind."

"Yeah. It looks like the guy was sitting in the backseat of the truck and reached around and cut Carl's throat from behind."

Rachel shuddered. "God, like he was hiding back there or something?"

"That's what it looks like. Carl had been at the tavern over there on

150 all evening. He left about midnight to drive home and Andy found him about a quarter to one. And the cops didn't find any other tire marks at the scene, so it doesn't look like he stopped for a breakdown or anything like that. Either somebody flagged him down, on foot, or somebody was in the car with him when he left the bar. In the backseat."

"Oh, Jesus." Rachel covered her mouth with her hands.

"Yeah. Think about that next time you get in the car."

Rachel was in desperate need of normality. Susan had half a dozen interviews to transcribe for her oral history, so she volunteered to help. She drove into Warrensburg, checking the backseat of the Chevy carefully before she got in, suppressing a creeping dread. She saw a sheriff's car on the highway into town, heading north as she went south, but otherwise no sign of any massive law enforcement mobilization. The land looked barren and sterile, scoured by a bitter wind.

I can do this, thought Rachel. If the military people can do it, if the Iraqi doctors can do it, I can do it. She had seen people whose job it was to contend with violent death get into a zone where they were able to function no matter how bad the things they saw got to be. She had never known how they did it, and she had hoped never to have to do it herself. Now she was feeling for that zone.

I got off easy in Iraq, she thought, and this is my test.

The wind whistled around the eaves of Susan's house, but it was warm inside, with the radiators hissing and a pot of tea on the table and Brahms on the stereo. Rachel and Susan took turns at the laptop, straining to interpret the reedy voices coming from Susan's recorder. It was really a one-woman job, but if it went more slowly with frequent interruptions for laughter and digressions, it also was less tedious. They had talked about Carl Holmes's death on the phone in the morning, and it had not been mentioned again; Rachel silently blessed Susan for her restraint.

"The hard part was being so lonesome, with Bob so far away and nobody but small children to talk to. There were days when I just went and hid in a closet and cried." Rachel punched the Stop button on the recorder and her fingers flew over the keys. She finished the entry and said, "Boy, is that a common theme."

"No kidding," said Susan from the kitchen, where she was taking brownies out of the oven. "I know men have the tough part in a war, but the women aren't far behind. Imagine trying to function like that, your husband out there in mortal danger somewhere, and here you are trying to keep a family together, run a farm, whatever. Those women were heroes, too."

"Tell me about it. And these days a lot of the military people in Iraq are mothers with children at home. Try that one on for size." Rachel punched the button. *"And it was the lonesomeness that made trouble for some folks, too. When the cat's away the mice will play, you know."*

"Oh, yeah, this was interesting," said Susan, bringing in the brownies. "Old Greta Swanson can still dish out the malicious gossip, seventy years later."

"Not me, goodness, don't get me wrong. But it happened. Farmers didn't get drafted, because they got an occupational exemption. A lot joined up anyway, but there was a lot that didn't. So there was a lot of lonesome wives and a lot of healthy young farmers around to make mischief. And then when men came home there was bad blood sometimes."

"That would do it," said Rachel. "Come home from the war and find out your wife had been sleeping with the guy that didn't go? I'd be peeved, too. Come to think of it, that was pretty much what happened to me." She bent to her typing.

Susan waited for her to finish and shoved the brownies toward her. "Try one of these. It won't mend a broken heart, but it'll keep you from wasting away. Want me to take over?"

"Sure." Rachel yielded the chair to Susan and moved to the other side of the table, mouth full of brownie. The anecdote had hit too close to home. Suddenly stricken, she sat and ate, staring out the window at the leaden sky, determined not to tear up. She was aware of Susan shooting covert glances at her as she listened, then typed. "Don't worry," Rachel said. "I'm not going to cry."

"Cry if you want to. Nobody here's gonna mind." Susan finished typing and started the tape again. *"I don't think Gus Holmes ever really believed Carl was his son."*

Susan punched the Stop button, and she and Rachel stared at each other across the table.

"Oh, my God," said Susan. "Is that a coincidence, or what?"

Rachel frowned. "Go on. What did she say?"

Susan started the tape. *"Nancy had Carl just under nine months after Gus got home from the army. Some people said the baby was early, but others said it looked like a fine healthy nine-month baby. Whatever Nancy thought about it was between her and Gus, but Gus was awfully hard on that boy, and on Nancy, too. And there was a young fellow that went off to California about that time, that some said was run out of town by Gus Holmes. But nobody ever knew what the truth of the matter was."*

"California," said Rachel.

Susan punched Stop. "Huh?"

"Who went out to California about that time?"

Susan blinked at her. "Is this a riddle? I give up."

"That's too much coincidence," Rachel said, feeling a chill creep up from her core.

"What, for God's sake?"

"That's about when he went out to California. Otis Ryle. The father."

"I don't know if it means anything."

"I don't either. I just thought you should know. I mean, this just keeps coming up. All of a sudden the Ryle family is everywhere."

"But this Mrs. Swanson didn't remember the name of the guy that went to California, right?" Roger said.

"No, but I went and asked my Aunt Helga about it, and she remembered it. She says she heard the gossip at the time. Gus Holmes and Otis Ryle Sr. had some kind of feud, and some said it was because Otis had been a little too familiar with Nancy Holmes while Gus was away at the war. She'd forgotten about it until I asked, but she was pretty definite."

A few seconds went by in silence. "The implication being that Otis Jr. knocked off Carl because . . ." Roger let the sentence trail away.

"I don't know what the implication is, Roger. I don't mean to be one of these nutcases who pesters the police with every brainstorm. I was just struck by the connection, that's all. It's just fucking *spooky*, if you'll pardon my language. There was a connection between Ed Thomas and the Ryles, and now it turns out there was a connection between the Holmeses and the Ryles. I don't know if it means anything, either. Maybe it just means that in a farm community everyone's connected. I just thought whoever's looking into this should know."

"You're right. You did the right thing. I don't mean to shoot you down. I'll pass it on, for sure."

"It's probably meaningless, I know."

"But maybe not."

"Yeah, maybe not. And if not . . ."

"I know where you're going."

"Where am I going?"

"If Otis Ryle is going around killing people because of old family grudges, then we better be busting our asses to find out about any more old Ryle family grudges."

"Because they'll tell us who he's going to kill next."

"Bingo," said Roger.

18 |||||||

"I'm not going," said Rachel. "I didn't even know the man. Besides, if you think Ed's funeral had media coverage, wait till you see this one. And they'll be all over you."

Matt sighed. "I know. But I have to go. Dan's my best friend."

"Give him my best. I just can't face it, Matt."

Matt stood nodding slowly, necktie dangling from his fingers. This was the second time in a week Rachel had seen Matt stuffed into his suit, and she was starting to take a distinct dislike to the garment. "Come out to the house afterwards, anyway," Matt said. "Jim's having people in after the funeral. Just friends."

"Jim Holmes that we went to school with? He's related to Carl?"

"Nephew. You didn't know that?"

"I had no idea." Holmes was a common name in the county, an Anglicization of the Swedish Holm, and they were scattered everywhere. Everyone's connected, Rachel thought. "OK, I can do that. Yeah, that would be good."

Matt put on his tie and jumped in the truck and was gone. Rachel locked the door behind him, cleaned up the kitchen and then puttered around the house, tidying. She stood at the south windows in the living room looking out at the far scattered farms. How many times had she seen these fields go through their cycles, from snow cover to green peeking up through black earth to midsummer sumptuousness to harvest and back to quiescence? A finite number, less than twenty if you got down to it, and yet she had an impression of an endless idyllic childhood behind her, rooted in this familiar earth. The memory had comforted her in far places. And now it was barren and sinister, a wasteland of ice.

She heard Billy stirring upstairs. He must have come in sometime late in the night, when she and Matt were asleep. His hours had gotten more and more eccentric, and he and Matt seldom crossed paths. Rachel wandered toward the kitchen. She had taken to fixing breakfast for Billy when he appeared, enjoying a half hour of easy companionship before he disappeared on mysterious errands. Since their shared tipple in the attic they had settled into an odd complicity.

She heard the shower running and took her time with the breakfast; when Billy appeared she had an omelet and fresh coffee and hot buttered toast waiting for him. Billy came in with wet shining hair and two or three days' stubble on his chin. He halted, looking at the breakfast laid out on the table, and said, "Damn, Aunt Rachel. You don't have to do this, you know."

"I know. I don't mind. Gives me something to do."

Billy sat down. "Well, I appreciate it. Whoa, what's in here?"

"Onions, peppers, Swiss cheese. You want jam or honey for the toast?"

"Uh, jam's fine."

Rachel fetched it from the refrigerator. "You growing a beard?" The whiskers coming in accented his fine cleft chin rather nicely, Rachel found.

"Nah, just too lazy to shave. Where's Dad?"

"Gone to the funeral."

"Ah, yeah." Billy ate in silence while Rachel poured herself a cup of coffee. "It's fucked up, ain't it?" Billy said. "This guy running around killing people."

"That's one way to put it."

He shot her a sharp glance. "I'm sorry. Don't mean to rake it all up. You feeling OK?"

She shrugged. "Every day it gets a little better."

"Yeah. When Mom died, I remember it was just misery for a long time and then after a while I would wake up in the morning and think, It doesn't hurt so much today."

Rachel stared at him over her coffee cup, thinking that compared to what Billy and Matt had gone through she really couldn't complain. "So. Who was that girl that came looking for you the other night?"

His face went blank and Rachel knew she had blown it again, stepped over the line. He chewed, eyes on his plate, and said, "Nobody special. There's this bunch down in East Warrensburg I hang out with sometimes. I don't know what they were doing up this way."

"I don't mean to pry into your private life. Just curious. When you don't have a lot going on in your life, you get interested in other people's." She smiled, trying to make light of it.

Somewhat to her surprise he smiled back. "Lot of fish in the sea, Aunt Rachel. Just because it didn't work out with one guy doesn't mean it's all over."

"No, I suppose not."

"Not that it's a very big sea around here."

"Well, I doubt I'll be settling here." She watched him eat for a few seconds. "What about you? You ever think about leaving?"

"All the time." The glance he gave her was grave, intense. "Gotta get some money together first."

She waited for elaboration but it didn't come. "Got an idea about where you'd go?"

Billy shrugged, scraping at his plate. "I used to think about New Orleans. Friend of mine went down there for Mardi Gras one year, said it was amazing. But now there ain't much of it left, after the hurricane. California, maybe? And Seattle's supposed to be cool. I don't know. Anyplace there's jobs, I guess. It's a big country."

"It sure is." Rachel was suddenly thrilled with the possibilities. She remembered being nineteen and not believing in limits. "I could help you maybe. If money's the only thing stopping you, I could float you a loan. I've got plenty saved up after the life I've been living."

That got his attention, she could see; she watched him start to take the notion seriously, maybe for the first time. But she could see it scared him a little, too. "Cool," he said finally. "I might have to think about that."

That put an end to it for the moment. Billy finished his breakfast and disappeared while Rachel cleaned up. When he came down again he had on his hooded sweatshirt and denim jacket. "Gotta roll," he said. He paused at the top of the steps, momentarily awkward, lips parted. "You'd really lend me money?" he said.

Drying her hands, Rachel took a few steps toward him. She had been fighting off second thoughts ever since her generous impulse had carried her away, and she knew it was time to set the terms. "Sure," she said. "But I'd want to talk about plans first. You really ought to finish school. You could go somewhere else to do that, of course. I think I'd want a commitment to go back to school, even if it wasn't right away. But if you had a plan and needed more support than your father could give you, of course I'd be happy to help."

Billy nodded, frowning faintly. Then his expression eased and he said, "For an aunt you're fuckin' awesome, you know that?"

Rachel had to laugh. "That's the first time anybody's said that to me."

"Hey, believe it." Billy grinned at her and then he was gone, out the back door.

Rachel stood still, listening as the Dodge started up and then tore away down the drive. She was stunned at what she had felt when Billy smiled at her, dark-eyed and unshaven and moving with his feral grace: Out of the blue she had felt a pang of physical desire, sharp and explicit, the first stirring of lust she had felt for many weeks. Brutally she suppressed a vision of her nephew's bare torso, strands of wet hair lacing his broad sinewy shoulders.

You need to get a grip, girl, she told herself. On top of every-thing else, not least the utter delusion involved in reading anything into that smile, that's *incest*. Rachel walked across the kitchen to the sink and stared out across the fields, then hid her face in her hands. You're pathetic, she thought. You are forty-three and have been reduced to fantasizing about young men half your age. Young men *related* to you.

After a moment Rachel took her hands from her face and heaved a great sigh, knowing she was perfectly capable of keeping a lid on her libido and acting with decorum around her nephew; all he was was the trigger. She turned away from the window and forced her mind to practical matters, meals to plan.

Two minutes later she had to shove the cookbooks away and close her eyes again. It had shaken her. Having dodged the question through-out her long period of celibacy, Rachel now knew with certainty she was not going to be able to forgo physical love forever. Men neglected and betrayed you, but the animal inside you needed the animal inside them.

If only, Rachel thought, you could be content with the animal part. Sometimes it was a burden to be human.

--- --- --- --- --- --- --- ---

Rachel drove east, noticing farms and their outbuildings as they passed. He's close, she thought. He's here somewhere, waiting for nightfall. She had grown up on this land and knew many of the people who lived in these houses, but now she was aware of how many farms could fill a few square miles, how many strangers there had always been on the fringes of her community. That small white house with a single red-painted shed in a grove of trees, half a mile to the south: Who lived there? Rachel had no idea.

Jim Holmes lived a mile or so north of Ontario, on a farm that looked middling prosperous, with a couple of grain bins and a barn that could use a coat of paint but had a recently replaced sliding track door. Rachel sat in the car for a moment after joining a dozen or so cars parked on the grass along the drive, reluctant to go in. The feeling of appalled dread had taken hold of her again, and she did not expect it to be relieved by mingling with people who had cared for Carl Holmes and would be dazed and wounded by his slaughter. She got out of the car.

In the kitchen were women she knew, tending to food: Karen Larson was there, along with other women of her generation, and Jim's sister Sherry. The greetings were subdued. "I'm so sorry," Rachel murmured, stepping back from a hug with Sherry.

"It's a shock," said Sherry, looking baffled and hurt. "I mean, God, why? It's just so . . . *evil*." Words failed her. Rachel allowed herself to be steered into the living room, where the main gathering was.

Rachel had been to a few funeral gatherings in her time, and she sensed instantly that this one was different. There was none of the closure, the unstated relief that prevailed when an elderly person passed on. The mood here was sullen. Men stood in knots, muttering; women held the couches, regarding the men warily. Matt nodded at her from across the room, standing with their cousin Steve. Some faces there were familiar from the basketball game: Tommy Swanson, Bobby Jacobs, a couple of others. Rachel's entrance had been noted, but nobody was in the mood for cheerful reunions. She made her way to where Jim Holmes stood, rubicund and heavy but recognizably the boy she had known twenty-five years before. She made her condolences, and Jim said, "You came home at a bad time. Too bad you had to land in the middle of this."

"Oh, Jim. It's so awful. I'm sorry. You must have been close to him."

Jim shrugged. "I guess. He never had no kids, so he kind of spoiled his nieces and nephews. He was the rowdy uncle who always did fun stuff like give us rides on his motorcycle. He was a character."

That brought a rumble of agreement from the company. "Here's to him," a man said, and bottles were raised.

Tommy Swanson said, "You were the one found Ed Thomas, weren't you?"

Rachel nodded. "I'm afraid so."

"And your brother found Carl?"

"Somebody else found Carl. Matt just got the call."

"Still. The police must be all over you."

"That'd be about par for the course for the cops around here," said Jim. "Waste their time messing with Rachel and Matt instead of tracking down this maniac."

"They brought in all these experts from Peoria and Springfield and God knows where, and they still can't find their own asses to wipe 'em."

"They come and search your outbuildings yet?" said another man. "They did mine."

Tommy nodded. "They had the dogs out the other day, down by the creek. Going through the woods."

"If they haven't found him it's because he ain't around," said the first man. "I think he's got himself a room in Peoria or someplace, comes up here at night to go hunting."

That set off a general debate. Rachel extricated herself and started across the room toward Matt, but before she got there she found herself looking down at a frail elderly woman in a wheelchair and, sitting next to her at the end of a sofa, Dan Olson. "Hey, Rachel," he said.

"Danny." She halted and stared at him, caught speechless. He was in a sport jacket but without a tie, cowboy boots showing beneath the cuffs of new blue jeans; he looked freshly groomed and almost civilized but wore a gaunt, brooding look. "Hi," she said, and was embarrassed by her inanity.

"You know my Aunt Peggy?" Dan cocked a thumb at the woman in the wheelchair. She wore a shiny gray wig that looked about as convincing as a Halloween mask over glazed eyes in a thin wasted face. She had a tube up her nose. She was clearly in pain, physical or psychic or both.

Rachel bent to take her hand. "I'm so sorry," she said. "What an awful thing."

The woman quivered with effort, and from her throat came a ragged whisper. "It's *horrible*." A tear gathered at the corner of her left eye.

Dan reached out and patted her hand. "They'll catch him, Aunt Peg. They'll get the son of a bitch."

Rachel was paralyzed. Dan caught her eye and for an instant his expression softened. "I'll catch up with you in a bit," he said.

Rachel fled to join Matt and Steve in their corner.

"Ain't this fun?" Matt said.

"It's unbearable."

"I'll tell you one thing," said Steve. "If these guys had any kind of idea where to find Otis Ryle, they'd be getting a lynch mob together. You gotta wonder what the cops are doing. How hard can it be to find this guy? I know I'm about ready to put in a call to the folks I know down in Springfield, get a little action."

Matt said, "It's a manpower issue. They can't even find all the meth labs stashed out here."

"Well, they better find this asshole fast. Becky's scared to go anywhere at night. My kids are freaking out, too. Tina came and jumped in bed with us last night. She hadn't done that since she was four years old. Fucking terrified." Steve was glaring out over the room. "Jim and Tommy were talking about organizing patrols. Or an escort service or something, make sure our wives can make it home safe."

"Vigilantes," said Matt. "There you go."

"Don't knock it," said Steve. "If the cops can't do anything, it's up to us."

Get me out of here, Rachel thought. She said, "I'll see if they need help in the kitchen." She edged through the throng, snagged briefly by Becky and the other women but cutting the conversations short, her feeling of oppression mounting toward panic.

In the hallway she came face to face with Dan, emerging from a bathroom. "How you doing?" Rachel said.

His eyes went past her into the living room. "I gotta get the fuck out of here."

Rachel's heart leapt. "Me, too. Can we slip out a window?"

Dan cast a look over his shoulder, placing a hand on Rachel's arm. "I don't know about that, but there's a side door through the den here."

19 ||||||

They went and sat in Dan's truck, which was parked a hundred feet from the house, screened from it by another pickup. Dan started the engine and when it was warm he turned on the heater. The view out the windshield was to the south, the Ontario water tower rising in the distance. "My aunt can't catch a fuckin' break," Dan said. "She lost both her kids, now this."

"God, I'm so sorry."

"Carl was kinda rough around the edges, but he was good for her. Then she got sick. Jesus, that poor woman's had enough bad luck for five or ten people."

"What's wrong with her?"

"Cancer. In her throat. She can't hardly eat anymore, but most of the time she doesn't seem to be in a lot of pain. They give her good drugs. But we're coming up on the end. The docs give her maybe a month before we have to take her to the hospice. It ain't pretty."

"That's how my mother went. But I missed most of it."

"You were lucky."

"I wasn't there. And that still hurts."

"You had your reasons. You had your life to lead."

"Yeah, that's what I tell myself."

They fell silent for a while, listening to the whistling wind, watching bare branches toss. "I remember when Frank Hartfield got killed racing that train to the crossing. It was a shock and all, but it was also like, well, he had it coming, the dumbass. But this . . ." Dan shook his head. "It hurts. It just makes you feel sick."

Rachel tracked a flight of geese across the sky. "It hurts because it's a violation. An accident's different. This is an injury, it's personal."

Dan grimaced, rubbed his face hard, sighed. Looking out the windshield he said, "Are you having nightmares? I am."

"Yeah, I've had a few."

"I always thought I was pretty tough. But I'm not tough enough for this."

"Nobody is."

He turned to her, and all the irony was gone, all the cockiness and humor and bravado. Dan Olson was showing the years today, and all the hard knocks. "Remember growing up, being seventeen, eighteen?"

"Barely."

"Remember how you felt like you could do anything? I did, anyway."

"Yeah, I remember."

"I was gonna make it in football, play in the NFL, all that shit. And then, even after that, when I got cut, I was like well, OK, what the hell, we'll try something else. And I thought, You can always come back and farm. Christ. I used to be an optimist."

Rachel could feel it happening, with a strange detachment. We like them most when they're vulnerable, she thought. "Me, too. Up until not too long ago. I thought I was basically doing what I should be doing, having the life I should have. And then my job started to become impossible, my marriage went away. And all of a sudden I was a failure."

Dan put his hand over hers where it lay on the seat. "You're not a failure. You went out and conquered the world. Jesus, Rachel. You know how proud you made your family?"

Her head drooped. "Then why do I feel like I let them down?"

"Beats the shit out of me. I'm the one never amounted to nothing."

My turn, thought Rachel. She felt as if she were reading from a script. She lifted her eyes to Dan's and said, "Why, because all you did was raise three good kids? Isn't that plenty? You did what you were supposed to do."

They just looked at each other then, and Rachel knew it was happening, and she knew it was what she wanted even though just a few hours before she would have sworn it was never going to happen. The look went on until it was time to take the next step or get out of the truck, and she knew she wasn't going to get out into the cold.

They started to lean at just about the same time, and Dan's hand went to the back of her neck as hers went to his cheek, and as kisses went it was pretty good. Rachel didn't know how she'd done without this for so long. Yes, she thought, I want this.

They drew back just enough for Dan to say, "You want to come to my place?"

"I'll follow you in my car," she said, and then she got out into the cold.

- - - - - - - - - - - - - - -

I'm not afraid, Rachel thought. For the first time in days, I'm not afraid. I am lying in darkness in a strange house but I am not afraid.

Outside, the wind was still gusting, but it sounded far away and ineffectual. Here in Dan's bed she was warm, naked under blankets with his breath on her shoulder, his arm across her belly, a leg crooked over hers. There was just enough light coming in through a window to show the contours of the room, the shapes of a dresser and a desk, a heap of clothes on a chair. The red figures on the digital clock by the bed said 7:34.

Here I am, she thought, in Danny Olson's bed. She smiled in the dark. She was not afraid, and, for the moment at least, she was content.

There were many potential disasters lurking in an unplanned dash for the bedroom, and none of them had come to pass. His house, though barely noticed in passing, was tidy enough; Dan himself had been calm and in control in the preliminaries. Disrobing had involved no more than the usual awkwardness and had revealed no unpleasant surprises; the still-powerful chest and shoulders diverted attention nicely from the slightly expanded middle. Rachel's flare of anxiety with regard to mechanics had been defused by the casual production of a condom from a drawer. And then she had finally been able to abandon herself.

It was never as good as you dreamed, but sometimes it wasn't bad. It was good to be wanted; it was good to be held and touched and taken. Dan was un-self-conscious and reasonably practiced and patient and finally passionate to about the right degree. Rachel had had plenty worse.

This will do, she thought, this will do for the time being.

She thought Dan had dropped off to sleep and was loath to stir and wake him, but his breathing changed and he shifted, rolled onto his back and cleared his throat and said, "You think the party's still going on over there?"

She gave it a token breath of laughter, and he rose up above her supported on an elbow. "You just took one hell of a lousy day and turned it around about 180 degrees. Make that a lousy week."

"Hasn't been a great month, has it?"

"It's basically sucked for a while around here."

Rachel worked her head into the crook of his arm. "Maybe it's bottomed out. It can only get better, right?"

"Let's hope so."

"This helps."

"Sure does." He kissed her and then rolled onto his back and pulled her to him and lay there just holding her. He didn't seem to need to talk any more than Rachel did, and she was grateful.

They got up after a while, and he put on a pair of sweat pants and a flannel shirt and found her a bathrobe. They went down to his kitchen, and he heated a can of soup and made grilled cheese sandwiches under the broiler and got a couple of beers out of the refrigerator. "Romance," he said. "I was going to lay in some caviar and champagne but the food mart at the truck stop was fresh out."

"Who needs caviar when you have a hunk of cheddar? God, I was hungry."

"I could thaw some pork chops. Perk of the job. I get all the hog meat I can eat."

"No, this is perfect." She looked around the kitchen, seeing ancient, battered linoleum and grout missing between tiles. But there were no dirty dishes languishing in the sink, no smells, and the floor looked as if it got washed once in a while.

"It's a dump, I know," said Dan. "Hasn't been remodeled in about fifty years."

Rachel shrugged, looking out the window over the sink at trees in a hollow behind the house. "It's cozy. It reminds me of our kitchen before Margie remodeled it."

"It's just like it was when I was a kid. I guess it's nostalgia. I want everything to be the way it was."

"Boy, do I understand that. Ever since I got home I've been feeling it. I want my mom and dad back, I want to be twelve again. I want to be taken care of."

He smiled at her. "I got a feeling you don't need much taking care of."

"OK, comforted maybe. I want somebody to tell me it's all right." She reached out and put her hand over his where it lay on the table. "This helps."

He took her hand. "You sure are beautiful," he said.

She reached up and ran a knuckle over his cheek, which was beginning to need a shave. "That's good to hear once in a while. Thanks."

"Don't know how you could doubt it. Don't you have a mirror?"

"Keep talking, Romeo."

"I remember you when you were a freshman. I remember thinking, give her a couple of years and she won't be too bad. But then I graduated and missed it."

"Oh, terrific. 'Not too bad,' huh?"

"And then I saw you once when you were home from college, and I thought, Jesus. Matt's little sister turned into a knockout."

There was never any good response to that kind of thing except to smile demurely and avert one's eyes. "And here we are."

She knew she could stay the night if she wanted, and she also knew it would be a bad idea. Dan seemed to be on the same wavelength, which was good. Please, she thought, let it be easy for once. Let it be just a nice casual fling, a port in the storm, no complications. I'm due for a break.

When she had showered and dressed, Dan was back in jeans and boots and in the kitchen, cleaning up. "I'll follow you home," he said.

She stared at him, startled. She had forgotten what was out in the night. She drew a deep breath and said, "If you think you should."

"I do." He turned, drying his hands. "I don't like the way it happened to Carl. The guy must have waylaid him somehow, got him to stop. If he's out there tonight, you shouldn't be driving around alone."

Rachel nodded. She almost told him about the gun in her purse, but she realized that would be just posturing; she was a lot happier relying on Dan Olson for protection than on her dubious skills with a firearm. "OK. You want to come over for a while, hang out with me and Matt?"

Dan grinned at her. "You think we could keep our hands off each other?"

She had to smile. "Maybe not. Come to think of it, I might be a little embarrassed."

He took a couple of steps and she was in his arms. "Let's say good night now. You know where I live. Matt's got my number."

As a seal on the evening's proceedings, the tone was perfect. The embrace was well calibrated, fervent but not crushing. The kiss was terrific.

- - - - - - - - - - - - - - - -

Rachel flicked her headlights as she turned into the drive. Dan gave a couple of quick honks in response and went on west. She pulled the Chevy up at the back steps, cut the engine and lights, and just sat there for a short while. There were lights on in the house and Matt's truck was there. Rachel was in good spirits but there were sober realities to return to.

She cast a wary eye around as she got out of the car, but she did not feel frightened as she covered the few steps to the door. It would take a while for the night to be benign again, but the malevolence had receded a step or two.

Inside she found Matt sitting at the kitchen table. She halted in the doorway. "What's wrong?"

There were two empty beer bottles in front of him and a third in progress. Matt had changed out of the suit and sat at his normal place at the table, but something about the slump of his shoulders told Rachel that something more than postfuneral depression was bothering him. No, she thought. Not again.

"Have a nice time?" Matt said.

His tone was not hostile, exactly, but it wasn't a friendly inquiry. Rachel stepped forward and laid her purse on the table. "Yeah. We did. I hope we didn't make a scandal."

"I don't think anybody noticed except me." Matt took a drink of beer. "I thought this wasn't going to happen."

"So did I." Rachel sat down. Here we go, she thought. "Matt, what's wrong?"

He looked up at her and said, "Billy's in jail."

20 |||||||

"He got scooped up with a bunch of other lowlifes at a bar in East Warrensburg, after a fight. Apparently he took a swing at a cop."

"Oh, no." Rachel put a hand to her face.

They sat in silence. Matt drank beer and said, "Beyond the underage drinking, they got him on aggravated battery. I don't think anybody's going to cut him a break this time." He looked up at Rachel but his eyes quickly fled hers.

"Where is he, Warrensburg?"

Matt nodded. "Dearborn County jail. Not the institution I hoped my son would graduate from."

The clock ticked a few more times; Rachel frowned. "So what happens next? Can't we get him out on bail?"

"He's got a court date next month. He wanted me to come bail him out. I told him no."

Rachel sat frozen. "You told him no?"

Now Matt looked at her. "I'm through, Rachel. I've had enough. It's time for him to face the consequences."

She nodded a few times, slowly. "You don't think criminal charges are consequences?"

He made a dismissive noise. "Sure. Whatever. I'm just done, Rachel. I just couldn't go down there and bail the damn kid out. I'm too God damn angry. I give up. He's an adult and I can't do anything with him, or for him, anymore. He's made his bed and all that."

Rachel sat and watched Matt drink for a while. When he finished the third bottle he sat staring at the empty, a defeated man. Rachel had not moved, had not taken off her coat. Finally she said, "I'm not trying to undermine you, Matt. I would never second-guess you about how you handle Billy. But it seems harsh to me to let him sit in jail for a month. Even real criminals get bailed out. If I drive down there and bail him out with my money, would that be a problem for you?"

He gave her a sharp look and said, "Don't bring him back here."

Rachel nodded. "He can probably find a place to stay."

"I'm through with him."

"You're angry and nobody can blame you. But don't do anything you'll regret while you're so mad you can't see straight. He'll always be your son."

"Fuck, you get along with him so well, you try handling him for a while."

Rachel stood up. "I think we're through trying to handle him. Like you said, he's an adult now. You're right to kick him out. It was probably past due. But don't write him off. Not yet."

Matt threw up his hands in surrender. "Whatever. Go bail him out if you want. You'll need a hundred bucks. But I don't want to see him."

- - - - - - - - - - - - - - - -

Crisis on top of crisis, thought Rachel, heading south on the highway toward Warrensburg. Her tryst with Dan already seemed like a hallucination. It had given her a glimpse of the well-being she had once taken for granted, but the effect was fading. The menace was back; it had cost her an effort to go back out into the night and get into the car.

I'm all right on the highway, she thought. It's the back roads that are dangerous. That's where he is. Back there where we live.

The lights of Warrensburg ahead had never looked so welcoming.

Dearborn County had built a new jail and courthouse complex in the eighties; Rachel had never been in it. She had never bailed anybody out of jail, either. She had heard you could use a credit card these days, but to be on the safe side she stopped at an ATM at a drive-through bank. She found the county building, which looked more like a post office or a high school than a jail, and parked on the street.

Just in time she remembered the Smith & Wesson in her purse. She extracted it and put it in the glove compartment. She got out, locked the car, and went in.

Inside was the expected fluorescent glare with desk and uniformed officer behind it. Rachel was directed down a hall to an office, where she explained herself to a couple of sheriff's deputies who appeared startled to see her. They were happy to take her money, gave her paperwork to fill out, and then sent her back into the hall to wait. Half an hour later Billy appeared, ushered through a metal door by a stone-faced deputy.

He looked as if he could use a shower and a good night's sleep but did not appear to have been beaten, Tasered, gang-raped, traumatized or particularly intimidated. He did not seem surprised to see her. "Does he know you're doing this?" was the first thing he said.

"He knows."

Billy barely slowed; he looked as if he knew his way around the building. She followed him out into the night.

Rachel started the car and said, "You got a place you could stay? Your dad's kind of mad at you right now."

"To hell with him. I'm done with him."

Rachel looked out the windshield for a while. "I'll tell you the same thing I told him. Wait till you calm down before you make any decisions about the future of your relationship."

"I'm calm. I've just had five hours to calm down."

"OK. That's all I have to say. Where am I taking you?"

Billy heaved a sigh. "Just a second." He pulled out his cell phone and punched in a number. "Hey, I'm out," he said. "Can I crash at your place for a while? I been kicked out of my house." He listened for a moment. "You have got to be fucking kidding me," he said. "Well, that's just fuckin' great. All right, I'll be there in a little bit." He clicked off and said, "East Warrensburg. Go out Main Street." He shook his head as Rachel put the car in gear, then let his head fall back, eyes closed.

"What now?" Rachel said.

"Somebody trashed my car. Probably the dudes that jumped us. Slashed the tires, smashed the windows. It ain't going nowhere for a while. I am like, messed *up*."

Rachel drove in silence, fighting the urge to try to fix things. Offering him the Chevy was a nonstarter; she needed it, and it would enrage Matt. A small cash loan made more sense, but she knew even that was better kept secret from her brother. "I can lend you a little money," she said.

A few seconds passed and Rachel was having second thoughts, thinking about tough love and foolish indulgence. Billy said, "Thanks, I really appreciate that. But I'll be OK. I got a place to crash for a while, and I'll figure something out. You're not responsible for any of this shit."

That was indisputable, and Rachel found nothing to say to it.

Warrensburg had never seemed big enough to Rachel to have a suburb, but there it was, on the wrong side of the interstate and hard by the railroad tracks, not much of a town with not much of an excuse for being there beyond having been cheap land near the county seat. East

Warrensburg was a haphazard grid of curbless blacktop streets laid out on wooded ground that was too broken by streams to be much good for farming. Beneath the trees, widely spaced, were flimsy ranch houses dwarfed by their garages, tumbledown shingle-sided shacks and a few mobile homes that had come to rest, with a paltry block of storefronts passing for a downtown. Two of the storefronts were bars, and their neon beer logos were the only sign of life. "Slow down a second, will you?" said Billy. "This joint here, that's where it happened. I want to look at my car."

There was a graveled lot just past the building, and as Rachel slowed she saw that one of the three cars parked there was Billy's Dodge, slumped low on four flat tires, the windshield spider-webbed and long scratches running the length of the body. "Shit," Billy breathed as Rachel eased to a stop. "Those pricks."

"Oh, Billy. I'm sorry."

"Fuck it. You win some, you lose some."

"Who were you fighting?"

"Just some assholes. Some Mexican guys. There's Mexicans moving in around here and there's a lot of fights. Stupid shit." He pointed. "Go up to the end of the street here."

Rachel pulled out. "Did you really hit a police officer?"

"I didn't know he was a cop. Somebody grabbed me from behind and I just turned around and swung. I thought it was one of the guys that jumped us."

"Well, if you were in the middle of a fight, a judge might consider that a mitigating circumstance. You'll need a lawyer."

"They'll give me one. I ain't spending any hard-earned money on a lawyer. And my dad sure as hell won't."

Rachel gave it a beat and said, "I might."

"Save your money. I'll take my chances. Make a right here."

Rachel followed Billy's directions to the edge of town, not a far stretch in any direction, where a fairly primitive-looking ranch house, a featureless box with a roof, sat at the foot of the railroad embankment with light showing behind curtains, a satellite dish on the roof and a Dodge Challenger parked on the lawn. When she eased to a stop Billy already had the door open. "OK, thanks," he said.

"Billy."

That stopped him with one foot on the ground. "What?"

Rachel had opened her mouth to deliver another platitude about parental love and reconciliation, but stopped herself in time. "You'll need some stuff, won't you? Clothes and things? Let me know what you need and I'll bring it by."

"Yeah, that would be good. Just go up to my room and throw some clothes in my backpack. Look in my dresser. And maybe the closet, a couple of shirts. And my toothbrush."

"The blue one, in the bathroom."

"Yeah." He got out of the car and bent to look in at her. "Thanks."

"You're welcome. I'll try and come by tomorrow. Be good." Rachel watched him as he walked up to the house and rapped on the door. She was curious to know who was taking Billy in, but he disappeared inside without her getting a glimpse of the person who had opened the door. Rachel turned the car around at the end of the street and headed back.

It was not a nice-looking town, even with darkness hiding the detail; her headlights swept over junked vehicles and derelict sheds and sagging porch roofs. It depressed her to think of Billy washed up here, nowhere else to go. There were so many things to depress her that her mind fled them all.

It startled her to think that she had been lying in Dan Olson's arms just a few hours before. Suddenly she wanted him. She wanted to be in that embrace; she wanted to laugh at that easygoing charm. Going home to deal with Matt's drunken gloom was not appealing. But it was past midnight, and she knew the best way to ruin a nice comfortable fling was to push it too hard too fast.

The interstate offered a quick way back to the northern part of the county; she had passed an entrance ramp on her way out of Warrensburg. If she got off at the next exit fifteen miles north she would be close to home.

Flying past the sleeping farms, passing long-haul semis rolling through the night, Rachel became aware that her stomach muscles were clenching, her anxiety level rising. The dread was returning as she approached the part of the county that was most familiar to her, the area where she should have felt most comfortable. She had the same feeling she had always had flying back into Baghdad after furloughs, feeling the pall descend.

Just keep going, Rachel thought. All the way to the junction with Interstate 80 up at the Quad Cities; go east and you will be in Chicago in three hours. You can get a room at the Drake, sleep all day tomorrow, go out for a nice meal on Rush Street in the evening and think about what to do with your life. You can leave this bad dream behind.

The gas station at Alwood was an oasis of light. Rachel put on her signal and eased onto the exit ramp. The food mart was open twenty-four hours a day and briefly she wanted to pull in, go inside and buy something, just to talk to someone, just to put off heading away into the darkness. She had four miles to cover along roads where the only light would be from her headlights.

You have a gun in the glove compartment, she thought. Nobody can hurt you. Just drive home and go to bed. She rolled past the gas station and turned south onto the county blacktop.

The bright lights receded in the mirror. She passed a couple of houses set back from the road and then there were only distant points of light, the farms widely spaced in the rolling land of the north part of the county. Under her headlights the road dipped and rose. Rachel's heart had accelerated. She was hunched forward, leaning over the wheel, concentrating on her driving, prey to a chaos of images crowding at the edges of her mind, intense and conflicting: coyotes tearing flesh, sweet carnal indulgence in the dark. Integration and disintegration, repulsion and lust, horror and ecstasy. None of it seemed real.

You need to sleep for about a week, Rachel told herself.

She had just topped a rise when the tire blew, the sudden juddering and the tug on the wheel unmistakable. Rachel swore, corrected the swerve of the car, and coasted to the bottom of the hill. She came to a stop and sat in shock for a moment, looking out at the little patch of road and ditch in the radius of her headlights and the vast blackness outside it. "Shit," she said.

From the feel of it, it was the left front tire that had gone. A few seconds' reflection told her that drunks barreling home along country roads were still a more likely peril than escaped madmen, and she pulled the car to the side of the road, two wheels in the shallow ditch. Now it was decision time.

On the morning she had cleaned out the car, she had made sure there was an inflated spare in the trunk. What she had neglected to provide was any kind of light. She was going to have to change the tire in the dark, by touch, on a deserted country road not too many miles from where a psychopath had cut a man's throat by the side of the road a few days before.

Call Matt. Rachel pulled her purse across the seat toward her. He can be here in fifteen minutes.

Matt's drunk. He's passed out in bed by this time.

Call Dan. Dan lives less than two miles from here. Rachel reached into the purse.

She had the phone in her hand when she stopped. If she called Dan, it was an admission of weakness. It was relying on a big strong man for help. And in the past Rachel had sweated blood to prove she could handle a crisis.

Change the damn tire, she told herself.

Rachel let go of the phone, turned off the headlights and cut the ignition. The world became very dark and very quiet. Remembering the drunks, she turned on her emergency flashers. You are going to have to get out of the car and do this, she thought.

She opened the glove compartment and took out the revolver. She held it in her lap, telling herself that the odds against Otis Ryle coming along in the old blue Ford pickup just as she was changing a flat tire were overwhelming. And there was nothing about schizoid personality disorder and psychopathic narcissism that made a man bulletproof. And yet the night was black and Rachel knew that the things it hid were real.

Get out of the car and change the tire.

She popped the trunk and got out of the car, leaving the gun on the driver's seat and leaving the door slightly ajar. She looked up and down the road; there was just enough light from a feeble moon, reflected by the snow, to show her the lay of the land. A stream passed under the road through a culvert just ahead; the streambed was wooded, brush and small trees black against the pale slope beyond.

A man could hide in there, Rachel thought.

Heart pounding, Rachel moved to the rear of the car and raised the trunk lid. She shoved junk aside to get at the cover of the wheel well. She froze when she heard the car approaching, behind her.

Rachel spun to see the glow of headlights over the rise. She watched for a few seconds, long enough to determine that the car was coming along slowly, unlike a speeding drunk.

Like a man cruising for victims? Rachel hurried to the driver's side, tore open the door and snatched the gun off the seat. The car was a few seconds from topping the rise.

Get in the car and lock the door, Rachel thought. Then she had a vision of roadside collisions and after a second's hesitation ran around the car and made for the ditch. The car was just topping the rise when she hopped across it and, in full panic now, made for the streambed.

Rachel slid down the short slope toward the stream and, lying on her belly, twisted to watch the approaching car come slowly down the hill. She held the gun out in front of her, aiming at nothing, her thumb on the hammer ready to cock it.

You are a fool, Rachel thought. Your imagination has run away with you.

In the next instant she thought, He will follow your footprints in the snow.

The Chevy's flashers were lighting the night in hypnotic pulses. The other car slowed and eased to a halt behind it. Rachel exhaled heavily and let her head sag. The rack of emergency lights and the sheriff's department logo shone intermittently in the flashes.

She watched the driver get out and walk along the side of the Chevy. A flashlight came on and played over the inside of the car. The man holding the light walked to the front of the Chevy and shone the light on the ground in front of it, then beyond, over the verge of the road. In his other hand he held a gun at his side.

Rachel had regained her voice. "Officer?" she called.

The light jerked toward her. "Rachel?"

Rachel let go a single sob of relief. "Roger? Oh, God."

21 |||||||

Rachel clambered up out of the streambed.

"Are you all right?"

"I'm fine. I was just scared. I had a flat tire."

"I can see that. Do me a favor, will you? Just take your finger off the trigger of that gun, will you?"

"Oh, shit. I'm sorry Roger, I was scared. Here, take it if you want it." She held it out toward him, grip first.

"That's OK, I just don't want any accidents." Roger holstered his gun. "What are you doing out here?"

"I was on my way home from the interstate. Oh, God, am I glad to see you."

She was close enough now to make out his features in the eerie light; he was peering at her with concern. "You sure you're OK?"

"I'm fine. Let me . . . let me put this away." Rachel went and put the gun in her purse on the car seat. "I was going to change the tire and then when I heard you coming I got scared. I mean, maybe it's silly, but . . ."

"It's not silly." Roger was shining the light into the brush across the road. "It's not silly at all. He's still out here somewhere. You got a spare?"

"In the trunk. I can change it. I just needed a light."

"I'll do it, don't worry." He went to the back of the car and shone the light into the trunk.

"I can do it, Roger."

"I know you can. But I'm happy to do it for you. Here, hold the light, will you?"

Rachel obeyed; she was not in a mood to stand on feminist principle. She watched as Roger got out the spare and laid out the tools.

"This tire's had it," he said.

"It's an old car. They're probably all about to go."

Roger bent to his work. Rachel held the light and occasionally looked off into the darkness, up and down the road and off into the trees. She was reassured by Roger's presence but her nerves were still twanging. "I thought you worked days," she said.

Roger grunted softly, tugging to loosen the old tire. Rachel wondered if he had heard her and was about to repeat the question when he said, "We're all working overtime these days." He pulled the damaged tire free, pushed it away and looked up at her, squinting in the glare from the cruiser's headlights. "Extra patrols. Us and the State Police. Especially at night."

Roger stood up, his knees making a cracking sound. "Because that's when he comes out," he said.

Matt was gone when Rachel came down in the morning. Sleep had attenuated the hallucinatory quality of the previous evening. Today she was just a woman under stress who had added the complication of an affair to a life in disarray. She felt neither remorse nor elation regarding her roll in the hay with Dan; she had needed it and it would probably happen again and when the time came it would be over. Her feelings for Dan had survived the night unchanged; there was a connection there, but she had no illusions. It was a fling, and a well-managed fling could do a woman a lot of good. The trick was the management.

She ate breakfast in front of the television set, surfing the news shows. The national and international news was depressing and the local stations had nothing new on the Dearborn County killer. Rachel looked out the window at the sunlit, wind-scoured landscape and found that the terrors were manageable.

Rachel cleaned up and then went upstairs to Billy's room. In a closet she found a canvas tote bag and then foraged for the things she had promised to bring him. When she had found them she paused, looking around the room. The books on the shelves were a motley assortment of science fiction, graphic novels and high school classics; a rack held a few dozen CDs whose covers looked like advertisements for tattoo parlors. A computer sat on a makeshift desk formed by an old door resting on milk crates. A baseball bat and glove rested in a corner, traces of a boy who had vanished.

Rachel sank onto the unmade bed, distracted. Her heart was heavy with what had happened to her family. She had grown up with the unshakable idea that the Lindstroms were successes: They had a prosperous farm, they were pillars of the community. They did well in school, married well and lived to a contented old age. They produced no black sheep, suffered no tragedies.

Rachel knew that her obscure feeling of guilt was irrational; her parents would have died, her sister-in-law would have killed herself and her nephew would have gone off the rails even if she hadn't gone halfway around the world to marry unwisely and fail in her career. But the idea she couldn't shake now was that she had run away and failed her family.

She sighed and rose; she could start atoning by making sure Billy had what he needed in exile. She went and found his toothbrush and put it in the bag. On her way out, she took a flashlight from a drawer in the kitchen and put it in the glove compartment in the car.

She made good time down the interstate to East Warrensburg. In daylight the town was no more prepossessing than at night, though she could see there was a nicer end of town like anywhere else, where the houses were a little bigger, a little better kept. People had to live somewhere. She managed to find the street that dead-ended at the railroad embankment and pulled up in front of the slovenly ranch house.

It didn't take much to make a slum, Rachel thought, looking at it. What passed for a yard showed bare patches and crushed beer cans; a car muffler leaned against the side of the house next to a stack of cinder blocks and a stray tarp crumpled haphazardly. The Dodge Challenger was gone, replaced by a big Silverado pickup that had seen better days. A curtain in one of the windows moved and fell back. Rachel grabbed the tote bag and got out of the car.

She spotted a doorbell but before she got close enough to push it the door opened. Rachel was not surprised to see the girl standing there; she had been topping the list of Rachel's guesses. She looked better without the heavy makeup, a little healthier at least, but she didn't look especially friendly. She still looked underfed and her hair could have used a wash. Today she was wearing an oversized white T-shirt over purple tights. The shirt came almost to her knees and said *SEX REHAB DROPOUT* in big letters. "You're Billy's aunt," she said.

"That's right. I've got some things for him."

"I'll take them." The girl held out her hand.

Rachel hesitated. Looking past the girl she could see a couch with a TV remote lying on it, and beyond that a life-sized liquor store cardboard cutout of a woman in a bikini brandishing a six-pack of beer. Some trailer-trash Rembrandt had added nipples and pubic hair with black marker. "Can I talk to him?" Rachel said.

"He's still in bed."

"Ah." Rachel nodded. She was on the point of handing over the bag and fleeing, but suddenly she was irked: She was not going to be turned away by this slattern without getting a sense of who her nephew had taken refuge with. "I'm sorry, do you think you could go wake him up? I'd really like to talk to him."

She thought for a moment she was about to get the door slammed in her face, but after stiffening and throwing a glance behind her the girl shrugged and stepped back, beckoning Rachel in. "I can try," she said.

She closed the door behind Rachel and walked back through a kitchen divided from the living room by a counter, disappearing through a door. Rachel had halted by the door, staring at the man who was sitting at the kitchen table, smoking a cigarette. She had last seen him sneaking out of the shadows near her back door, casting a glance over his shoulder. Light did not improve his looks; he had long stringy blond hair and pale sleepy-looking eyes. Prominent cheekbones and a massive jutting jaw gave him the angular rough-hewn cast that had struck Rachel; he had a face made for mug shots.

"Don't just stand there," he said. "Make yourself to home." He had the drawl, and a blaring voice that he didn't bother to modulate much.

Rachel took a few steps toward the kitchen, taking in the living room as she went: a television set the size of a small billboard, an armchair with multiple burned spots and a coffee table on which a deck of cards lay scattered in a pool of spilled beer. The place depressed her; it smelled of smoke, beer, dope, unwashed laundry and dirty dishes. It was overheated and she was uncomfortable in her coat. "I won't trouble you too long," she said.

"Ain't no trouble. Want a beer?" He had one going in front of him, in a can, not the first of the day to judge by the empties on the counter. He was wearing a flannel shirt open over a T-shirt, the sleeves rolled up to reveal tattoos in blue ink on his forearms.

"No thanks. I'm driving."

He laughed. "That don't never stop me." His heavy-lidded eyes had looked sleepy at first; now, as they sized Rachel up from head to toe, they looked impudent. "You're his aunt, huh?"

He scared Rachel a little, but she was getting used to being scared; she had also had plenty of experience with men trying to intimidate her, from sour old deputy chiefs of mission to thuggish tribal sheiks. She looked directly into the pale eyes and said, "I am. And who are you?"

"Me? I'm what the cat drug in." He sucked on the cigarette.

Rachel nodded, giving him her coolest smile. "You live here?"

"Shit, no. I been thrown out of here. But the lady that done the throwing ain't here right now."

"I see. Who does live here?"

"You're kinda curious, ain't you?"

Rachel returned the stare. "Yeah. I'm curious."

He grinned, showing crooked teeth. "I guess Billy does, now."

"With her?" Rachel nodded toward the back of the house.

"Her and her mom. The Bitch, we call her."

Rachel nodded, looking around. "I can see why you like it here," she said.

She thought for a moment that she had made the mistake of mocking somebody who was smart enough to get it. But he only said, "It ain't bad. You should come around some time when you can stay a while."

And Rachel realized with a shock that the sleepy look was not intended to intimidate so much as seduce; this specimen was coming on to her.

Her astonishment struck her dumb until the door at the back opened. "He's getting dressed," said the girl, coming back into the kitchen. Her eyes flicked from Rachel to the man and back.

"Thanks." Rachel turned. "I'll be waiting outside."

"Shit, sit down and have a beer," said the man. "Don't be that way."

"Thanks but no thanks," Rachel said, making for the door. "I'm in kind of a rush." She let herself out.

Outside in the cold she shook her head. You have got to be kidding me, she thought. Do I look like the type who sleeps with Neanderthals?

The enormity of his presumption appalled her, then made her stifle a laugh. She thought of Dan suddenly, six three and two-hundred-something, linebacker sized.

I have a man who could wipe the floor with you. Rachel leaned on the car, surprised at the atavism of her reaction. Cavemen fighting over a woman, she thought. But it felt good to think of Dan, swatting the punk like a fly. It felt good to think of him, period.

The door opened and Billy came out. His hair flew in the wind as he came to meet her. "Jeez, thanks. I appreciate it." He took the bag.

"Billy, who the hell is that guy?"

He gave her a shamefaced look. "That's Randy. I know, he's kinda hard to take sometimes. Did he say something to piss you off?"

"No, he was pretty friendly, actually. Would his last name be Stanfield by any chance?"

Billy nodded. "My dad warned you about him, huh?"

"He mentioned him. Who's the girl?"

Billy shrugged. "Just a friend. Kayla. She's cool."

Rachel nodded vaguely and they stood looking at each other, Billy shivering in the wind. "Billy. My offer stands. You come up with a plan to change your life, I'll fund it. I'll loan you what you need to get started somewhere else. I haven't done anything else for this family for twenty years, so it's time. But you have to have a plan."

He stared gravely at her for a long time, then his eyes fell. "I ain't going nowhere till my court case comes up. But I'll be thinking about it. And I really, truly appreciate it, Aunt Rachel. Believe me, I do."

"All right, then." Impulsively she grabbed him in a quick hug.

His arms went around her briefly and then he pulled away. "Thanks for this shit."

22 |||||||

Somebody had put up decorations in Aunt Helga's room: a nativity scene on the dresser, a string of lights around the window, a tiny Christmas tree with needles made of foil on an end table. Steve was in attendance today, lounging in a chair by the window, one leg crossed over the other and tapping his fingers nervously on the arm of the chair. "Matt waited too long to crack down on the kid," he said. "I always thought he was too easy on Billy when he was little. Seemed like whenever there was a tussle, Billy always got his way. And then when Matt tried to rein him in, it was too late."

That was met with silence from Helga and Rachel, who was not getting the solace she had hoped to find here. "I'm not in a position to judge," Rachel said after a moment.

"Matt didn't spoil that boy any more than your daddy spoiled you," Helga said, peering at her son. "You got your way plenty."

Steve shrugged. "OK, whatever. I'm just saying."

"I think Billy's hurting," said Rachel. "I think he blames Matt for his mother's death. So he's trying to get back at Matt."

"How in the hell can he blame Matt?" said Steve.

"For moving back to the house after our mother died. Margie didn't want to leave the house they'd started out in when they were married.

Matt thinks that made the depression worse. He's still second-guessing himself about it."

"A woman likes to take pride in her home," said Helga. "It's like a farm. You put work into it, build it up, it's something you can call yours."

"Still, to kill yourself because you had to switch houses? That's a little extreme."

"I think there was a little more to it than that," said Rachel. There were times when her cousin Steve irritated her; he was one of those men whose views were as unshakable as they were unreflective. "She was depressed. She was on medication for it. The move was just a pre-cipitating factor." She was dealing with a couple of skeptics, she could see. "Anyway, you don't have to be a psychologist to recognize pain. And Billy's in pain."

After a silence Steve said, "Well, I'm sorry for him, then. But he's still got to straighten up and fly right. You don't get any points with the law for being in pain."

"Of course not. I think Billy's going to be OK. He's got some grow-ing up to do, that's all."

"Let's hope he doesn't have to do his growing up in jail."

That brought conversation to a halt. Rachel was on the point of tak-ing her leave when Helga said, "She made a lot of trouble, you know."

Rachel blinked at her. "Who, Margie?"

"That's right. Did you know the sheriff took Matt in and ques-tioned him about it? There was a lot of talk for a while about how he could have shot her and made it look like she killed herself. Anybody that knew him knew it was ridiculous, of course. That sheriff's a fool."

"Poor Matt. That's horrible."

Steve said, "They had to at least take a look at it. Something like that, it has to at least cross your mind the husband could have done it. Out there, no witnesses around, he could get away with it, easy. I bet it happens all the time."

"Steven. How can you even think such a thing?"

"Jeez, Mom. I'm not saying Matt did it. I'm just saying the cops had to be suspicious. They had to take a look at the possibility. They wouldn't be doing their jobs if they didn't."

"It's ridiculous." Helga waved the notion away, handkerchief clutched in her knobby hand. "That poor girl wasn't strong enough for the burdens she had to bear, and she killed herself. That's all there was to it."

Except for the pain she left behind her, Rachel thought, but chose not to say.

--- --- --- --- --- --- --- ---

The sheriff's department cruiser was parked next to Matt's pickup when Rachel got home, and her heart sank a little. She sat in the Chevy for a minute before going in, telling herself there was no reason her conscience should be uneasy with regard to Roger just because she had wound up in bed with Dan. She didn't owe anybody any explanations.

She did, however, owe Roger a word of thanks. When she came into the kitchen Roger and Matt were sitting in silence, coffee cups in front of them, as if waiting for her. "Hello there," said Roger, smiling. "Tires holding out OK?"

"So far. Thank you so much for helping me last night." To Matt she said, "Did Roger tell you how he rescued me?"

"Yeah," said Matt. "Who says chivalry's dead? I'd have let you change the damn thing yourself."

"I didn't want to chip a nail," Rachel said, playing along.

"I was happy to do it," said Roger. "It was something to do on a boring shift."

Rachel hung up her coat and got a mug from the cupboard. Matt said, "Roger's just filling me in on what to expect with Billy."

Rachel poured herself a cup of coffee. "And what can we expect?"

"Probably probation," said Roger. "Nobody's gonna put him in jail for a bar fight."

"Not even for hitting a cop?"

"Not unless he went after the cop on purpose. Which it doesn't seem like he did. But he's gonna need a lawyer, for sure."

"I'll take it out of his college fund," said Matt.

Rachel sipped coffee. "He says he's willing to go with the public defender."

Matt and Roger traded a look. "That could work," said Roger.

"Suits me," said Matt. "Maybe a little jail time would be good for him, who knows?"

"I don't think it does anybody much good," said Roger. "But probation's been known to get a kid's attention."

Matt scowled at him. "Man, that's a great credential to have when you're applying for a job, a criminal record."

"Could be a lot worse," said Roger. "If he gets probation it won't look all that bad on paper. Of course, he's got to stay out of trouble from now on."

"I wish I could guarantee he would."

"He's not your responsibility anymore. And like I keep telling you, you could have done a lot worse. There's successful prominent citizens in this county that raised more hell when they were young than Billy has."

Matt sighed. "You been a good friend, Roger. I appreciate everything you've done."

"I just try and look out for my friends." He looked across the table at Rachel. "How are you?" There was no smile today, crooked or otherwise.

"I'm fine, Roger." He knows, she thought. Matt told him. "Anything new in the investigation?"

"Which one?"

"The murder investigation. Otis Ryle."

"Well, there's two investigations. There have been two murders."

She blinked at him. "I guess I've been assuming they were done by the same guy."

"And they probably were. But they're still two different murders and two different investigations. You start assuming things, you can assume yourself right up a blind alley sometimes." Roger took a drink of coffee, frowning as if he were framing the opening words of a lecture. Then he grinned. "Not that the detectives ever tell me what they're thinking. They still got us out beating the bushes for Otis Ryle, that's for sure."

Rachel waited a second or two and said, "You never answered my question."

"What, whether there's anything new?" He waved a hand vaguely. "Like I said, the detectives never talk to me. The task force is set up in a room over at Warrensburg PD, and they go running in and out of there like they know what they're doing. Last I heard they were waiting on fingerprint results from Carl Holmes's truck. And they had talked to everybody that was at the bar with him that night. But I don't know that they had anything they were really excited about. I think they're going on the assumption that Ryle, or whoever, is still out there, armed and dangerous."

Outside the sun was getting low in the sky, the light starting to go. The three of them sat not looking at each other. Rachel shuddered. "I want it to be over."

"It'll be over before too long," Roger said, pushing away from the table. "Whoever it is, he's got too many people looking for him and too much that can go wrong for him. He's just about done."

"Let's hope so," said Matt.

"Gotta run," said Roger, standing and reaching for his cap. "Keep the doors locked."

- - - - - - - - - - - - - - - -

"Go ahead and do something with Dan tonight if you want. Don't hang around here on my account." Matt popped open a beer and tossed the cap into the trash can.

Rachel set the skillet on the stove. "I already told him I was staying in tonight. I'm making *côtes de porc à la moutarde*."

"More frog food, huh? What is it?"

"Pork chops. With mustard sauce."

"Well, why didn't you say so?"

"Because then it would be just pork chops. We'll have a feast and settle down in front of the TV. Or we could play Scrabble if you want. There's something we haven't done in a while."

Matt stood with his head slightly aslant, looking at her. "Trying to make sure poor old Matt doesn't get too gloomy?"

Rachel opened the refrigerator and pulled out the pork chops. "We're all pretty gloomy these days. It's as much for me as it is for you." She slapped the meat down on the counter and turned to face him. "I'm looking for my family, Matt. I've been home for two weeks, and I still feel like I'm a stranger. I've got a lot of catching up to do."

He thought about that for a while and then nodded. "OK. Want some help?"

"I'll let you do the dishes."

"Oh, yeah, I get the fun part. All right, call me when it's ready."

Rachel set to work, making a production of it; she needed something to absorb her. Along with the pork chops she made potatoes *boulangère*, potato and onion layers baked in the oven; she sautéed green beans with garlic and made a green salad, and she opened a bottle of a good California pinot noir she had found in Warrensburg.

"Nice," said Matt, once they were installed at the table. "I love these potatoes. Margie used to make something like this."

They ate in silence for a while. Finally Matt said, "I miss her. I miss her a lot sometimes. But I'm over the guilt. I can be philosophical about it." He drank some wine. "Mostly."

"Billy says it was just brain chemistry."

"Well, I'm glad he understands that now. He told me after it happened it was me that killed her."

"God, I'm sorry."

"It wasn't much fun. I even had the cops in my face for a while."

"That's what Aunt Helga said. I went and saw her today. Steve was there."

"He goes to see her, does he? I thought he'd written her off."

Rachel gave him a sharp look and Matt waved a hand. "I shouldn't talk. Steve and I have had our issues, that's all. Not my favorite cousin, but he's OK."

"What happened?"

"Nothing much happened except that we had a difference of opinion." Matt poured himself more wine with great concentration. "Steve got on the ethanol bandwagon a couple of years back, went around trying to get everyone to sell their land to DAE or contract to sell them all their corn. And I'm not convinced ethanol's not a house of cards. Right now a lot of it depends on federal subsidies and mandates. It's not completely economically viable. But these companies that get the subsidies are putting up plants all over the place, selling towns on the jobs they create and all that. And the next time Congress monkeys with energy policy or gas prices go down, the plants will close and the jobs will disappear. But Steve wasn't having any of that. I think he had some kind of financial stake in it somehow, he never really told me. And you know Steve, he's always right. So we don't get the families together for dinner too much anymore."

"Mm, that's too bad."

"I got cut off from a lot of people, to tell you the truth. People shy away from a bad-luck family. They're full of sympathy but the truth is, you scare them. They stop coming around and you don't see them as often. They drift away and never come back."

Rachel thought of Dan saying how many friends Matt had and wondered how good those friends could be. He was gazing at the tabletop and Rachel sat there thinking how much she loved him and how helpless she was to make anything better. "I'm sorry, Matt."

He came out of his reverie with a shrug. "It's OK. You learn who your real friends are. Dan, for sure. And Roger." Matt laughed, shaking his head. "Shit, old Roger, the doofus. We were never really pals when we were kids, but he's turned into a good friend. All this shit with my family, Roger's been there. You have serious trouble in your family, it's good to have a friend who can mediate with law enforcement agencies." He shot Rachel a look with mischief in it. "Anyway, if you had to pick two guys to fight over you, you picked two good ones."

"I didn't plan any of this."

"Nah, I know. I'm kidding."

Rachel sipped her wine and said, "Did you tell Roger about me and Dan?"

"He asked. He'd heard about it from somebody. I guess somebody did notice you sneaking off yesterday."

"Was he angry?"

"How the hell should I know? We didn't really talk about it. You and I haven't really talked about it."

"Not much to say. It just kind of happened."

"Your love life is your business, Rachel. If it's what you want, I'm happy for you."

"It's a fling. That's all it is."

"Well, Dan's a good guy. We been friends a long time, seen each other through some rough times." When the silence stretched on, Matt's eyes rose to meet hers. "Dan had a hard time with the divorce. There was a lot of anger. I pulled him off a couple of guys, walked him around the block to cool down a few times."

"Do I want to hear this?"

Matt dismissed it with a flop of the hand. "Dan's fine. He's mellowed. He's realized that fire that made him such a great football player doesn't do much for you off the field. And he never took it out on Sandy, if that's what you're thinking."

"I wasn't. But that's good to know."

"Dan's a good man. You could do a lot worse for a fling."

"That's my impression." Rachel set down her glass. "Roger probably thinks I lied to him last night. I told him I was on my way home from the interstate, which was the truth. But he probably thinks I was coming back from Dan's and just didn't want to tell him."

"Jesus, Rachel. Give yourself a break. He'll get over it."

She sighed. "I know he will. Poor Roger."

23 |||||||

Rachel wasn't entirely sure why she wanted to talk to Roger; perhaps just because it made her feel safer to have an armed officer of the law nearby. And while she knew she didn't owe Roger or anybody else any explanations, her conscience was bothering her a little. At best she knew she looked awfully fickle. If there was going to be an ongoing friendship there, he deserved a little attention. She called Roger on his cell phone to see if he could meet her for lunch.

Roger was on duty but said he could meet her in Warrensburg for coffee at three o'clock. "Afternoons can get busy sometimes. I might have to skedaddle. But unless there's a sudden outbreak of agricultural criminality I can probably make time for a cup of coffee." They agreed to meet at one of the franchise family joints along the highway at the north end of town, famed for its pies.

Rachel got there first and watched as Roger came in and dallied by the entrance with the hostess and one of the waitresses. They evidently knew him and were pleased to see him; Rachel knew that for obvious reasons restaurant people loved having cops in the place, but watching body language and facial expressions she thought there was more to it than that. For all his homeliness Roger had a certain rough charm; he smiled easily and he listened. Women saw that Roger was not going to put the moves on them; he made them feel safe. Rachel felt a brief pang of remorse.

"Hope I didn't keep you waiting," he said, laying his cap on the table and sliding into the booth.

"I just got here. How are things out there?"

"Quiet so far." He was scanning the place, not meeting Rachel's eye.

"No sign of escaped madmen?" She tried to make it sound light.

The waitress arrived with coffee and menus before Roger could answer. Rachel had already ordered coffee, and now following Roger's lead she indulged herself and ordered a slice of pecan pie. When the waitress had gone Roger said, "If he's still around, he's laying low. He only comes out at night."

"And what are the chances he's still around?"

He grinned suddenly, his mouth twisting. "If I could answer that, they'd give me a medal." The grin vanished. "Nobody knows, Rachel. And if they tell you they do, they're lying. Just like after the first time, he could have left the area or he could be hiding out in somebody's barn. He could be right here in Warrensburg. If he is still here, I don't think he's necessarily driving that truck anymore. I think he's got himself another vehicle, or we'd have spotted him by now." He took a sip of coffee. "I also think he's got help."

Rachel stared at him. "Somebody's hiding him?"

"That would be my guess. I don't think he's living in the woods and eating rabbits. Somebody has to be buying the food, helping him keep out of sight."

"That's appalling."

Roger nodded. "I think when we get this guy we're going to find out some interesting things."

"You mean . . ."

"I don't know yet what I mean. I just think he has to have some help, that's all."

"Somebody he knows from before?"

Roger frowned into his coffee. "Possibly. Maybe somebody he can terrorize. An elderly person, for example. Psychopaths are good manipulators sometimes." He raised the cup and looked at Rachel over the rim. "But it's all guesswork. The only thing we know for sure is, two people are dead."

The pie arrived in the depressing silence that followed. It wasn't much of a consolation. Rachel washed down a swallow with coffee and despite a voice in her head screaming at her to keep her mouth shut said, "You probably heard about me and Dan."

Roger stabbed at his pie, his face a blank. "I heard a rumor."

"The rumor's true. I just wanted you to know that I wasn't lying when I told you I had no intention of getting involved with anyone. This thing with me and Dan just kind of happened, suddenly. It caught me by surprise."

Roger shrugged. "It's none of my business."

"I know. But I didn't want you to think I'd had my eye on Dan all along and was putting you off with excuses. It was just, I don't know. Chemistry, the moment, whatever. It just happened. I hope it doesn't affect our friendship. That's all I'm trying to say."

Roger chewed, swallowed and drank coffee, frowning faintly. He set down the cup, clasped his hands like a pastor about to deliver a homily and looked at her. "Rachel, you don't owe me any explanations about your personal life."

"It's just a fling. I'm going to be leaving again in a few weeks anyway."

"OK. Like I say, you don't have to explain."

Wretchedly, Rachel returned to her pie. She realized she didn't really want it and shoved it away. "Thanks for understanding."

He made a gesture of dismissal. "Dan's a good man."

"So are you." Abruptly Rachel was on the brink of tears. Oh God, no, she thought. Don't make a scene over this.

Roger was staring at her, apprehensive. When she had managed to stabilize herself he smiled again, the old crooked smile. "It's all right, Rachel. Really it is."

She flashed him a smile. "I don't know where that came from. I'm a wreck."

"You been through a rough time."

"I'm so scared. This thing, these killings. I'm this close to just leaving, going back to Washington or wherever. But that would be running away from my family again." She had to look away out the window, at an ugly commercial strip in a depressed town, under a lowering winter sky. "I just want to feel safe again. I want Billy to be all right. I want Matt to be happy. I want my childhood back. I want all kinds of things I can't have."

Roger shoved his plate away. "And I can't give them to you. All I can tell you is, I'll do what I can to help."

"I can't tell you how much I appreciate it, Roger. Matt, too. He's very grateful for the support you've given him."

Roger was frowning again, avoiding her eyes. When he looked at her the sympathy and the charm were gone, replaced by a hard opaque look. "I'm working overtime to help you feel safe again. We all are. But right now I have to tell you something that's going to make things worse."

"What do you mean?"

"Remember when we talked about trying to predict who Ryle would go for next, from the quarrels his family had been involved in?"

"Sure."

"Well, I been doing a little snooping, asking around among people who might remember that far back. I talked to Dick Thomas, Ed's brother."

"Yeah?"

"He told me about the feud between the Ryles and the Thomases. There was bad blood because the Thomases had wound up with land that used to belong to the Ryles. Dick said all that happened was, they bought it from the bank when the Ryles got foreclosed. But he said Otis Ryle, now this was the father, the one who went out to California, blamed Ed and Dick's father somehow, accused him of scheming to get the land."

"Yeah, I heard about that."

"Well, what you didn't hear was that your dad got involved."

In the silence that followed, Rachel stared at Roger and felt the freeze creep up from her entrails. "My dad?"

"You knew he and Ed were friends."

"Sure."

"Well, Dick says your dad and Otis Ryle got in a fight once, just before Otis took off for California. Dick wasn't there but Ed told him about it. He said your dad was basically just taking Ed's side in the feud, but Otis had a nasty temperament and it came to blows. According to Dick, your dad gave Otis a thumping and Otis went away making threats. But then nothing happened and before too long Otis left town."

Rachel had worked through the implications before Roger stopped talking. "And it probably means nothing at all. Except that Otis's son grew up to be a psychopath. And there's a possibility he's going around killing people to settle old family scores."

"It's possible."

"How would he know my dad was involved?"

"He probably wouldn't. And it's probably a stretch to think these killings have anything at all to do with things that happened before our Otis Ryle was born."

"But two people are dead who had issues with his father."

"There it is. The last thing I want to do is scare you for no reason. But I thought I ought to tell you. It wouldn't be right to keep it from you."

"No. I appreciate it."

"Matt needs to know, too. You both need to be extra alert till we find this guy."

Rachel suppressed a sudden urge to laugh. "This is not real. This is too stupid."

Roger's look was suddenly intense. "It probably is, yeah. But the stakes are real high. I don't have to tell you that."

"No, you don't."

"So even if it's stupid, you need to be real careful. Lock the doors, all of that. Stick close to people."

"Check the backseat before I get in the car."

"That, too." Roger waved at the waitress and reached for his cap. "We're gonna catch this guy before too long, Rachel. Soon. But we haven't yet." He settled the cap on his head. "He's still out there, and he's close."

Rachel sat by herself in the booth for a little while after Roger left. Outside, the light was going and along with it her morale. She floated on dark waters, fighting currents of depression and little eddies of panic. It was time to go out and get in her car and drive home, and she didn't have the strength.

She was surprised by the force of the desire that took her at the thought that Dan would be off work by now. Suddenly her resolve to keep him and the romance at arm's length was vaporized by the memory of his mouth on her body. Her fingers brushed the cylinder of the revolver as she dug in her purse for her cell phone.

He answered after the second ring. "What are you doing after work?" Rachel said. Suddenly she was sure she was being needy and shameless and pathetic.

"Whatever you want me to do," Dan said. "I'm broad-minded."

"Want to have a drink? I'm in Warrensburg."

"Hot damn. Can you hold out where you are for a while? I just got off work. I'll need to stick my head under the pump for a second before I break the land speed record getting down there."

It had been a long time since Rachel had experienced this, having her spirits lifted so abruptly by the sound of a man's voice. "Take it easy. I can kill time here. Just tell me where to meet you."

"Give me an hour. You know where Duffy's is?"

Duffy's was a tavern just off Main Street that had been dingy and disreputable the last time Rachel had been around. Since then, it had been bought by somebody with deep enough pockets to redecorate and expand it into a beer-and-burger joint with multiple TV screens, a sound system playing generic rock music not quite loud enough to drown out conversation, three pool tables and two waitresses. It was moderately full, and Dan stopped a couple of times to shake hands and slap shoulders as he made his way down the room toward the booth where Rachel sat.

When he reached her he bent to kiss her, not making a production of it but lingering just long enough to show he didn't care who was watching. "This is where the local yuppies and rich folks drink," he said, sliding onto the bench across from her. "I damn near got in a fight with Sandy's lawyer in here one night just after the divorce."

"Good thing you waited."

"No shit. If I'd run into him a week earlier I'd be living in a hog house."

When he had ordered a drink, Dan reached for her hand across the table. "So. How you holding up?" He had shed the up-tempo bonhomie and he looked a little worn, a little tired, but pleased with the company.

Rachel returned the squeeze of his hand and released it. "I'm hanging in there. No nightmares for a couple of nights, and I can stay up after Matt goes to bed without getting freaked out by every little noise. But I'm still scared. And getting scareder. Roger says my dad once got in a fight with Otis Ryle's father."

"So?"

"Well, one theory is, Ryle's settling old scores."

Dan frowned and said, "I think that's horseshit. I think he's just a fuckin' head case. I think Ed Thomas and Carl were just unlucky to cross his path."

"I hope you're right. I'll still be scared till they catch him."

Dan nodded, looking grave. "It sucks, don't it? I get up in the morning and it takes me a few seconds to remember, and then all of a sudden I feel sick. I think about Carl and . . ." He broke off, looking away and shaking his head. "My aunt's taking it real bad."

"I'm so sorry."

"Ah, hell. I didn't bring you out to get you all depressed. You look nice tonight."

"Thanks."

"What are you guys doing for Christmas? Matt going anyplace?"

"He hasn't mentioned it. I was hoping to have a nice quiet homey type of Christmas. I think Emma and her husband are coming up from Peoria. I don't know if Billy will be involved. But then we weren't going to talk about depressing things."

Rachel took a sip of her drink and her eyes went to one of the muted TV screens above the bar. "Oh, my God," she said.

The set was tuned to a Quad Cities station and showed a talking head with the line at the bottom of the screen reading *Dearborn County Nightstalker: Hideout Found?*

24 |||||||

Dan twisted to follow her look. "Holy shit. Let's hear this."

He slid off the bench and went to the bar, Rachel following. "Can you turn up the news here?" Dan called to the bartender.

The barkeep gave him a dirty look but produced a remote from under the counter and began to study it as if it were the Rosetta Stone. "Come on, genius," Dan muttered. On the screen the image had changed to show a Dearborn County Sheriff's Department cruiser parked by the side of a gravel road. A couple of deputies and a man in plain clothes holding a clipboard were standing next to it, looking off into a stand of trees.

The sound came on, just audible above the music. Dan and Rachel leaned over the bar, straining to hear. "Illinois State Police detectives found traces of recent occupation in the barn, including stockpiled food and bedding materials. But it is the discovery of remnants of burned clothing near the barn which makes investigators think they may have found the place where escaped murderer Otis Ryle, suspected in two recent killings, has been hiding."

The older of the two detectives who had sat at Matt's kitchen table a few days before appeared on the screen, saying, "His clothing would have been bloody after either of these two killings, and burning it would be the best way to get rid of it."

The screen cut to a view of an old barn, swaybacked and unpainted, seen through trees. "Where the hell's that?" said Dan. "You recognize it?"

A voiceover said, "Investigators are analyzing tire tracks found near the barn to see if they match the truck stolen from the scene of the first murder. The killer is believed to be in possession of the truck. It was hoped he had left Dearborn County, but after the latest killing, police are warning residents that he may have chosen to go to earth in the area, where he lived as a child."

A shot of corn stubble in empty snow-dusted fields followed. "The abandoned barn near Regina, Illinois, is on land recently purchased from an absentee owner by a local agribusiness company. They say to their knowledge the barn has not been in use for at least twenty years."

The next face to appear on the screen was one they knew. "I'll be damned," said Dan.

Frowning at an off-screen interviewer, Mark McDonald was saying, "This is a parcel we just bought, from an owner down in Florida who hasn't lived on it since she was a child. The barn's derelict. We were planning to tear it down. Whatever was going on in there before we acquired the land has nothing to do with Dearborn Agricultural Enterprises."

"Oho," said Dan. "Caught you, you son of a bitch. Hiding a murderer in your barn."

The report had caught the attention of the drinkers along the bar and somebody said, "I wouldn't put anything past those bastards."

"Him in particular," said somebody else.

On the screen the anchor was back, saying, "Illinois State Police and Dearborn County sheriff's deputies raided the site this morning after receiving an anonymous tip, officers say. They found tantalizing clues, but no trace of Ryle."

"What kind of clues was that?" said a drunk at the end of the bar, struggling to focus. The news program had moved on to the next story and the bartender muted the set.

Dan shook his head. "It's horseshit. They don't have anything."

Three stools down the bar a man said, "What I want to know is how the cops let him get away. I mean, what they should have done is just sit on the damn place till the guy came sneaking back and then slapped the cuffs on him. Don't go raising a ruckus, making a big production of it, just to get your face on TV. All this fuss and Ryle's still out there."

His neighbor said, "It does seem like they're taking their sweet time about reeling him in."

"I mean, how hard can it be? They know what he's driving. And there can't be that many abandoned barns in this county."

"Let's go," said Dan. "There's nobody here knows anything more than we do."

Back in the booth he took a drink of beer and stared past Rachel for a few seconds. "He's not sleeping out in an old barn," he said finally. "Not in this weather. He's got a place to go. He's got friends."

"That's what Roger said. He thinks maybe he's moved in on some old person, somebody easy to manipulate."

Dan nodded slowly. "That would make sense. He wouldn't even have to have moved in. All he needs is a key. There's houses that are empty but not derelict. They're not abandoned. They're waiting for a renter, whatever, they been empty for a few months but the owner's still coming by to cut the grass, check the doors and windows. There's plenty of houses like that. If the detectives are smart, that's what they're looking at."

"You should talk to Roger."

"Ah, they don't need my help. They know what they're doing." He took a drink of beer and said, "Hey, listen. What would you say about getting away for a couple of days, just you and me? I got some vacation time coming and we could go somewhere. There's some nice places over by the river, we could rent a lodge with a fireplace, go cross-country skiing, hike, just lie around by the fire, whatever."

Rachel hadn't seen that coming. "Sounds nice," she said, after a moment, less than emphatically.

"Rushing things? Going too fast?"

She gave him a frank look. "Truthfully? I don't know yet. The other day was like grabbing a lifeline. You don't think, you just grab. Now we're back on shore and we're both old enough to know there's more to this than jumping into bed. What I can tell you for sure is, I'm leaving again, probably in a few weeks. This is just a visit. Factor that in."

He nodded once. "Not everything has to be all serious and complicated and long-term. I don't have any illusions about your life and mine. But I think we could have a nice few weeks."

That was pretty much what Rachel had been hoping to hear. This time she was the one who reached for his hand. "Give me a day or two on the getaway, OK? Right now I can't think past what I'm going to have for dinner."

"You hungry?"

"Not especially."

After a finely timed pause Dan said, "What do you feel like doing?"

Probably exactly what you want to do, Rachel thought. She remembered driving in along Main Street from the strip, looking at the scattering of businesses that were hanging on. Why not? she thought. I am an adult and not accountable to anybody and most of all not ready to be driven back out into the dark countryside. She gave Dan Olson a cool look and said, "I want to drive out Main Street, buy a pint of bourbon at the liquor store, and then check in at the West End Motel for an hour or two. I've never had an affair in a sleazy motel."

"Hot damn," said Dan. "I swear, you must be reading my mind."

- - - - - - - - - - - - - - - -

Soon I will be ready to face the dark countryside, Rachel thought, sitting up in bed. Right here, right now, I feel safe. A car purred by in the street outside. The faint light coming in around the edges of the curtains showed ghostly outlines: bed, armchair, desk, TV. The darkness concealed the frayed cushions, the peeling laminate, the missing drawer handles. But the sheets were clean and the plumbing worked, and the room wasn't going to do much harm to her credit card bill. Rachel listened to Dan's even breathing for a time and then swung her feet to the floor. She went and used the toilet and drank a glass of water and then came back and sat on the side of the bed. She held the pint bottle of bourbon up to the light and saw it was nearly empty; she set it back down. She didn't want any more to drink. She pulled her legs back onto the bed and clasped her knees to her chest.

I have gone halfway around the world, seen strife and suffering and joy and love and pain and loss, and wound up back here in a shabby motel room on Main Street in Warrensburg, she thought. With Danny Olson. Of all the exotic adventures she had had, this was the last one she would have predicted. Yes, she thought. Lying around by a fireplace with this man for a couple of days sounds pretty good.

Beside her Dan stirred, coughed, cleared his throat. "Remind me next time to skip the booze."

Rachel smiled in the dark, sliding down to rest on an elbow, running a hand through his hair. "You didn't seem to be impaired very much."

"I'm impaired as hell now." His great brawny arm snaked out and pulled her down on top of him. "My mouth feels like an asbestos recovery site and somebody's been pounding nails in the back of my head."

Rachel lay in his arms, refusing to think beyond the next hour. He was massive and warm and apparently pleased to be holding her, and for now that was all she needed. After a while Dan said, "I must have done something right this year. Here I was expecting the usual lump of coal and instead I get you. And it ain't even Christmas for a week yet."

Rachel burrowed deeper into his embrace, luxuriating in the warmth of skin on skin. "A present that unwraps itself. A special bonus."

He laughed, his chest heaving under her cheek. "Damn, you're something. Say something in French for me."

"*J'ai faim.*"

"That sounds sexy. What's it mean?"

"It means 'I'm hungry.'"

"For real? Me, too. We could hit the pancake house out on Gunderson."

"Pancakes at ten o'clock at night?"

"They go good with coffee. I'm gonna need a couple of gallons."

The South Asian clerk in the motel office did not seem at all surprised when they checked out. They climbed into their separate vehicles and wheeled out onto the street. Pancakes at ten o'clock at night proved to taste much as they did in the morning, though Rachel went for decaf to wash them down. They made small talk, Rachel laughing at Dan's scattergun humor. And then there was no more avoiding it.

In the parking lot they stood where the Chevy and Dan's truck sat parked side by side, keys in hand. "Well, it ain't very romantic, but I can think of a few dates I've had that would have gone a lot better if we'd had separate cars," Dan said. "You want to lead or follow?"

Rachel had given it some thought: Did she want an escort home? She could ask Dan in for a nightcap; Matt would still be up and it would be a cozy end to the evening. But there was the potential for awkwardness, as well: Her instinct was to keep this intimacy insulated from her brother's friendship with Dan.

And there was her independence to consider. She had enjoyed the tryst but perspective was returning, a sense of how far and how fast she wanted this relationship to go. "I can make it home by myself. It's a straight shot up 150. It's faster for you to take 34 over to the interstate."

"I just thought I'd offer. You seem a little jittery, that's all."

"I am a little jittery. But there's not far to go once I get off the highway. I'll be all right."

Dan gave her an appraising look and nodded. "If you say so. I don't mind following you."

She stepped into his embrace. "Thanks. But I'll make it." They kissed, making it last. Rachel pulled away and said, "That was fun. I'm living out a twenty-five-year-old fantasy."

"Man, that's pressure. I gotta live up to your image from twenty-five years ago?"

"You're doing fine." Her hand lingered on his cheek as she left him.

Driving up 150, Rachel felt the dread starting to creep back, stronger than the afterglow from lying in Dan Olson's arms. "I don't want to think about that," she said out loud. Lights passed by in the dark, inhabited farmsteads scattered across the endless acres, and occasionally a hulk glimpsed in the dark, a barn or maybe a house with no lights showing.

When she turned into the driveway of the farm, her heart sank. A couple of lights burned in the house, but Matt's truck wasn't there. She parked the Chevy near the back door and sat with the engine idling.

She put her hand in her purse and felt for her cell phone, instead finding the revolver. I am not going to play the frightened child again, she thought. She pulled her hand out of her purse and cut the ignition. She sat still until she became conscious of the rearview mirror and caught her breath, suddenly aware of the darkness behind her. She twisted abruptly on the seat to look over her shoulder. There was nobody there, only the familiar expanse of lawn stretching toward the road, into the darkness.

Damn you, move, thought Rachel. Either drive down the road to Clyde and Karen's again, or rein in your imagination and go into your house and go to bed.

Rachel remembered hearing a sergeant in a convoy on the way in from Baghdad airport say that everybody was afraid and that the trick was to learn to function with fear.

All right, then, function. Rachel took a deep breath and opened the car door. She got out of the car, locked it and then swept the farmstead with a look, seeing nothing but familiar things, made sinister in the light from the halogen lamp high on its pole. She hurried to the back door, unlocked it and slipped inside, locking it behind her.

The overhead light in the kitchen was on, casting its light down the steps to the back door. From the yard, Rachel had seen that a lamp was on in the living room. The rest of the house was dark. It's empty, she thought. There's nobody here. He doesn't break into houses; he waylays people on the road. Anyway, how could he know where you live?

She stood listening for a long time, her back to the wall beside the back door. She heard nothing but the hum of the refrigerator, the ticking of the kitchen clock, the miscellaneous creaks of an old wooden house.

Rachel slid her hand back into her purse and gently released her keys. She shifted her fingers a little and found the grip of the revolver. She pulled it out.

Start at the top of the house and work down, she thought. You will have to check the attic. You will have to check every closet; you will have to look under all the beds. You will have to go down into the dark basement and check every nook and cranny. Keep your back to the wall.

She went up the steps into the kitchen, scanning, holding the gun out before her. She set her purse on the table and stood listening.

And if he's in the basement and comes softly up the stairs behind you while you're in the attic? What if he is waiting by the circuit breakers, ready to plunge the house into darkness and come swiftly after me with the knife before I can find a flashlight?

Rachel's heart was pounding. The rational part of her mind knew that the house was empty, but the part that had seen Ed Thomas's arm in the mouth of a coyote was stronger.

I can't do this, she thought.

Rachel took a deep breath. Plan B, then. When your lines are too extended, you pull back on a secure position. Gun at the ready, she went briskly down the hall toward the lighted living room. Halfway along the hall was the door to the den, closed.

I can't search the whole house, but I can barricade myself in the den. Provided he is not waiting for me in there.

At the door to the den, Rachel put her left hand on the doorknob, raising the revolver with her right. She turned the knob and shoved the door open, violently. She jumped into the middle of the room and spun, ready to fire at point-blank range into Otis Ryle's face.

25 |||||||

The room was empty. There was only the neatly made cot, the computer, and the mess of papers on the desk, the bookshelves, the armchair, the dresser Matt had moved down from upstairs.

Panting, nearly sobbing, Rachel shoved the door shut and tossed the gun onto the seat of the armchair, quickly wrestling the chair over to block the door. When the door was secure she picked up the gun and flopped on the cot with her back to the wall, holding the gun with both hands, assuring herself there was no room for anyone to hide behind the curtains, no closet, nobody crouched under the desk, no threat, no sign of danger, no justification for her panic. She was a hysterical woman sitting on a bed in an empty house with a gun in her lap, trying to breathe deeply.

"Get a *grip*," she said out loud. In a minute she had steadied her breathing.

Rachel leaned over to lay the revolver carefully on the desk. She closed her eyes and let her head fall back against the wall. Slowly her breathing steadied. The old house creaked as the wind probed the eaves, and slowly Rachel became sure that she was alone.

Eventually she opened her eyes and swung her feet to the floor. Her gaze wandered about the room. The quarters were cramped, with the dresser and the cot out of place in what had been their father's study, but it was tidy and she could see how Matt would be comfortable here, cocooned in his monastic cell.

Rachel rose and stepped over to the desk. The screen saver on Matt's computer had been drawing her eye inexorably with its geometric shapes in hypnotic motion. She knew better than to go poking around too deeply on other people's computers, but if she could call up a game of solitaire it would be a welcome sedative. She sat and nudged the mouse next to the keyboard. The screen saver vanished to reveal a headline: *Mexican Gangs Penetrating Heartland.*

The article was on a news aggregator site Rachel had looked at a few times. She reached for the mouse to minimize it. *Mexican methamphetamine producers have extended their reach into the Midwestern states,* she read.

Like we don't have enough to worry about, Rachel thought. She positioned the cursor over the minimize button.

The gang, known in Mexico for decapitating rivals and leaving the heads as messages, has chased out local producers in many areas.

Rachel clicked and the article disappeared. Enough, she thought. Leave me alone.

She was scanning the desktop for the game when she was startled by a faint tweeting noise somewhere in the house; it took her a moment to recognize it.

Her cell phone was ringing.

Rachel wrestled the chair away from the door and picked up the gun. She took a deep breath, flung open the door and hurried down the hall to the kitchen. She laid down the revolver and managed to get her phone out of her purse and focus on Matt's number on the display. She stabbed at the phone with her thumb. "Matt?"

"The one and only. You at home?"

"Yeah. Where are you?"

"I'm standing by the side of the road, all messed up."

"What's wrong?"

"I put the truck in the ditch."

Rachel sagged back against the refrigerator, closing her eyes. "Where?"

"About a mile south of Alwood, on West 300. I was coming home from the bar."

The sound of Matt's voice had broken the spell of her fear, but now she could hear the careful diction, the hint of slurring. "Matt, are you drunk?"

A soft chuckle came through the phone. "I might have had one or two too many. Actually what happened was, I dozed off for a second. I'm awake now for sure, but the truck's staying where it is till I can get a tractor over here."

"Oh, Matt. Are you all right?"

"I'm fine. I just need you to come get me. I'd hitch a ride, but there's not too many people out tonight."

And suddenly Rachel saw him, standing alone in the dark by the side of the road. "Matt, call the police. He's still around here somewhere. Otis Ryle."

"Call the cops so they can come and charge me with drunk driving? No, thanks."

"Matt, you're in danger. I'm going to call 911."

"Dammit, Rachel. You're four miles away. You'll be here faster than any sheriff's deputy can get here. Just come get me for God's sake."

Rachel gave it two seconds' thought. "OK, I'll be right there."

"I'm on West 300 about a half mile north of Jack Swanson's place. Look for a truck in the ditch and a shit-faced farmer."

"Get in the truck and lock the doors. I'm coming." Rachel killed the phone. She threw it into her purse and dug out her keys. She stuffed the gun in after the phone, put on her coat, and made for the back door.

Outside, the night was just as empty as before. Function, she told herself. She got the car door open, tossed in her purse, got in and started the car. She spun her tires on the gravel pulling away from the house.

She knew exactly where Matt was, and she knew it shouldn't take her more than a few minutes to get there. She knew that he was less than a mile from where Carl Holmes had had his throat cut by the side of the road.

I didn't check the backseat when I got in, Rachel thought, and almost panicked. Her eyes went to the mirror in spite of herself. The car was locked the whole time you were in the house, she told herself. Function.

The asphalt spun by under her headlights. Rachel realized she was going almost sixty, too fast for these roads at night. "Function," she said out loud, slowing for a turn. Her lights swept over a ditch, the border of an empty field. Beyond the arc of her headlights was black night.

Uphill and down, the country dipping and rising, pockets of woodland lurking in the hollows just beyond the range of her lights. One more rise, and then her lights caught the big Ford pickup, slewed off the road into a deep ditch, lying nearly on its side. Rachel braked.

There was no sign of Matt. As she approached she veered toward the truck and her high beams shone into the cab. It was empty. Rachel came to a stop. Frantically she scanned the eerily lit cone of road, ditch, brush and field her lights showed her. "Matt, where are you?" she said aloud, in a quavering voice.

He climbed up out of the ditch from behind the truck, zipping up his pants, squinting in the lights. Rachel sagged on the seat, exhaling. She rolled down the window. "Nice parking job."

Matt stepped onto the road, walking carefully. "Thanks. Kind of a tight fit, but I got it on the first try. Hear that?"

"Hear what?"

Matt halted, a hand raised. In a lousy Bela Lugosi voice he said, "Listen to the voolves, de children of de night."

Now she heard it, coming clearly through the chilled air, audible above the muttering of the Chevy's engine: a distant cacophony of barking. "Dogs?"

"Coyotes. Probably fighting over a kill."

Rachel shivered. "Get in, will you?" She rolled up the window.

Matt walked across the front of the Chevy and got in, collapsing onto the seat. He patted Rachel on the thigh. "Thanks for coming to get me."

"You sure you're OK?"

"I'm fine. Just . . ."

"What?"

Quietly, he said, "Disgusted, that's all. Disgusted with myself."

Rachel was checking her mirrors, conscious of the vast night behind her. "Is there a place to turn around up here?"

"Hell, just go up to the next road and head west to 500."

"All right." She had already put the car in gear. "Weren't you terrified? He's out here somewhere."

"Who's that?"

"Don't kid me. Otis Ryle."

"Ah, fuck him."

"Matt, Roger says he could be targeting us. You and me. He says Daddy got in a fight with Ryle's father, years ago."

"Yeah, I know."

"You know?"

"Roger called me to tell me about it. I think it's a load of crap."

They reached the top of a hill and Rachel could see the lights of Alwood far ahead, the gas station by the interstate exit brightly lit. "I don't know how you can be sure."

"None of this has anything to do with Otis Ryle's childhood or his father or any of that. He's just a sick bastard who got away from the loony bin. They'll catch him inside a week. You watch."

"God, I hope you're right."

Matt was silent as they approached a crossroads, letting her slow and make her turn. As they headed west he said, "Finding Carl was bad enough. Ed, I can't imagine. I'm sorry it had to be you."

"Actually, can we not talk about it? I'm close to freaking out here."

"Sorry."

She drove, leaning forward over the wheel. The road revealed itself under her lights, coming at her out of the darkness. Rachel drew a deep breath, glanced sideways at Matt. "Growing up, I never, not once, felt isolated or scared living out here. There was always a friend a few minutes away by car, and if there was no car there was always the telephone. I loved living in the country. Even at night, it never scared me. Now? All that out there terrifies me." She flapped a hand at the darkness speeding by.

Matt let a few seconds pass. "They'll catch him and then it will be all right."

"Maybe. But right now it scares me to death." Rachel was concentrating on her driving, leaning forward, tensed.

"He's not a frickin' werewolf. He's human. Anyway, whatever he is, he can't catch a moving car."

Rachel came over a rise. The road dipped into a hollow, and at the bottom of the hollow was a swirl of motion, things flashing in the sudden glare, resolving as she hit the brakes into a frenzy of animal movement, three or four coyotes nipping and slashing at each other, in front of a car parked across the road, blocking it.

Rachel braked hard and came to a stop fifty feet from the car. "Christ," said Matt.

Caught in her headlights, the coyotes barked and scattered, leaving the car shining in the lights and the man leaning on it. "Oh, my God," said Rachel, her heart thumping as she stared, trying to make sense of what she was seeing. "Is he all right?"

"He doesn't look good, does he?" said Matt.

The man was leaning against the driver's-side door of the silver Lexus, facing them, head tilted a little, right hand draped casually over the side mirror, the left dangling at his side. One of his trouser legs was torn, revealing the shaft of a cowboy boot. "Holy shit," said Matt, opening his door. "He must have got bit." He was out of the car and trotting toward the man.

"Matt, be careful!" Rachel could still see coyotes, milling at the edge of the light. She eased forward, her brights lighting up the car and the man sagging back against it. She saw a long coat with a fleece collar, blond hair shining in the headlights. When she was twenty feet away she put the car in Park and got out. Matt had reached the car but had stopped, staring. "Who is that?" Rachel said. "I've seen him somewhere."

The man hadn't moved. His eyes were closed; he looked as if he had dozed off on his feet. "It's Mark McDonald," said Matt. "What the hell's wrong with him?" McDonald's legs didn't seem to be supporting any of his weight. He was resting on his heels, the soles of his cowboy boots showing; he ought to have slid down the car and come to rest on his rump.

"What's holding him up?" Rachel said, barely able to force the words out of her constricted throat.

"I don't know," Matt said. Rachel watched as her brother stepped slowly toward the motionless figure, heard him call McDonald's name. She saw Matt reach toward the lapel of the long coat and she saw how the coat was parted unnaturally, somehow held away from McDonald's chest. She watched as Matt pulled one of the lapels aside to expose the three sharp points of the pitchfork just protruding from McDonald's chest and then she was screaming for him to get in the car and Matt was stumbling away from the corpse.

"He didn't bleed much," Roger said. "That's good. It means he died fast. Probably one of the tines went right through the heart."

Matt and Rachel had wound up in the backseat of his cruiser, watching while state cops in their Smokey hats and Dearborn County sheriff's deputies milled in the glare from their congregated vehicles. She was grateful that a State Police car had parked so as to block her view of the car where Mark McDonald still hung skewered.

"Terrific," said Matt. "That's a relief." Since their interview with a sheriff's department investigator who had come out from Warrensburg, he had mostly been sitting motionless, staring straight ahead.

"Could have been a lot worse," said Roger. "He must have been dead when he was propped up like that. Would have hurt like hell if he was still alive. Once he was dead all our guy had to do was haul him up to the car, shove the handle in through the open window, get in on the other side and run the window up to hold it tight." Roger shook his head. "Just for show. Sick son of a gun."

Rachel wanted to get on the interstate and drive till she ran out of gas and then get out of the car and run across fields until she dropped. She had not wanted to come back here, but the sheriff's deputy who had shown up at the Alwood truck stop in response to Matt's call had insisted they get in his cruiser and guide him to the spot. The other cops had come wailing out of the night shortly after that.

"Don't worry," said Roger. "You shouldn't have to wait around much longer. There's a forensic guy on the way from Warrensburg, but he won't need you. I think our guy's just waiting for an OK on the radio from the ISP guys to let you go."

"They won't let us go," said Matt.

"Why not?" said Rachel.

"They'll need to ask us why it's always us that finds the bodies."

Roger turned to look at them over the seat and said, "There's always a reason. There's a reason why Rachel went over to Ed's place and found him, and there's a reason why you got called out and found Carl. And there's got to be a reason it was you tonight. But it doesn't mean you had anything to do with it."

"Tell your detective that. I think he wants to slap the cuffs on us. But there's no way anybody could know where I was going to put my truck in the ditch. And that's what determined our route. So he wasn't laying for us. He was just laying for whoever came along."

"That's what I figured," said Roger, turning again to look out the windshield. "He parked Ed's truck across the road to get McDonald to stop. You can see the tire marks on the shoulder." Roger shook his head. "He got him to stop and he got him out of the car. But that's the part that's hard to figure."

A few seconds passed. Rachel said, "Why?"

She could just make out Roger's long face in the gloom as he twisted to look at her. "He got McDonald from behind. But there's no cover here. Even before McDonald got out of the car, he should have been able to see if there was any threat. But he got stabbed in the back." Roger shook his head slowly, looking out at the night, patches of snow showing faintly on the dark slopes. "How does this guy always manage to get behind people?"

26 | | | | | | |

Rachel awoke to sunlight glowing on smooth, worn floorboards. She sat up with a start, and the blanket slid off the sofa and onto the floor. She gazed about the living room. The house was quiet. She was fully clothed except for her shoes; the last thing she remembered was sitting with her feet drawn up on the couch, Matt's arm around her, watching something stupid on wee-hour television. She had been too disturbed to go to bed, and she had needed to sit there with her big brother's arm around her, trembling.

Rachel rose and walked to the window. Outside it was a bright clear day, the branches of the oak etched black against the hard blue heavens. Over everything lay a pall of dread. It's all spoiled, Rachel thought. I'll never be happy here again.

She had been numb with shock the night before, but she was clear-headed enough in the morning light to know that it was time for decisions. She found Matt at his desk in the den, shuffling scratch paper and stabbing at a calculator with the eraser end of a pencil.

He glanced up from his work. "Sleep OK?"

"Lost consciousness for a while anyway, thank God. Don't you ever sleep?"

"I got my four hours."

Rachel laid a hand on his shoulder. "Sorry I was such a wreck last night."

Matt patted her hand. "I wasn't thrilled myself."

"Why us, Matt? What's going on?"

He sighed, staring out the window. "The luck of the Lindstroms, that's all. The odds are catching up with us after four generations of good fortune."

"I found one, you found one, we found one together. Who's going to believe that's coincidence?"

"It's not coincidence. Roger's right. There's a reason." He slapped down the pencil and turned to look up at her. "Look, Ed didn't have any friends but us. So who else is going to find him but somebody from our family? And then Dan and I are first responders, so that's why we found Carl. As for last night, we were the only ones out because I had to try and drive home drunk from the bar. All this whole thing means is that we're plugged into the community and there's a God damn psycho loose in the community."

"Is that what everyone else will think?"

"Who gives a shit what anyone else thinks? Now, will you be available to ride on the tractor with me over to pull the truck out?"

Rachel exhaled, squeezing Matt's shoulder. "Can I have breakfast first?"

"Sure. I don't think the truck's going anywhere."

Rachel was settling down to coffee when her cell phone rang. She retrieved it from her purse and saw Dan's number on the display. She felt a little flare of warmth, an ember still glowing under a layer of ash. "Hi."

"Did you hear?"

Rachel closed her eyes. "I didn't have to hear. Matt and I found him."

There was a frozen silence. "Jesus Christ. You found McDonald?"

"Yeah. Matt put his truck in the ditch coming home from the bar and I had to go get him. Coming back we found McDonald. We were up all night with the cops."

A faint exhalation came through the ether. "Oh, Jesus Christ. Oh, Rachel, I'm sorry."

She tried a laugh, which was not convincing. "It wasn't your fault."

"Are you OK? Matt OK?"

"As well as can be expected. We're functioning."

"How did you . . . Where in the hell did Matt go off the road?"

"Oh, I don't know. Let me see. We were on West 300 and then we turned west on, it must have been about 1200 North. I'm not sure. The first, no the second road north of Jack Swanson's place. And he was at the bottom of a hill, maybe half a mile west of where we turned."

There was another silence. Dan said, "It sucks. Even if McDonald was a prick."

"'Sucks' hardly covers it. I'm a basket case, Dan."

"Ah, Jesus, Rachel. This is messed up. Are you all right? I can ditch work if you want, come over to your place."

"Actually, I'm OK. Matt's here. And we're expecting more cops. And more media. It won't be a lot of fun. But maybe later would be good. I'll call you."

"OK." A pause, and then Dan said, "Look, Rachel. Roger's full of shit, with this thing about Ryle targeting you. There's no connection between Ryle and McDonald, couldn't be. McDonald moved in here from Texas, ten or fifteen years ago. So this has nothing to do with Otis Ryle's dad picking fights or any of that nonsense. That's all horseshit. It's just a fucking madman running around."

"So we're all at risk. He's right here, on top of us. Look at where the killings have been. Ed Thomas northwest of Ontario, Carl Holmes east of Rome, and now McDonald, just south of Alwood, right? They're all three here in the north part of the county, within what, ten miles of each other?"

"Yeah, that occurred to me, too. He's hiding out somewhere around here. But that means they gotta catch him soon. I mean, they have to. He's not invisible. He's eating and sleeping somewhere. And they got every cop in the state of Illinois after him. He doesn't have much time left. I bet you."

"God, I so hope you're right. But that's no guarantee."

"I know, Rachel. Keep the doors locked."

Rachel heaved a great sigh. "I'm past that stage, Dan. I decided when I woke up, I can't live out here till they catch him. I'm too much of a wreck. I'm going to see if I can go stay with Susan in Warrensburg for a while. If I can convince Matt to come with me, so much the better. And you. You're alone out there. You're not that far from things."

"No, but I got a shotgun and a thirty-aught-six at home. He shows up at my place, he's roadkill."

"Don't let the guns make you cocky."

"Don't worry. I'm looking over my shoulder all the time. Listen, I gotta go. I'm at work. But I want to see you, Rachel."

"I want to see you, too. Let me give you a call when I figure out what I'm doing with my life for the next few days."

They made their good-byes, and Rachel sat holding the phone for a few seconds, feeling dazed and hollowed.

Matt came down the hall from the den, carrying a coffee mug. Rachel said, "Matt, I'd like to go camp with Susan in town if I can, just until this is over. I'm too scared to be here while that man's on the loose. I don't suppose I can convince you to go someplace safer, too."

He gave her a look, eyebrows raised. "Like where?"

"I don't know. Someplace less isolated."

He cocked his head in the direction of the Larsons'. "Who's going to watch over Clyde and Karen?"

"All right, I know it's not practical. I'm sorry, Matt. I'm just too frightened."

He pulled out a chair and sat, giving her a thoughtful look. "Do what you have to do. But I'm staying here."

"I'm sorry."

"For what? After what you've been through, I'm surprised you're still in the state."

Rachel put her face in her hands and suddenly she was crying, softly. "I wanted it all to be like it was. I wanted to come home and be babied."

"And we let you down."

She reached for his hand. "Nobody let me down. It's just bad luck."

Matt squeezed her hand and released it, pushing away from the table. "The luck of the Lindstroms," he said.

"We'll put you in Michelle's room," said Susan, leading Rachel up the stairs. "It's become the guest room by default, since Abby still comes home on break and Jason's room has never really recovered from darts in the wallboard and paint schemes out of Marvel Comics."

"I'm sure it'll be perfect," said Rachel, leaning against the weight of her overnight bag.

And it was: clearly a girl's room, but neutralized by the disappearance of knickknacks and favorite toys, a cozy nook under the slope of the roof with floral wallpaper and white-painted built-in bookshelves, with a window on the quiet street below. Rachel tossed her bag onto the bed and sank down beside it. "I love it."

"I put out towels for you in the bathroom at the end of the hall, which is all yours, at least till Abby gets home next week. Greg and I have our own."

"I don't know how to thank you, Susan."

"My God, it's the least I can do. I can't believe what you've been through." Susan came and sat beside her. "I'm worried about my parents out there. I think it's a great time to go spend a couple of weeks in Florida, but Daddy's too cheap. He's like, 'I'm not letting some maniac run me off my land.' He thinks he's John Wayne or somebody, waiting for the Comanches. But he's locking the doors and not letting my mom go anywhere by herself."

"I'm terrified for Matt, too. He's being stoic, a perfect Scandinavian male. He hasn't shown any emotion about it at all. He's gotten very good at suppression, I guess."

"He's probably in denial. Nobody believes it can happen to them."

"Until it does. *I* believe it." Rachel shuddered.

Susan's arm went around her. "You're safe here."

"It's awful. I was never this scared in Iraq. Never. Of course there I had the U.S. military to protect me."

"Well, we're almost to that point here. The radio this morning said they're bringing in more state police for the task force. I think it's only a matter of time before they catch him."

"They have to find him first," said Rachel.

Aunt Helga was asleep in her chair when Rachel came in, head canted over awkwardly and mouth slightly open, her sunken breast heaving just perceptibly. Rachel lowered herself quietly onto the chair by the window and waited, glad of the chance to sit and be utterly vacant for a moment. Her gaze wandered about the room: the pictures on the shelf, the slightly rumpled bed, the Christmas cards crowded together on the small table. This is my future, she thought. Except there will be no grandchildren to visit. She drew a deep breath, remembering her aunt's contempt for self-pity.

Perhaps ten minutes went by. Helga stirred and opened her eyes. It took her a few seconds to focus on Rachel. "How long have you been there?" Helga said.

"I just now sat down. I'm sorry to wake you."

"Oh, don't be sorry. I have all the time in the world to sleep." The old woman collected herself, locating handkerchief, paperback book and glasses in her lap. She peered at Rachel. "You don't look well, honey."

"I've been under a lot of stress."

"Have they caught the Ryle boy yet?"

"Not yet. There was another murder last night."

This brought a sharp look. "Who got killed?"

"A man named Mark McDonald. He lived up near Alwood." For a moment Rachel considered telling her what had happened, but she found she had no stomach for it. "He wasn't from around here originally, so it doesn't look as if this one was part of whatever vendetta Otis Ryle's engaged in."

Helga blinked at her. "Well, there were some McDonalds that lived south of Ontario when I was young, but I don't know what became of them. All the Scots that settled around here, that's never been a particularly common name."

"Well, the vendetta theory is just a guess anyway. I'm starting to believe he's just a madman."

"But I believe I remember John Black's daughter married somebody named McDonald about twenty years ago. Though I don't think the marriage lasted."

Rachel frowned across the room at her. "John Black? Is that Roger Black's father?"

"Yes, Roger was his son, I think. And the daughter was Marcia."

"I know Roger. That's funny, I was just talking about Marcia with him the other day. He told me about how she sold all the land he was supposed to get."

"I recall hearing about that. And then she moved away."

To Texas, Rachel thought. She said, "And she married somebody named McDonald?"

"Yes, I think so. But I doubt it's the same one."

"No, probably not. That would be a long shot."

They sat without speaking for a time, not looking at each other. Helga said, "Are they sure it's this Ryle who's doing all the killing?"

Rachel roused herself. "I don't know that they are. But when a homicidal maniac escapes and then people in the area start getting murdered, the maniac is a good first guess. How many madmen are there likely to be running around at any given time?"

The look Helga gave her was steady and grave, with no hint of irony. "More than we really want to know, honey. More than we could stand to know."

27 |||||||

There was a missed call on Rachel's cell phone; the number was Roger's. Rachel brought up the voice mail. *"Hey, Rachel. It's Roger. Just wanted to bring you up to date on things. I could have coffee again this afternoon if you want. Matt says there's reporters looking for you, so keep your head down. He had to chase away a few today. Call me if you want to meet."* Rachel thought about it for a second with the phone in her hand and then punched Call.

They went for the same place, at four o'clock this time. "But no pie," Rachel said as she slid into the booth opposite him. "I'm having dinner at Susan's in a couple of hours." Something in Roger's look froze her. "What?"

"You haven't heard from Matt, huh?"

"What happened?"

Roger frowned at his coffee cup. "Nothing to panic about. But the investigators from the task force decided they needed to sit him down for a longer talk. He's over at WPD right now."

"They arrested him?"

"They brought him in for questioning. They haven't charged him with anything, and I don't think they're going to, because they don't really have anything. But they couldn't really ignore the fact that he was on the scene for all three of the killings."

Rachel sat with her eyes closed and a hand over her face until she felt Roger's touch on her arm, gently. She looked him in the eye and said, "He didn't have anything to do with it. That's stupid, it's ridiculous."

Roger nodded, looking grave. "You don't have to tell me. But they have to take a hard look at him. Just because of circumstances."

Rachel inhaled sharply; suddenly queasy, she almost bolted for the bathroom. She managed to steady herself and said, "I know Matt. I know people we love aren't perfect, but you know what they're capable of. Matt's not capable of anything like that."

"I agree with you. I think they'll put him through the wringer and cut him loose."

"They're going to railroad him, aren't they? They're already suspicious because of what happened to Margie. I know there was talk at the time. They're already prejudiced against him."

"Rachel." Roger had raised his voice just enough to get her attention. "If Matt didn't do it, they can't charge him. They can't charge him without evidence. And they can't charge him if he's got alibis. And it sounds like he's got a good one for last night, anyway. There's several people that can put him at the bar for a couple of hours before you found McDonald."

A waitress appeared and Rachel managed to order coffee. "I'm sorry. I'll try to act like a grown-up. So Matt's got to be in the clear for last night, right?"

Roger cocked his head slightly, a gesture of reserve. "Probably. The forensic guys found tire tracks on the shoulder last night that matched the ones at Ed Thomas's house. It looks like Ed's truck was used to block the road to get McDonald to stop. But . . ."

"But what?"

"They don't know when McDonald was killed. Apparently rigor mortis was starting to set in when the forensic guys looked at him, which means he'd been dead for a while when you found him. And since cold retards rigor, he could have been killed pretty much anytime yesterday afternoon or evening."

"What, you mean he'd been sitting out there for hours?"

"Could have been. There's not a lot of traffic on that road. Or he could have been killed earlier, stashed somewhere, then set up after dark."

"So Matt's not in the clear."

"Rachel, I don't think Matt did it any more than you did. But right now they have to look at anything that comes up. And Matt jumps up at them, big time."

"I know. I can't blame them."

Roger's look softened a little. "Anyway, with McDonald being the victim it's looking more like a random thing again. Nothing to do with old Ryle grudges. I don't know if that helps."

"Not really." She sighed and stared out the window at the leaden sky. Ask him, Rachel thought. Ask him if McDonald was his brother-in-law. Instead she said, "We're in the danger zone, aren't we? It's all happening right out there where we live. Everyone I know is in danger."

Roger nodded, his frown deepening. "North central Dearborn County is where it's at, yeah. But we got more manpower from the state police, extra patrols. There's still a lot of land out there, but he can't hide forever. I think when we get a break it'll be because somebody stumbles onto something. Some citizen, I mean. It's bound to happen sooner or later. But that worries me because that immediately puts that citizen in danger. Whoever's doing this, one more won't bother them."

They were interrupted by the arrival of Rachel's coffee. When she had doctored it Rachel said, "Whoever. You don't think it was Otis Ryle?"

Roger held his mug in both hands as if to warm them. He frowned into his coffee for a few seconds and said, "It could be. That's been the most likely scenario ever since he went missing from the prison. But there's some funny things about it, if it is him."

"Like what?"

Roger set the mug down, clasped his hands and gave Rachel a piercing look. "Well, to start with, look at what he was in jail for."

"For killing his wife and kids."

Roger nodded. "For dismembering them and partially eating them. That's the work of a very sick man."

"I think we're all on the same page there."

"You know how he actually killed them?"

"No, Roger, I somehow missed that."

"He strangled them. And then he dismembered them with a kitchen knife and a hacksaw."

Rachel nodded. "And?"

"So look at what happened to our victims. One was killed with a sledge hammer. And then cut up with a saw." He put a hand on Rachel's arm. "I'm sorry to go through this."

"That's OK. Go on."

"That was the only case of dismemberment. And there was no suggestion of cannibalism."

"Thank God."

"The other two, one had his throat cut and one was run through with a pitchfork. Three different methods, only one dismemberment, no strangulation. Now, it's perfectly possible Ryle did them all. People can learn, people improvise. But serial killers usually have a preferred methodology. They like to do things the same way. And these three killings are all improvised, and every one's different. And another thing."

"What?"

"What's his motive?"

"Does a sick person need a motive?"

"I think so. Even a sick person needs a motive. In Ryle's case, whatever weird psychological kick he got out of cannibalism, along with whatever it is makes guys kill their wife and kids, which happens a lot. If it's Ryle out there doing this, why's he doing it? What kick's he on now?"

Rachel sat looking Roger in the eye, the bottom of her stomach dropping out. "So what are you saying, Roger?"

"I'm just saying there's no guarantee Otis Ryle did these murders, that's all. He might have, but it's not for sure."

Outside, the light was going, traffic purring along the strip with the headlights on. Rachel heaved a great breath. "Have you talked with the detectives about this?"

"Oh, they've been thinking along these lines all along. But they're happy to let the media play up Otis Ryle."

"So if not him, who did them?"

"Well, that's the question, isn't it? I don't know. Not yet."

Rachel shoved her mug away from her. "But that's even worse, if it isn't Ryle. If somebody . . . somebody else is doing this."

"Somebody sane, you mean?" Roger smiled, and there was nothing charming about the crooked grin. "Yeah, that's a lot worse, isn't it?"

"For God's sake, stop," said Greg Stevenson. "We don't scour the stovetop more than once a month. Don't go raising the standards around here or it'll mean more work for me."

Susan's husband was a large hearty man whose hairline was creeping back as his waistline pushed outward; he had bright mischievous eyes and a chin that would be double in another year or two. He had confounded Rachel's stereotype of mild-mannered accountants with his bluff humor and a steady stream of wicked local gossip over dinner. The act had distracted them all from thoughts of Matt in an interrogation room.

"Just trying to earn my keep." Rachel replaced a burner grate and went to the sink to rinse out the sponge. "Besides, my mother drilled that one into me. 'If I can see it, the mice can smell it,' she used to say. She ran a tight ship."

"So did my mother, but she's not here."

"Don't bother," said Susan, coming into the kitchen. "He can't be taught. We've been fighting for twenty years about the right way to load a dishwasher."

"What she means is, she's been doing it the wrong way for twenty years." He snapped the dishtowel at Susan's rump.

"You can be replaced, you know," she said, leveling an index at him.

"You don't know how lucky you are," said Rachel, drying her hands. "I never saw my husband in the kitchen except to yell at the cook." She hung up the towel and looked up to see her hosts waiting for more. "Different culture."

"Sounds like my kind of household," said Greg.

Susan rolled her eyes. "Yeah, well. Rachel, I'd love to tell you we play intricate games of skill or read improving books after supper, but the truth is, we generally flop on the couch and watch TV. There's plenty of room for three."

"Sounds perfect. I just need to make a couple of phone calls."

"OK. You'll know where to find us."

Rachel watched them go, suppressing a brutal pang of envy at the happy mediocrity of their domestic life, then sat at the kitchen table with her phone and punched in Matt's number, without much hope of getting him. She wondered if he was in a jail cell. She got his voice mail and left a short message just touching base, then called Dan.

"Yeah," he said after a couple of rings.

"It's me."

"Hey, how you doing?" Dan's voice had everything she ought to want in it—concern and tenderness—but Rachel realized she had been longing for the usual jauntiness. She had been moving in a fog all day.

"I'm OK. Make me laugh, will you?"

"All right, I'll show you my college transcript some time."

"Nice try. Did you know the police took Matt in for questioning?"

"Yeah, he just told me all about it."

"He's with you?"

"He just left. The cops cut him loose about six and he came straight to the bar."

"Thank God. I just tried to call him."

"I think he turned his phone off. He just walked out of here, actually. You need to talk to him? I can run after him."

"Not really. I just wanted to make sure he's OK."

"He's fine. It was all bullshit, and they knew it. They just needed to look busy."

"How did Matt take it?"

"Laughed about it. He's OK. A little drunk, maybe."

"Terrific. He's going to wind up in a ditch again."

"Hey, Matt's the best drunk driver I know."

"Seriously, Dan. I'm starting to worry a little about Matt's drinking."

"Ah, I'm just bullshitting. He had a couple of beers, that's all. What are you up to?"

Rachel relaxed a little. "I'm hanging with Susan tonight. I need a nice quiet evening. I was thinking tomorrow might be a good night for a date, though. Dinner and a movie, an old-fashioned kind of date."

"Where I get you home before midnight and kiss you on the doorstep, with Matt standing there in the doorway with a baseball bat, you mean?"

"Well, we can negotiate that part. But the dinner and the movie, that's for real. You up for it?"

"Hell, yeah. I'll give you a call when I get off work."

"Sounds good. And listen."

"What?"

"Be careful going home tonight. Be real careful."

"Actually, I think we're OK out here. You wouldn't believe the number of cops out driving around this part of the county tonight. I think they got it covered. That son of a bitch comes out of his hole tonight, he's gonna get stomped on."

"That would be good. Be careful anyway."

"Oh, I will. Tell Susan hi from me and I haven't forgotten about that pencil she lent me in study hall back in 1981, will you? I know I owe her."

He hung up before Rachel could come up with a wisecrack, and she sat staring at the phone in her hand for a few seconds. A lifeline, she thought. That's all he is. In three months you might be ready to move on. But for the moment he's a pretty good lifeline. I was due for something good to happen, and this is good. She put the phone away.

She joined Greg and Susan ten minutes into a drama that showed implausibly handsome crime scene technicians collecting evidence on a sex killing that had occurred off-screen. To Rachel the whole thing looked thin and phony. After the show they went back to the kitchen and Greg made Manhattans for everyone. "We allow ourselves one cocktail a night," said Susan. "This month it's Manhattans. We're working our way through the bartender's guide."

"I'm amazed you can limit yourself to one," said Rachel. "In Baghdad, with all the stress, there were people that put away amazing amounts of booze, every night. I knew if I ever started I would wind up an alcoholic, so I went completely Carry Nation, didn't touch a drop for months. And then when I got back to Beirut with Fadi I would drink like a fish."

They wound up skipping the next TV show, hanging at the kitchen table while Rachel told them about Baghdad and Beirut and eventually, over a mutually agreed-upon second drink, the crashing and burning of her marriage. "Thank God there were no kids," said Rachel. "That's the one thing we did right."

In the heavy silence that followed, Rachel's cell phone could be heard faintly purring. She went and pulled it out of her purse and saw a number she didn't recognize on the display. "Hello?"

"Aunt Rachel?"

"Billy? What's up?"

"I need your help, Aunt Rachel. I need it bad."

"What's wrong?"

"You got the Chevy, right? You could come and pick me up?"

"Uh, sure. Where are you?"

"Right now I'm out in the middle of fuckin' nowhere. But what I need is, if you can swing by where I was in East Warrensburg and grab my stuff, I can tell you where to come and get me."

"What's going on?"

"I'm in deep shit and I got nobody else I can trust. I need you to get me to Peoria tonight if you can."

Now she could hear the edge in his voice, the desperation. "Billy, if you need help, I'll help you, but are you allowed to leave the county while you're out on bail?"

"Christ, if that was all I had to worry about. Look, it's a long story. I'll tell you all about it, but right now I just got to get out of the cold and then have somebody come and get me and take me the hell away from Dearborn County."

Rachel flicked one glance at Greg and Susan's baffled looks and said, "All right, Billy. I'll be there as fast as I can. Where am I meeting you?"

"Get my stuff from Kayla's house first and then come up 74 and get off at Alwood. Then it gets a little complicated. You got a pencil, I'll give you directions."

28 ||||||

Rachel made one wrong turn in East Warrensburg, but in a town that size you can never go too far wrong, and she pulled up in front of the long low ranch house by ten thirty. The curtains were drawn but there was light behind them. Rachel took a deep breath and got out of the car.

She rang the doorbell and waited, looking around at the scattering of lights in the darkness under the trees, houses jumbled just close enough together to qualify as a town, people keeping their distance from one another. Somewhere not too far away, somebody was playing country music, loudly. The door opened.

"Can I help you?" The woman standing there with a cigarette in her hand looked as if she had been pretty not that long ago, before hard living or maybe hard usage had worn her down; the tobacco and the whiskey Rachel could smell on her breath hadn't helped.

"I'm so sorry to bother you," said Rachel. "Billy Lindstrom asked me to come by and pick up his things."

All Rachel got in response was a little frown and a series of blinks. She was about to launch into explanations when the woman said, "He's cuttin' and runnin', is he?"

Rachel groped for an answer and said, "All I know is, he called me and asked me to come and get his things. I'm sorry, I should introduce myself. I'm Rachel Lindstrom, Billy's aunt." Rachel held out her hand.

The woman gave it a good look first before she stuck the cigarette in her mouth to shake it. "I'm Deanna. What happened, him and Kayla had a fight?"

"I really don't know. All Billy told me was to pick up his stuff and come and get him."

"Decided he was too good for us, is that it?"

Rachel sensed class resentment at work and groped for an answer. "I got the impression he was in some kind of trouble."

Deanna took a drag on the cigarette and stepped back to let Rachel in. "Well, I'm sorry to hear that. Compared to some of the riff-raff Kayla's drug in here, Billy wasn't too bad. I thought maybe he'd get Kayla straightened out a little, but I guess that's asking too much."

The television was on, emitting unidentifiable generic reality-show babble; a DVD cover bearing the image of a bloodied saw blade lay in the middle of the floor. "I think Billy has enough work to do getting himself straightened out."

They stood for a moment assessing each other, and then Deanna shrugged and said, "Well, easy come, easy go. Come on back and see if you can find his stuff in the mess." She led Rachel back through the kitchen to the door in the rear where Billy had emerged the last time she had been here. At the end of a short hallway Deanna pushed a door open and gestured Rachel in.

The mess wasn't that bad: There was an unmade bed and a pile of clothes on a chair, but the floor was mostly visible and the dirty dishes were neatly stacked on a bedside table. On the wall at the head of the bed was a poster depicting a woman dressed in black leather standing in a cemetery, with the legend *Thanatos* at the bottom. "OK," said Rachel.

She had packed Billy's things to begin with, so she didn't have too much trouble identifying them. She found the tote bag in the closet and began filling it. "Don't forget the bathroom," said Deanna. "He's got some shit in there."

Rachel retrieved his toothbrush; there was a can of shaving cream and a package of disposable razors on the sink. "Are these Billy's?"

"They ain't mine," said Deanna. "We don't have nobody around here that shaves but Billy." Rachel stuffed them into the bag.

At the door Rachel checked her urge to rush out into the clean cold air. She turned and said, "Thank you for taking Billy in. His father and I appreciate it."

Deanna was crushing her cigarette out in an ashtray that hadn't been emptied in a while. She looked up and said, "He's got a father that's still interested in him, that's more than my Kayla's got." The look in the eyes under the fake lashes was sullen.

Rachel didn't have much to say to that. She left, closing the door behind her. She went to the car and got in behind the wheel, tossing the bag on the passenger seat. She reversed and swung around and made a beeline for the road back toward Warrensburg.

In five minutes she was on the interstate and in fifteen she was pulling off at Alwood, the gas station sign floating high and bright in the night. She rolled past it to the edge of town and pulled over to the side of the road, looking out into the darkness beyond the range of her headlights. She sat still for a time and then switched on the dome light, reached into her purse and pulled out the sheet of notepaper on which she had written Billy's directions. She scanned them again. They were simple enough and she didn't really need the paper, but she was stalling.

The problem was the fear. Dan had assured her there were police on the roads tonight, but Rachel hadn't seen any. The house Billy had described to her was about three miles from where she sat, if his directions were accurate: south and a little east. He had said it was hard to find, which meant it was isolated and not on a frequented road. Rachel was trying hard not to let her imagination run away with her, but the prospect of exploring the remoter corners of Dearborn County at night with a killer, sane or otherwise, demonstrably at large, had reduced her to paralysis.

She laid the paper on the seat and reached into her purse for her cell phone. She hadn't asked what bar Dan was camped at, but there was a chance he was just a few blocks away, here in Alwood. And if not, he was probably at the bar at the Rome crossroads on 150, a ten-minute drive away. It was time to call for the cavalry.

Dan answered on the second ring. "I need your help," Rachel said.

There was no joking this time, maybe because he had picked up on her tone of voice. "What do you need?"

"Billy called. He's in some kind of trouble and he wants me to come and pick him up. Right now I'm sitting at the side of the road in Alwood. He said to meet him at an old abandoned house around here somewhere. He gave me directions. But I'm too scared to go look for it alone."

There was a pause of maybe three seconds. "What the fuck is that kid up to?"

"I don't know. He said he was in deep shit and he couldn't trust the cops and he needed to be taken to Peoria. I went by his girlfriend's house and got his stuff and now I just have to go find him. But I'm too chicken to go by myself. I just can't do it. Is that ridiculous?"

"No. That's not ridiculous at all. Sit tight. I'm right here in Alwood. Where are you exactly?"

"I'm right at the edge of town, on what is it, East 200 maybe. A couple of hundred yards past the gas station."

"Give me five minutes," said Dan, and hung up.

Rachel let the phone drop to her lap, closing her eyes and exhaling in relief. She rested for a moment, listening to the gentle idling of the car, and then opened her eyes and put the phone back in her purse. She turned off the headlights, switched on the hazard blinkers and then turned off the ignition, bewildered as she did so by the sudden slight rocking of the car and the eruption of swishing, thumping and creaking noises from behind her. Her hand was still on the key when her shocked awareness registered the presence of somebody in the car with her.

Rachel screamed. A hand in her hair jerked her head back and an instant later the knife was at her throat.

The physiological responses overwhelmed anything resembling actual thought: All her brain could come up with was an adrenaline surge and muscular contractions. A voice in Rachel's ear said, "Surprise."

Terror does not facilitate speech: What came out of Rachel's mouth with each breath was merely wind through the vocal cords, a rapid high-pitched "Huh, huh, huh" that communicated nothing except distress. Her mind, however, stabilized to the point where she could think: I am going to die now. She had a brief pitying vision of a woman with her throat cut bleeding all over the seat of a car, and the voice said, "I think we'll just start her up again and put her in gear, don't you?"

"Huh, huh, huh, huh . . ."

"Calm the fuck down, will you? I ain't gonna hurt you." The pressure of the knife blade on her throat eased and her hair was released. "Less you fuck with me. Now turn on the car and let's move. We ain't waiting for your friend."

"Huh, huh, huh. Oh, God." Rachel was amazed to find that her throat was not cut and strove to control her breathing. "Oh, God. All right, all right."

"Just take it easy and get this car started. We're going to see Billy, OK? You get me to where Billy is and nobody gets hurt. Fuck with me and I'll kill you, you got it?" The knife edge pressed on her throat again, lightly, then receded. "Now let's go."

"All right, all right." Rachel reached for the key in the ignition.

She was still in full adrenaline surge, which made fine motor skills problematic, but she managed to get the car started. "Here's the deal," the voice behind her said. "You get me to where Billy is, I'll let you go.

You fuck with me, I'll kill you. I got every cop in the State of Illinois looking for me already, so one more crime don't mean shit to me."

Rachel knew now who it was behind her; the voice had finally registered. "Take the car," she said. "Just take it."

"I don't think so," said Randy Stanfield. "I don't want you running back there for help. What I want is for you to take me to Billy. Hand me those directions." Rachel hesitated, then stiffened as the knife touched her again. "Come on, I heard you looking at the paper. Give 'em here."

Rachel felt for the paper in the dark and handed it back over her shoulder. Stanfield snatched it. "We'll pull over so I can take a look somewhere up ahead. For now just get this fucker moving."

She managed to turn on the headlights and put the car in gear. Pulling onto the road, she headed south into the darkness, quickly leaving the lights of the town behind. Function, she told herself, fighting hard to order her thoughts. What will Dan do when he doesn't find me? He will call me on my cell phone. When I don't answer, he will . . . what? She came up against a blank wall. Beneath her headlights the black asphalt came flowing out of the darkness.

"Not too fast now. We don't want no accidents." The blade was not touching her throat, but his hand was resting on her shoulder blade, clutching the knife.

I didn't check the backseat, Rachel thought. The one time I was too distracted, too hurried, he was there and I had left the car unlocked. She remembered looking into the darkness under the trees from Kayla's doorstep; he had been there and she had missed him.

Function, she thought. Her heart rate and breathing had stabilized at crisis levels; she was in control of the car though driving stiffly, gripping the wheel hard. This is the trouble Billy was running from. So whatever you do, you can't take him to Billy.

"Pull over."

Rachel obeyed, easing to a stop on the shoulder. "What do you want with Billy?" she said, her voice quavering.

"Me and him got business." The knife went away and the dome light came on, and then quickly the knife was back, in Stanfield's other hand. There was a pause, a rustle of paper, and then the light went off and Stanfield said, "Let's go. Looks like your first turn's up here on the left."

And that is that, she thought. He knows where Billy is and we are running out of time. She pulled back onto the road and accelerated. The road rose in front of her.

There is a revolver in my purse, Rachel thought.

"Slow down," said Stanfield. "Here it is."

Rachel braked at the top of a hill and turned left onto a gravel road. She was already on unfamiliar ground, disoriented with no landmarks visible in the dark. The numbered county roads at one-mile intervals overlay a less than regular system of blacktopped major roads and graveled minor ones, mostly at right angles but with local anomalies, roads that didn't get used or maintained much, and here and there a road to nowhere. Exploring these roads while learning to drive, Rachel had once been hopelessly lost within three miles of her home. This one was taking her into the rolling, intermittently wooded country to the north of the creek. The road dipped and something scuttled across it in the headlights.

In Rachel's purse, her cell phone rang. "Leave it be," said Stanfield. "We got enough for a party already."

"He'll come looking for me."

"Let him." They were approaching a stop sign. Stanfield said, "OK, this is East 400. Lemme see, go straight here and then make the first right about, should be a half mile ahead."

Rachel looked up and down the county road as she crossed it but saw no lights. She took a deep breath. "We're not that far from the interstate and you can be miles away before I can hike anywhere to get help. Why don't you just forget about Billy, let me out and take the car?"

"Why don't you just keep your fuckin' mouth shut and drive? I told you, I got business with Billy. Once I'm done with him, I'm gone. Here's your turn."

Rachel turned south and the road dipped again, dropping toward the creek. There were trees on either side now; she hadn't seen a house for the past three-quarters of a mile. Gravel and ice in the potholes crunched under her tires. She slowed as the road bottomed out. Just ahead her lights shone on the low steel guardrails of a bridge where the road crossed the creek. "Turn here," Stanfield said. "This has gotta be it."

"Turn where? There's nowhere to turn."

"Just past the bridge, on the left there."

Rachel rolled slowly across the bridge, peering into the dark. On the other side of the bridge she saw it, a narrow dirt track that led down off the road. She turned onto it, her headlights sweeping across brush on a rising slope and falling on tree trunks as she straightened out, casting long shadows across the snowy ground. "This doesn't look like a road."

"Close enough," said Stanfield. "Go slow."

Rachel didn't need to be told; she could make out twin tracks over the rough ground, but it wasn't much of a road. The track took them along a flat strip of land, the creek visible through the trees. Rachel's heart had begun to beat faster again. Make a quick grab for the gun as he's getting out of the car, she thought. If he doesn't cut your throat first.

"Whoa," said Stanfield. The knife moved away from her throat. "There it is."

29 |||||||

"Shut it down," said Stanfield. Rachel doused the lights and cut the ignition.

The darkness took her by surprise. It took a moment for her eyes to adjust, snow reflecting the light of the new moon just enough for her to make out what was in front of her.

The house squatted dark and defunct at the end of the track. A house that was lived in always gave signs: parked vehicles, children's playthings, a light behind a curtain on a cold night. This house was dead.

It was a square frame house that somebody had built on a slight rise fifty feet from the creek in the faith or delusion that the water would never rise enough to cover the bottom of the hollow entirely. The house would be invisible from the fields above it and invisible from the road because of the trees.

"All right," said Stanfield, his voice a low murmur in Rachel's ear. "Here's what's gonna happen. First off, give me the keys."

Rachel pulled the keys out of the ignition and handed them back over her shoulder. When the keys left her hand she let it fall onto her purse, resting with her fingers just touching the grip of the revolver.

She gasped as the knife blade pressed against her throat. "Just take your hand out of there, sugar. You ain't gonna be needing that phone."

Rachel raised both hands. "Don't hurt Billy." She barely had the breath to say it.

"Don't you worry about Billy. You just take care of yourself. You got a flashlight in this car?"

"In the glove compartment."

"Give it to me. Move slow and keep your hand away from that purse."

She leaned over, opened the glove compartment and pulled out the light. She handed it back to Stanfield and he flicked it on and off briefly, testing it.

"Cool. Now listen good. You're getting out of the car. You're gonna get out and run back the way we came. Just take off running and don't stop. You read me?"

"Uh-huh." Now, Rachel thought. Open the door, start to get out, and grab for the purse.

Abruptly Stanfield reached over the seat and snatched the purse. "I think I'll keep this back here with me. Now get out."

Despairing, Rachel closed her eyes. Help me God, she prayed. Help me and help Billy.

"Go on, get out."

She opened the door and got out into the cold. Her feet crunched on the snow. The back door of the car opened and Stanfield said, "Take off, move."

Rachel ran. She ran stumbling over the rough ground, thinking now of getting back to a main road and flagging down help. Where were the cops Dan had said were all over the roads? She ran for fifty feet or so and stopped to look back. She could just make out a dark shape next to the car. "Keep moving," Stanfield rasped. The car door closed with a soft click.

Rachel ran back to within fifty yards of the bridge and stopped to look back. The house was out of sight but she could see flashes of light through the trees. She waited for a few seconds and then began trotting back toward the house. The light disappeared.

She stopped to listen. She thought she heard the creak of a door, very faintly, and then there was silence. She began to run again, faster.

She reached the car and clawed at the rear door handle. She tried the driver's-side door, found it locked as well, tried both doors on the other side, and sobbed in frustration. Stanfield had locked the car. She could make out her purse with the gun in it on the back seat.

Rachel dashed into the woods by the side of the track. It took her precious seconds to find a fallen limb small enough to handle but big enough to break a window. She ran back to the car and swung the limb at the rear window. It hit the glass with a thump and the limb broke in her hands.

There would be rocks in the creek bed. She could hear a murmur of water under ice somewhere in the dark beyond the car. She ran toward it. She slipped on the bank and slid down to the stream. On her hands and knees she felt for rocks in the mud and ice. She managed to pry loose a grapefruit-sized stone and scrambled back up the bank. She slipped again and fell on her face and then froze as the door of the house fifty yards to her left burst open and the flashlight beam came dancing crazily across the snow as somebody ran at top speed away from the house.

As panicked steps neared the car the flashlight was jettisoned and the skittering light caught a flash of Stanfield's pale hair. The flashlight bounced a couple of times and came to rest with the beam pointing off into the woods. Stanfield skidded to a halt at the car and jabbed at the lock with the key, tore open the door and jumped in. The engine caught and roared, the car reversed in a tight curve, the lights came on, blinding Rachel, and then the Chevy spun its tires in the snow as it fought for traction, swinging around toward the bridge and straightening out, picking up speed.

Rachel watched the taillights as they receded through the trees, reached the bridge and vanished as the car tore away south along the road. She listened until she could hear nothing but the murmur of water in the creek behind her and then she got to her feet.

"Billy," she said, knowing she was going to have to walk into that dead house. She stumbled on the rough ground, got her balance, stepped onto the track. She walked to where the flashlight lay and picked it up. She switched it off and stood for a moment, listening. There was nothing but wind in the trees. She began walking toward the house.

There was enough light for her to make out its contours: It was a simple two-story cube, with a porch tacked on in front. Rachel had been looking for the gleam of windows, but as she drew near she saw that all of the windows had been boarded over, making the house a total blank, a light-eating mass in the dark.

There is no life in there, Rachel thought.

A dark shape to the right of the house, set back against the slope among the trees, drew her eye. It resolved itself into a shed, big enough to house a tractor and not much more. Even in the dark Rachel could see it was derelict, with gaps in the side where boards were missing and holes in the roof. She switched on the flashlight and trained the beam on the ground before her. She saw tire tracks in the snow, curving toward the shed.

Rachel took a couple of steps, letting the beam play along the tracks. Something stirred, deep down, black and malevolent. She had seen tracks like these before.

She had seen tracks like these, but they had not been in snow.

She gasped as a multitude of crows rose with a great flapping of wings. She could not at first make out what this was that they had been pecking at. The side of the barn was flecked with blood spatter. The chainsaw lay a few feet from her, the teeth clotted with bits of matter, the blade smeared dark red.

Here was the other arm, the watch still encircling the wrist, and a leg there with a boot at the end of it, and a lump here draped in shreds of flannel with buttons still fastened, and worst of all the head, Ed Thomas's head, perfectly recognizable despite its unaccustomed look of heavy-lidded boredom, impaled on a fencepost.

Someone had driven a truck through the mess, crushing a limb, leaving dark, faintly glistening tracks on the pale gravel.

"Oh Jesus, please. Dear God help me." Rachel switched off the flashlight but it was too late: Her memory was back, toxic and invincible.

She was hyperventilating. She desperately wanted to turn and run, but her limbs would not move. It took a few seconds for her mind to claw back from sheer panic, and make out the choices and the stakes. Function, she raged at herself. Billy needs you.

Rachel looked at the black faceless house to her left and then turned on the flashlight again. She followed the tracks the few steps to the shed. It had double Z-frame doors sagging off the hinges. She leaned close to a gap in the siding and shone the light through it.

First she saw nothing but the cracked concrete of the floor. The flashlight beam rose and passed over the tread of a tire, and chrome and steel gleamed.

Rachel held the beam steady on the back gate of an old Ford pickup, a pale blue in the dim light.

Rachel stared for a few long seconds. Then she abruptly switched off the light and jerked back away from the opening and around the corner of the shed. She sagged against the wall, gasping, her heart kicking.

Run. Nobody on earth could expect you to walk into that house, Rachel thought. The only sane thing to do now is to run until you find help. Nobody could fault you.

Except Billy. If he is still alive.

Function. Rachel switched on the light and ran it over the front of the house as she approached. It had probably been a standard frame house originally, but somebody had shingled the sides at some point, giving it a look of irredeemable poverty. The front door had been kicked in, reinforced, shot at, patched up, pounded on and scrawled on multiple times. Now it hung slightly open. Beyond it was darkness.

She paused at the foot of the front steps. I can't do this, she thought. I'm not brave enough. I'm not strong enough to walk in there.

Rachel mounted the steps. The porch was treacherous, with boards rotted and missing; she swept it quickly with the light and stepped carefully. She paused at the door, standing to one side so that only her face and the hand holding the flashlight would be exposed, and pushed the door open.

Her light played over a floor covered with grit, scraps of paper, an old sock, cigarette butts, crushed beer cans, clots of animal excrement. She made out the foot of a flight of stairs. She switched off the light.

"Billy?" she called, more weakly than she had intended, hardly loud enough to be heard ten feet away. There was no answer.

Rachel waited for a few heartbeats, listening, hearing nothing. She ducked quickly through the door and sank to her haunches with her back to the wall just to the right of the opening, waiting for something to come flying out of the dark.

Nothing came. Rachel inhaled the acrid breath of the place, the smell of vermin and decay and ash.

And something else: wood smoke. She squatted by the door and strained to make out shapes in the blackness. She listened as well, hearing the faint rustlings of mice or something worse. The loudest sound in her ears was that of her heart.

When she was still alive after half a minute Rachel stood up and held the flashlight to one side at arm's length, hoping that if anything leaped at the light it would miss her. She switched on the light and quickly swept the room.

People had lived here once; they had sat on these chairs that now lay splintered and hung pictures on these walls that had been gouged and defaced. The beam of the flashlight steadied on the words *STONE COLD KILLERZ* spray-painted on a patch of wall. She shifted the light and it fell on another inscription, in larger letters and sprayed with a less steady hand: *DEATH RAINS HERE.*

When Rachel was sure the room she was in was empty, she took a few steps away from the door. At the back of the room was a doorway into another room, only glimpsed in her sweep of the light. You are going to have to look, Rachel told herself. She went toward the doorway.

As she did, she became aware, beneath the terror, of something that didn't fit: It was warm inside the house. This rooted her to the spot for a long moment. That was impossible: The house should have been as cold as the woods outside.

When she put that together with the smell of wood smoke, it did nothing but increase her alarm. *Get out*, an inner voice screamed at Rachel. She drew breath and called out, stronger now, "Billy?"

There was no answer, and Rachel walked slowly toward the doorway at the rear of the room, jerking the light this way and that, the limited field of illumination inflating her dread of the darkness just outside it. To her astonishment she survived the trip across the floor, finding that every second she lived gave her strength to face the next one. Again she stood to one side while shining the light through: This was the kitchen, or had been; truncated pipes and scars on ancient linoleum showed where a sink had been. The light fell on a back door, planks nailed across it.

And there in a corner was the old potbelly cast iron stove, the faint glow of embers visible behind the slightly opened door. On the floor beside it sat a small stack of firewood, neatly split logs.

Rachel whirled around frantically at a soft creak behind her, crying out. The light shook in her hand, wildly sweeping the room. There was nobody there.

She waited for her breathing to steady and looked into the kitchen again, probing the corners now. There was a pantry in the far corner but the door was long gone; Rachel stepped far enough into the kitchen to shine the light inside the pantry.

She let out a single ragged cry and leaped backward. The man in the pantry just looked at her. Rachel stumbled over debris and fell heavily back against a wall, losing the light. Amazingly it survived the jolt as it hit the floor, coming to rest and casting its beam on the rear wall next to the stove. Rachel scrabbled in panic to retrieve it, waiting for the man to come and kill her. When she managed to train the light on the pantry, the man had not moved.

He sat where he had been sitting when her light first fell on him, with his back to the wall of the pantry, his knees pulled up to his chest and one hand trailing on the floor, palm up, at his side. He was not, after all, looking at her; he was in dreamland, his gaze going over her head to a spot high on the wall. Rachel held the light steady on him long enough to see that he was a man in middle age, balding and gray, wearing a hooded sweatshirt, and he did not look well.

Rachel was hyperventilating again, her heart threatening to punch its way out the front of her chest, the flashlight beam oscillating with the trembling of her hands. As the seconds passed and the man on the floor of the pantry did not move, it began to be clear to Rachel that he was never going to move again.

After a minute or two had passed, Rachel had calmed enough to struggle to her feet. She was scrambling to put together a picture, groping for a context that would make sense of the hysteria of the past few minutes of her life.

She had almost decided that in spite of everything she was in no imminent danger when a footstep sounded, soft but distinct, on the porch outside, and she heard the front door creak as it swung open.

Rachel flicked off the flashlight and sagged back against the wall, stress sapping the strength from her legs. Steps sounded in the front room, and light glowed faintly through the doorway. She had heard no car approaching. There had been no tires crackling on ice, no engine murmuring through the woods. And yet a person had materialized on the porch and was now coming slowly toward the kitchen. A beam of light came through the doorway and lit up the battered linoleum.

He heard me cry out, thought Rachel. He knows I am here.

She flicked on her light just long enough to find what she had stumbled over: a piece of wood, a wedge of split log about a foot and a half long and just thin enough to grasp with one hand. She switched off the light, stepped forward and bent to find it by touch, then retreated to put her back against the wall. The footsteps had halted at the doorway into the kitchen, the light playing over the walls and floor.

Rush at him, blind him with the light as soon as he comes through the doorway and then swing at his face, sharp edge first. With flight no longer an option, Rachel was ready to fight.

The beam of light swept the kitchen as the flashlight came through the doorway. Rachel flattened herself against the wall, waiting for the man holding it to take one more step.

"Rachel," said a voice. "Come on out of there. I know you're in there."

Rachel waited as the light swept her way and fell full in her face.

"There you are," said Roger Black.

30 |||||||

"Roger?" Rachel's voice wavered.

Roger had advanced into the kitchen, lowering the light so it no longer shone in Rachel's eyes. She in turn had clicked on her flashlight and caught Roger full in the face. He was in uniform with the fur-lined trooper's cap on his head, and as he squinted into the light he wasn't smiling. "You look a little shook up," he said. "Don't tell me your boyfriend ditched you."

Rachel understood nothing except that help had arrived. "Roger, where's Billy?"

"Don't worry about Billy. He's OK."

"Is he here?"

"He's not far away. I'll take you to him in a minute."

"Is he all right?"

"Billy's fine. Here's the guy you ought to be worried about." Roger jerked his light toward the body in the pantry.

Rachel quailed. "Who is that?"

Roger made a noise that might have been a grunt or might have been a soft laugh in the dark. "Don't you recognize him?"

"*Who is it?*"

Roger shined his light in the corpse's face. "That's the man of the hour, Rachel. The guy everybody's been looking for. This here's Otis Ryle."

In the silence Rachel could hear her heart beating, a steady muffled thump. She held her light as stable as she could on the waxen face. Now she could see it, the face she had seen on television and in the news photos. Bewildered, she said, "Is he dead?"

"He doesn't look too good, does he? Yes, I'd say he's pretty dead."

Rachel was working at it, fighting hard to jam things into a frame that made sense. "Roger, that guy, Billy's friend Stanfield, he hid in the backseat of my car and he had a knife. Just like it happened with Carl Holmes. And he was just here. He must have killed all these people."

"Now that's an interesting idea." Roger had wandered over to the pantry and stood examining the body in the beam of his flashlight. "Believe me, I'd love to hang this on Stanfield. But I'm not sure he's smart enough. Anyway, he's not gonna get very far. He's got three agencies looking for him tonight."

Rachel drew a deep breath, steadying. "Roger, what the *hell* is going on?"

"Come over here."

Doubt blossomed, black and cold. "Why?"

"So you'll understand. I want you to come over here."

"I don't want to."

Roger swung the light into her face and held it there for a few seconds. "Rachel. It's very important to me for you to understand this. Now come over here, please."

Rachel walked slowly across the kitchen, keeping her light on Roger. He was frowning at her, but it was a frown of absorption, concentration. "What?" said Rachel.

"Touch him." Roger bent over and laid the back of his hand against Otis Ryle's cheek. "Go on, touch him."

"Why?"

He grabbed her by the wrist and pulled her toward the body on the pantry floor. Rachel cried out and nearly lost her balance. "Touch him, Rachel."

She put out a trembling hand and brushed a cheek with her knuckles. It felt like a slab of frozen meat. She wrenched herself free of Roger's grasp and took a couple of steps back.

"What do you feel?"

"He's cold."

"He sure is, isn't he? Mighty cold."

Rachel took a step backward, toward the door. "So, he's cold. He's dead. So what?"

"If Stanfield killed him just now, he'd still be warm. And the house is warm. Somebody's been feeding that stove, and judging by the embers in there it's been going a while. Ryle shouldn't be *that* cold, even if he's been dead for a while." Roger shone his light in Rachel's eyes again and she squinted and turned her head.

"What?"

"He's *thawing*, Rachel. That's what Otis is doing here. He's thawing out. You know what that means?"

"What?"

"It means all the time these people were getting slaughtered, Otis was on ice. He had nothing to do with any of it. Poor Otis got framed."

Rachel managed to steady her light on Roger's face, and he was smiling his crooked smile. "That's crazy," she said.

"You bet it is. But it's God damn brilliant, too. If you want to kill three men and get away with it, a homicidal maniac on the loose is the best cover you could have. Of course, you've got to deal with the maniac first. You've got to catch him, kill him and put him on ice. Then when you're done with your business you can thaw him out and arrange for him to get found hanging from a tree or drowned in the creek, the crazy man finally committing suicide after the rampage. And who's going to question it?"

Roger fell silent, and Rachel wondered if he expected her to say something. All she wanted was to break out into the clean night air and run. "Who?" she breathed.

"Well, that's the question, isn't it? Let's try Stanfield on for size. He came running in here and then back out again in a hurry. What was that all about?"

"He was looking for Billy."

"And how did he know to come here?"

Rachel had to think for a second. "He didn't. That's why he carjacked me. He needed me to take him to Billy."

"So he didn't know Ryle was here."

"No."

"Must have been a shock. That's why he went tearing out of here again."

Rachel's knees were trembling; they could hardly support her. "Roger, what are you saying?"

"Well, let's think about it some more, Rachel. You remember that deer?"

"What deer?"

"The deer you found in the creek bed. The one the hunters had left."

"What about it?"

"What kind of shape was it in when you saw it? Was it all torn up?"

Rachel shook her head. "No. It was just skinned, just lying there."

"Did you think about that? Why was it still intact? If it had been a fresh kill there wouldn't have been much left of it within an hour of being left there. But the coyotes hadn't made much progress, had they?"

In the silence Rachel's heart kept cadence, time slipping away. All she could say was, "Why?"

"Because it was frozen. It had been dumped there, frozen, just that night, and hadn't thawed any in the cold weather. Now why would somebody dump all that fine venison?"

"I don't know."

"Come on, Rachel. Use your head. Somebody had to make room in the freezer."

Rachel stood in the dark in the evil suffocating air and fought it with all her might. "No," she said. "I don't believe that."

"You got a better story? I'm all ears."

"No. That's all wrong. I don't believe it."

A few seconds passed. Roger said, "OK, Rachel. Suit yourself. Let's go for a walk. I want to show you something."

"What?"

"Just follow me. Let's get the hell out of here." He stalked past her, lighting his way with his flashlight.

Rachel turned and went after him. "Where are we going?"

"We're going to take a little hike. Along the creek." Roger swung the door open and went out onto the porch, into the clean night air.

Rachel was close behind. "Roger, please. Can we please just go find Billy? Don't you have to report this or something?"

Moonlight on snow gave enough light, even under the trees to make it seem like high noon compared to the black pit behind them. Roger went down the steps. He said, "Don't worry, I'll call it in. But you have to see this first."

He was striding toward the creek, his flashlight beam playing over the ground in front of him. Rachel followed, a few steps behind him. "This creek runs clear across the northern part of the county," Roger said over his shoulder. "This is the same one that runs past your house."

"No," she said, trotting to catch up. "I don't believe that."

"Oh, it's true. And if you have a good sturdy truck, or for that matter a vehicle you don't really give a shit about, and take it slow, you can drive along it most of the way. Have to climb out to get around a few culverts, but it keeps you off the roads. You can move around in the middle of the night without being seen." Roger stepped down into the creek bed, his light showing the shimmer of water over rock, ice glinting at the edges. "Watch your step," he said. He led the way, stepping carefully, stone to stone, slipping once or twice and wetting his boots.

"Roger, where are we going?" Rachel was following, afraid of being left, missing stones and plunging into the freezing water ankle deep.

"We're going to see where this path leads," he said. "Come on."

Following the light, Rachel scrambled up the bank on the far side. Roger had turned to wait for her, the light shining on the ground.

She put her hand on his shoulder. "Roger, you're wrong, you have to be. I know my brother. Matt could never do that."

Roger halted at her touch and spun to face her. She could just make out his face. "Matt? Who the hell says I'm talking about Matt?"

Rachel stared at him in horror, then took two shambling steps back. "No, God, that's even worse. Not Billy."

In answer Roger said nothing, but froze suddenly and flashed his light into the trees. "Rachel," he said quietly. "Who knows you're here?"

In the silence she could hear only the gentle murmur of water and the sighing of wind in the trees. She found the breath to say, "Stanfield. He brought me here."

Roger flicked off the light, and the woods were very dark suddenly. Rachel heard Roger undoing the snap on his holster and easing his gun out. "And Billy," he said. "Billy knows."

Thunder and lightning, simultaneous and impossible, exploded in the trees, a few feet away. Rachel cried out, dropping into a crouch before she had made sense of it.

It was Roger's grunt of pain that told her it was a gunshot. Something moved in the darkness ahead, and a footstep crunched on snow. The cold, metallic sound of a slide being racked was unmistakable.

"Run," said Roger, his voice a ragged gasp. He staggered away from her, into the trees. Rachel spun and glanced off a tree, regained her balance and took off for the creek, the only clear space she could make out.

Another shot cracked; the flash lit the woods and shotgun pellets peppered the tree trunks. Rachel tripped and went sprawling. She scrambled to her feet, lurched forward and fell headlong into the streambed.

She lay dazed, listening, her left hand immersed in cold water. To her right she could hear someone stumbling through the woods, gasping every couple of steps. The slide was racked again.

Lie still, Rachel's instincts told her. She heard the second set of footsteps, steady and unhurried, moving away from her.

He's going to kill Roger, she thought. And I am going to lie here and listen to it.

Rachel hauled herself to her feet and looked into the woods. Snow covered the slope beyond the trees, just enough of a background to let her make out movement across the pattern of the black tree trunks. Roger was fifty feet away from her, heading toward the road, and behind him, quite close to Rachel but receding, a figure tracked him. Roger groaned as he went, listing to one side.

She climbed back up the bank, no conscious decision involved, knowing only that she could not lie still and listen. She stopped just long enough to orient herself as best she could, then trotted forward, desperately searching the ground.

There was snow under the trees as well, and she spotted Roger's black gun lying where it had fallen next to his flashlight. She snatched up the gun and whirled. It was an automatic; she had her finger on the trigger, hands trembling, and she knew there had to be a safety, but she didn't know where it was. She was already rushing after the figures ahead of her in the trees. "Stop!" she cried.

She found something that clicked under the pressure of her thumb, and she raised the gun, aiming high so as not to hit Roger by mistake, and squeezed off a shot. The strength of the recoil surprised her but she managed to hold on to the gun. "Drop that gun or I'll kill you!" she screamed, not expecting to be obeyed. She halted, shielded by a tree trunk.

Silence. Nothing happened for what seemed a long time, and then the footsteps ahead of her resumed, slow and steady, moving away.

Rachel had no training and no experience and no plan; she was propelled by adrenaline and instinct. She scrambled to her left, expecting shotgun pellets to come flying through the woods at her, slowing as she approached the bank of the stream this time so that she was able to slide down on her seat, more or less under control.

She ran along the streambed toward the road, crouching, making no attempt at stealth, hoping only to outflank the man with the shotgun and get between him and Roger. She slipped and fell, rose, stumbled over rocks, and then finally threw herself against the bank, gun raised, panting, and listened, scanning the dark woods.

Roger was no longer moving. She couldn't see him, but she could hear him, breathing heavily somewhere just to her left. Nothing else was stirring in the woods. Behind her was the soft trickle of water.

"Roger, where's your car?" Rachel called, softly.

Weakly, fighting for breath, Roger said, "Run, Rachel. Just run."

WHAM! went the shotgun, the muzzle flashing about a hundred feet away, pellets smacking into trees and kicking up snow.

Rachel raised the gun and squeezed off three quick shots at where the flash had been, hoping this time to hit flesh.

In response she heard only the sound of the slide being racked again.

"Roger, can you walk?"

"Forget about me. Just go."

"I'm not leaving you." She could see him now, a dark huddled shape on the ground, twenty feet from the stream bank. "Hang on, Roger. Do you have your radio? Can you call for help?"

Roger made a sighing sound. "Lost it."

"Well, somebody will hear the shots. I'm not leaving you."

"He'll kill us both."

A sudden rush of steps sounded in the darkness, and Rachel raised the gun, peering into the black. A dark shape cut across her field of vision, toward the stream, and then she could see nothing but heard quite clearly the sound of somebody jumping down into the streambed.

She saw him as he crossed the stream a hundred feet from her and she fired twice more. You're wasting bullets, she thought, watching him scramble up the far bank to disappear into the trees. She could see it all laid out before her, what was going to happen as he tried his own flanking maneuver, coming up through the trees on the other side of the stream.

He will expect me to pull back and protect Roger, she thought, and she was moving before thinking it through, crossing the stream herself to take cover under the opposite bank, nothing but an image driving her, the image of catching the man with the shotgun by surprise where he wouldn't expect to find her.

How many times have I fired? She didn't know; she didn't know how many rounds Roger's gun held. She knew only that it was time to start making the shots count. She could hear the man making his way slowly up the bank of the stream. Wait until you're sure, she told herself. She held the gun two-handed as she'd seen it done, with no clear idea of technique, left hand wrapped around her right wrist, elbows resting on the ground, waiting for something to shoot at.

I am outgunned, she thought. I don't know what I'm doing and he has a shotgun and Roger and I are both going to die. A great rage suffused her.

The dark figure came into view, stepping carefully through the trees. She could just make out the shotgun, barrel dipping slightly from the horizontal. Her grip tightened. Wait, she thought. Wait until you're sure.

When she was sure, she fired, and the instant she did it she knew she had missed. The figure leaped sideways and blended with the silhouette of a tree trunk, and Rachel fired twice more in panic. She saw the shotgun rising.

There was a rush of feet in the darkness, from her right, impossibly. The figure jerked away from the tree, the barrel of the shotgun making a dull thwack against the trunk. Rachel fired again, but there were two figures now, one swooping out of the darkness with something raised above its head. There was a sickening crack. The barrel of the shotgun drooped, the first figure swayed and began to buckle, and then after a second blow it toppled backward and fell heavily into the creek bed, the shotgun sliding down the bank.

Above it, the second figure stood with legs apart, grasping a tree limb two-handed. "Aunt Rachel?" he panted. "You OK?"

"Oh, God, Billy."

"Are you hurt?" Billy jumped down into the streambed.

Rachel could not find her voice. She held up a hand, the gun dangling in the other, and managed to say, "I'm OK. Roger's hurt. He's over there."

Billy dropped the tree limb and picked up the shotgun. Holding it with one hand, he pulled something from his belt with the other. There was a click and a flashlight came on. "Watch this fucker," he said. "If he moves, shoot him. You might want to shoot him anyway."

"Who is it?" Rachel's voice was full of dread.

The light played over the boots and denim-clad legs and the outflung arms, and Rachel knew before it reached the face framed in the hood of the sweatshirt.

"No," she sobbed as Billy's light fell on Dan Olson's face.

31 |||||||

"We couldn't save the arm," said the trauma surgeon. "We were lucky to save him, all the blood he lost." The surgeon was a gloomy-looking individual, perhaps because of all the ravaged flesh he had had to deal with. "I'm afraid his law enforcement career is over."

"Well, we'll fix him up with a nice pension," said the Dearborn County sheriff, who had been sitting with Rachel in a quiet lounge in the intensive care ward of St. Mary's Hospital in Warrensburg. "He's earned it." The sheriff was a tall, handsome man going nicely gray, and Rachel had taken a dislike to him because his every word was so obviously produced with an eye toward the public relations effect.

"When can I see him?" said Rachel.

"Try a couple of days from now," said the surgeon, already turning away. "Right now he's so far under he doesn't even know he's hurt yet."

When the doctor had gone, the sheriff steered Rachel by the elbow toward the double doors at the end of the hall. "We'll try to sneak you out a side door," he said. "There's a fair number of media people waiting downstairs."

"I'd like to see my nephew if I could." She was light-headed with lack of sleep and the aftereffects of stress and shock. She had bandages on her hands where the rocky streambed had lacerated them.

The sheriff frowned a little. "He's at the county building, being debriefed. I think they're still going at it."

"I hope you'll do a better job of keeping his name out of the papers than you did keeping his cover intact."

The frown deepened. "We're taking that extremely seriously. We're looking into how that happened. There was a violation of procedures somewhere."

Rachel let an icy silence be her only comment. When a deputy ushered her into an office in the county building twenty minutes later, Matt turned from a window with a cup of coffee in his hand. He looked haggard and worn down; Rachel would have sworn he had aged five years since she'd seen him last. He set the coffee down on a desk and they embraced. "How's Roger?" he said.

"He'll live. He lost the arm."

"Jesus."

"Billy saved his life by putting on a tourniquet. Billy saved my life, too. And he tied up . . . that asshole. Trussed him up with his shoelaces, neat as could be. Your son's a hero." Not least, Rachel thought, because he had refused to comply with Dan Olson's tearful pleading to kill him, a request Rachel would have been all too happy to grant. She had finally stumbled a few yards away into the woods to retch herself empty before returning to wait for the police.

Matt shook his head. "I wish I'd known. I wish Roger'd told me."

"I think the cops are usually pretty tight-lipped about informants. Except when they screw up and blow their cover."

"I'm still not real clear on what happened. Nobody around here will tell me anything."

"Because they're busy covering their asses." She reached for Matt's coffee and took a sip. "All I know is what Billy told me last night. He'd agreed to be a confidential informant for the sheriff's department, going after the meth networks in the county. He'd been doing it for weeks. Roger was one of the few who knew about it.

"Last night Billy got a text message from Kayla saying Stanfield was looking for him. Somebody'd blown Billy's cover, probably someone in the sheriff's department. When Billy got the message, he was at a house near Bremen with a couple of Stanfield's pals, meth guys he was hoping to set up. He figured he didn't have much time before they got whatever information Stanfield had, so he slipped out the back door and took off on foot.

"He didn't know who he could trust, so he called me. He was a couple of miles from that old house across the creek from Dan's place, so he made for there. He'd discovered the place when he worked for Dan that time, and as far as he knew, the meth guys didn't know about it. He had no idea Dan was using it for . . . his purposes.

"When he got in there and saw Ryle, he freaked out and called Roger. Roger came and got him and parked in a field a couple of hundred yards away, then went back to investigate. Meanwhile I had showed up with Stanfield. I'm just lucky Billy disobeyed Roger's orders to stay put at the car."

Matt looked past Rachel with a thousand-yard stare. "I can't believe it. I just can't fucking believe it about Dan. I will never, ever understand it."

"Believe it," said Rachel, her voice tight with disgust. "I was there."

"He's in confession mode," said the ISP detective, the older of the two who had sat at Matt's kitchen table days before. "He's spilling his guts. He breaks down a lot and cries, which slows things down. He's way into remorse at this point."

The detective sat across a desk from Rachel in an office at the Warrensburg Police Department, a gray-painted room with half a dozen desks, a couple of computers and a bulletin board with several layers of notices pinned to it.

"I'm sorry he feels bad," said Rachel. "So do I."

She felt as if she had been burned hollow and then filled with ice. She was beyond numb and into disembodied. She sensed she had perhaps two hours left before total collapse, and she was hoping to be at home in her bed before then.

The detective said, "Just in case it matters, he swears he had no intention of hurting you. It was Deputy Black he was after, because he knew he'd figured things out. He says he wouldn't have hurt you."

"That's good to know," said Rachel, coldly. She smoothed a stray flap of adhesive tape with a thumb. "How on earth did he run into Otis Ryle?"

"The company Olson works for has the pork contract for the prison. Olson delivers meat there every week. He just happened to be there on the day Ryle got hold of his bogus pass, and Ryle just happened to pick his truck to hide in. Ryle jumped him when Olson discovered him back there, and Olson won the fight. As in, he broke Ryle's neck. He was all set to call the police, and then he found Ryle's prisoner ID and realized who he had. He took him home and put him on ice in a big walk-in freezer he had and started to plan his campaign. It was damn quick thinking. He's pretty smart, whatever else he is."

"No, he's not stupid. Why did he dump the deer behind our place?"

"He says he wasn't trying to incriminate anybody. He was just looking for some place to dump it that wasn't right by his place. He'd parked his truck in some trees and was scouting on foot for a way down to the creek when you saw him on the road. He did a lot of this on foot, he says. When he killed Holmes, he hiked across country to the bar on 150 and crawled into the backseat of his truck. He knew nobody locks their vehicles around here."

"What happened the night he killed McDonald? He was with me that night. I don't know when he had a chance to do it." Rachel could still feel Dan on top of her in the creaking motel bed, grunting with pleasure.

"He'd actually killed him that afternoon. He'd arranged to talk to McDonald about a job with DAE, and McDonald came out to his house. He clobbered him on the head like he did the other two. They all three had skull fractures, by the way. None of them was conscious when the, uh, nasty stuff was done."

"That was nice of him."

The detective met her cold stare for a couple of seconds and then gave up and shrugged. "It's something. Anyway, he hid McDonald and his car in a shed, and then after he spent the evening with you he went home, shoved McDonald into his car, drove him to the spot he'd picked, and set up the show. He'd had Thomas's truck out the night before and parked it across the road at that spot, to leave the tracks. He wanted us to think McDonald had been stopped at random. But there was nothing random about it."

Rachel sighed. "And all of this was about his aunt, was it?"

The detective nodded. "It was all about her land. The land had come to her from her father, Olson's grandfather, that is. Her children had predeceased her, so when she married Holmes it meant the land would pass to him. And he had declared his intention to sell it off and go south somewhere. Olson said he had pleaded with his aunt to keep the land in the family, let him have a shot at farming it, but she just told him to talk to Holmes. She was sick by then and Holmes was calling all the shots. And Olson said he could see Holmes knew he had hit the jackpot and wasn't going to budge. So he had to go. If he died before the aunt did, the land would pass to Olson. And that's what would happen now if he wasn't going to spend the rest of his life in prison."

Rachel sat tight-lipped, contending with warring emotions. "And the other two were just to cover up."

"To sell the Otis Ryle scenario and to distract people from looking too closely at a motive for Carl Holmes. But he had reasons for picking both of them."

"And what would those be?"

"Well, with Mark McDonald he said he considered it a public service. A whole lot of people had gotten hurt in the elevator scandal. He was playing avenging angel."

"That would be a gratifying role," Rachel said. "And Ed Thomas?"

The detective's lips firmed, as if he were repressing a mild attack of gas. "It emerged that he and Mr. Thomas had . . . a history."

"What do you mean?"

The detective frowned at a pen he was fiddling with and then his eyes flicked up to meet Rachel's. "He said Ed Thomas molested him, repeatedly, when he was twelve years old and working for Thomas one summer."

Rachel closed her eyes. "Oh, God."

"Olson said he never told anyone about it. He was ashamed."

"Oh, poor Danny."

"Yes. I think that might account for the . . . savagery in the first killing."

When Rachel opened her eyes and took her hands away from her face, the detective was staring at her, a pensive look on his face. "Olson told me Thomas did do one good thing for him."

"What was that?"

"He said, 'He made me a better football player. You need rage to play football, and he gave me that.'"

Rage would help, Rachel thought as she stood at the south window in the living room looking out across the fields. It would help to be able to feel something besides this bottomless horror at herself and the world. Rage would burn her clean. But all she could summon was loathing.

She pulled away from the window and wandered through the house where she had grown up. Everything was muted, colors and sounds; Rachel had been moving in a fog for days. She collapsed onto the couch, inert, staring out at the branches of the old oak.

Well, wasn't that fun, she thought. You jumped in the sack with a guy you had always had the hots for, and damned if it wasn't pretty good. And then he turned out to be a killer who hacked three men to death.

What do you do with *that*? That's going to make intimacy problematic for a long, long time.

The pilot light of her optimism had gone out. Rachel had never given in to despair, but for the first time in her life she saw how a person could.

You wanted to be different, Rachel thought. You weren't going to be like everybody else, marry a strapping boy just like your father and wind up another farm wife staring out the window while you did dishes, wondering what was out there beyond the fields. You wanted distinction and you spent your life chasing it, all the way to a bunker in Baghdad and a bitter good-bye in Beirut. And then you came home and found a way to really distinguish yourself. You fucked the Dearborn County Nightstalker, and they'll be talking about you for fifty years.

The house was silent. Matt was gone on some errand and Billy was asleep. Rachel hauled herself to her feet. She walked down the hall into the kitchen. She needed something to occupy herself and there was an item of business she had been postponing. She reached into her purse lying on the kitchen table and pulled out the revolver. It lay heavy in her hand, a kilogram or so of brutal functionality in machined steel, sleek and lethal.

All you have to do is drive a half mile down the road and return it to Clyde, Rachel thought.

She shoved the gun back into her purse, put on her coat, grabbed the purse off the table and went out and got into the Chevy. She sat letting it warm up, the purse on the seat beside her. That would do it, she thought. It did it for Margie. Margie is through worrying about people's expectations. Margie put in her time and it's her turn to rest.

Somewhere far away, she thought. Drive until you are in a different county, so whoever finds you will be nobody you know. Find a place with a nice view. She put the car in gear, wheeled around on the gravel and headed out the drive. She hesitated for an instant and then turned left toward the Larsons'.

A place with a nice view and then an end. Matt won't have to find you; he'll be sad but he'll survive. The farm will survive. He'll plant in the spring and the seasons will change; Billy will go away and have a life somewhere and Matt will grow old in the house, standing at the sink looking out across the fields thinking of everything he has lost.

Rachel hit the brakes and jerked the wheel to the left just in time to slew into Clyde Larson's driveway. She pulled up at the door and sat for a moment, her heart pounding. When she was calm she turned off the ignition, picked up her purse and got out of the car.

In the kitchen she pulled the revolver out of the purse and handed it to Clyde, grip first. "I'm glad I didn't have to use it," she said.

"Me, too," said Clyde, taking it back.

Karen put a hand on her arm. "Are you all right, honey?"

Rachel nodded, eyes closed. "I'm all right. I'm OK now."

Clyde broke out the cylinder and froze for a second, then looked up at Rachel. "Where are the bullets?" he said. He showed her the empty cylinder.

Rachel blinked at the gun and then at him, bewildered. "I don't know."

Billy was sitting at the kitchen table when she got home, a mug of coffee and a plate of eggs and toast in front of him. Unshaven, he wore a ragged sweatshirt, his lank unwashed hair hooked behind his ears. He looked like a bad boy after a bad night. Rachel set her newly lightened purse on the table. "I took Clyde's gun back to him."

Billy nodded, his mouth full of toast. "That's good," he said. He swallowed and gulped coffee. "I'll get the bullets back to him one of these days."

Rachel sank onto a chair, weak-kneed. "Thank you," she said.

"No problem," said Billy. "Feeling better?"

"Getting there," she said. "Give me time."

Billy said, "I figured with you, brain chemistry wouldn't be a problem. But you sure as hell had a run of bad luck with men."

She closed her eyes briefly, exhaling. "Bad luck or bad judgment, maybe."

Billy considered that while he drank more coffee. "You can't be thinking like that. That's what my mom did, blame herself for everything. There's nothing wrong with your judgment. Sometimes people let you down, that's all. And it sucks, big time. But there's a lot of other people out there. You put it behind you and go find somebody else."

Rachel reached across the table for his free hand. She clasped it and squeezed and was gratified when he squeezed back. She said, "Next time I need somebody to sit with me for a good cry in the attic, I'll know who to call."

He smiled. "Hope it helped."

"It helped," said Rachel. "Big time."

"They have damn good prostheses these days," Roger said. "The doctors say I should be able to do pretty much anything I could before." His mouth twisted in the crooked grin. "Of course, I might have to give up on learning to play the violin at this point."

For now the prosthesis was still in the future and Roger's arm ended six inches below his shoulder, clad in a white cotton stump sock. He was sweating lightly from the exercises Rachel had watched him doing through the glass at the physical therapy outpatient clinic on Gunderson Street in Warrensburg.

"I had breakfast with Billy this morning," Roger said. "That's one smart kid."

"He is that."

"Best damn confidential informant we ever had, I'll tell you that. That boy has guts. What he went through over the last few months I wouldn't wish on anybody."

"He's glad it's over. He's thinking about going back to Macomb to finish up."

"He might want to get a little farther away from Dearborn County than that. There's a few lowlife types still on the loose around here that aren't big Billy Lindstrom fans. We busted a whole network of meth cooks thanks to him, but they got friends. Tell him to stay away for a while."

"I'll do that." They fell silent for a minute and then Rachel said, "I'm sorry, Roger."

His eyes widened. "Sorry? What do you have to be sorry for?"

"For everything. For what happened to you, for getting involved with Dan. For calling him that night because I was too chicken to go meet Billy by myself."

Roger waved it all away with his remaining hand. "Everything happens for a reason, Rachel. We might never have nailed him if he hadn't showed up like that. Anyway, you saved my life. Most people would have lit out of there as fast as they could. I've seen trained law enforcement officers run from gunfire. But you came back and saved my life. From here on out, every morning I get to wake up is because of you."

Rachel had to look away. After a minute she said, "Did you have any idea before that? Did you suspect anything?"

"I'd had a notion or two. As soon as I saw that deer down in the creek bed had been frozen, I started thinking about freezers, and hunters. Trouble was, there's a hell of a lot of both of them around here. So then I started looking at who lived near the creek. And that narrowed it down some. And when Carl got killed and people started talking about how hard it was on Peggy, I thought about her land, maybe because I'd been cheated out of land myself, and how Dan was going to lose it. And that was kind of uncomfortable, because I always liked Dan. I was rooting for it to be somebody else."

Rachel nodded, eyes downcast. "I can't even process it. I hate him and I'm grieving for him at the same time."

"Aw, Rachel." He reached for her hand and held it, gently. "You gotta remember, the good parts with Dan are just as real as the bad parts. It's OK to grieve for them."

"Thanks. That's a nice try." Rachel released his hand. "I'm leaving in a couple of days."

Roger's eyes held hers, his expression carefully neutral. "Going back overseas?"

"No, just to Washington, DC. I'm interviewing for a research position at a think tank."

"Wow. That's impressive. That sounds really interesting."

"It'll pay the rent, if it comes through. But I'm going to try to make it back here more often, for holidays at least. I never realized how much of my heart is here."

Roger nodded solemnly. "Well, when you're out there in Washington solving the world's problems, just remember. There's a one-armed man in Illinois who always . . ." Roger's mouth hung open for a moment and he frowned a little. "Who never forgot a prom date he had once in high school." Rachel waited for the crooked grin, but it never came.

- - - - - - - - - - - - - - -

"Try not to let eight years go by before you come see us again," said Matt.

"I promise," said Rachel.

The California Zephyr was sounding its horn somewhere around the curve, slowing for the station. Matt looked off into the distance and said, "Though I can understand if you don't want to get within a thousand miles of the place."

Rachel looked up at him gravely. "I'm glad I was here for it, given that you had to go through it. I ducked out on enough things."

"That's awful broad-minded of you."

Rachel frowned into a bitter wind, trying to put the words together. "I had this fairy-tale home I wanted to come back to, but that was just escapism. It's better to know it's a real place with real people. It's better to know there's no Utopia and no escaping."

Matt shivered, jamming his hands into his pockets. "Says you. I'll be in Montego Bay next week, and if that ain't escaping I don't know what is."

Rachel gave it a token laugh, and wiped her eyes, and then it was time for the embrace as the train pulled into sight. She clung to her brother as long as she could, and then, too soon, there was only the frozen land passing by outside the window, waiting for spring.

ACKNOWLEDGMENTS

This book could not have been completed without the generous help of Linda Bell, Dale Bjorling, Lowell Bjorling, Andrew Bowman, Nick Carlson, Howard Magnuson and David Salter. Any implausibilities or errors are strictly the fault of the author.

ABOUT THE AUTHOR

Sam Reaves was raised in small towns in Indiana and Illinois but gravitated to Chicago upon graduating from college and has been there ever since, when on US soil. He has lived and traveled widely in Europe and the Middle East and has worked as a teacher and a translator. He has published fiction and nonfiction as Sam Reaves; under the pen name Dominic Martell he has written a European-based suspense trilogy. He is married and has two adult children.